"So hissed. Her
hearing rd human's.

Haa er at ready.
He w egistered the
uniforms on the men of their hands.
The first two fell, and those higher up stopped and
tried to back up the stairs. It was the most foolish
move possible. A quick, aggressive charge down
would have overwhelmed those below and swept
them from the stairway with few casualties among
the guards. Momentum and gravity were on their
side.

Rama let out a blood-freezing squall, and Haakon
stepped aside to let her pass. She hit the packed
guards so hard and fast that the few who got off
shots hit only the air or their own men. She actually climbed up and over the first rank with a
liberal use of her claws and attacked those behind
from above.

The action that followed was too swift to follow, but Haakon saw chunks of uniform flying
with flesh still attached, and several guards vaulted
the rail to the floor ten meters below just to escape. Then the last two or three were showing
their backs, running full-tilt to get away.

Look for this other TOR book by John Maddox Roberts

THE CINGULUM

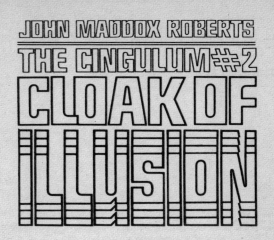

JOHN MADDOX ROBERTS

THE CINGULUM #2

CLOAK OF ILLUSION

A TOM DOHERTY ASSOCIATES BOOK

For my parents, Charles F. Roberts and Dotsey Scarborough Roberts, with love and gratitude.

CLOAK OF ILLUSION

First printing: August 1985

A TOR Book

Published by Tom Doherty Associates
8-10 West 36 Street
New York, N.Y. 10018

Cover art by Alex Ebel

ISBN: 0-812-55202-4
CAN. ED.: 0-812-55203-2

Printed in the United States of America

ONE

Timur Khan Bey selected an arrow. It was of traditional design: tipped with a barbed steel point, nocked with horn, fletched with real feathers. He fitted the horn nock to the silk string, laid the shaft along the right side of the bow, and settled the string against the jade ring he wore on the thumb of his right hand. The bow was of equally traditional design: a compound recurve made up of layered wood, horn, and sinew bound by glue. All of his shooting tackle was made meticulously by hand of natural materials.

The target hovered fifty meters from his balcony in the Black Obelisk. Ninety-nine arrows already bristled from it. This was his last shot of the day. He drew and released almost in a single motion, but this time something happened. In the instant that his thumb was about to release the string, a gong sounded in the office behind him. It caused him to loose the arrow a tiny instant too soon. The arrow nicked the edge of the target and flew off on a tangent. Soon it was lost to sight in the cityscape below, where it was likely to skewer some unfortunate citizen. No matter. What annoyed Timur Khan was that, for the first time in many years, he had missed.

He left the balcony and reentered his office, unstrung the bow and hung it on its peg. He moved with what was, for him, great haste. The gong was the one summons that made even the powerful Timur Khan Bey hurry. He went to his desk and punched the summons for his personal aircraft. He was a tall, spare man with black hair going somewhat gray at the temples. He had the narrow, high-cheekboned, small-nosed features common to the upper classes of Bahadur. He wore a tight-fitting black uniform that was utterly without decoration or insignia. His only visible weapon was a narrow dagger sheathed at his belt.

His office door opened at his approach and he walked out into the atrium. The two guards flanking the door fell in behind him. They wore uniforms identical to his own except for unit and rank insignia. They wore close-fitting black helmets that exposed little of their faces except eyes, nose, and mouth, and they wore knives and pistols at their belts. The three walked to the dock on the same floor and boarded the plane shuttle that awaited. The three men wore the uniform of the Black Tuman, the symbol of utter terror for all the worlds under the sway of the Bahadur System. Timur Khan Bey was chief of security for Bahadur and commander of the Black Tuman. The shuttle circled, gaining altitude, then headed south, toward the vast hunting estate called Xanadu.

The shuttle dropped them before an immense, pagodalike building of gold and green tile. Timur Khan and his guards left the craft and strode toward the building. Everywhere, there were soldiers in the green-and-gold dress livery of the Household Regiment. They made no move, said nothing, but their sullen hostility was evident. Like everyone else, they hated the BT's. Timur Khan noted the fact with satisfaction. Their hate was evidence of their fear, and fear was a thing he trusted.

He was met at the entrance by the steward, a liveried Han named Chiu Li. The man bowed deeply. "May I serve you, Noyon?" It was a formality. The man always knew when someone was expected.

"A summons to the Presence," Timur Khan said.

"Of course. The Khakhan is in the chess room. The Second Lady is with him." Timur Khan followed the elderly Han down a lengthy corridor covered with hand-knotted silken carpets. The walls were similarly covered. Timur Khan disliked this air of luxury. He was notorious for his exaltation of the abstemious habits of his ancestors. Small, exotic animals called from jeweled cages hanging from the ceiling.

Chiu Li preceded him into a room from which came a disagreeable scent of incense. Both men prostrated themselves with forehead to floor. "The Noyon Timur Khan Bey comes at your summons,

Lord,'' Chiu Li called. Far away, on a raised dais
at the end of the room, a man looked up. The
woman with him did not remove her attention
from the game board between them.

''Come here, Noyon,'' the man said. Timur
Khan rose and approached as the steward dis-
creetly withdrew. Twice more in his progress down
the long room, Timur Khan knelt and bowed his
head to the floor. He passed dozens of chess boards
laid out with games in progress. There were hundreds of them within the room. Every chess piece
was carved of some precious substance. The
Khakhan carried on games with the chess masters
of many worlds. Some of the games had been in
progress for decades.

Timur Khan bowed for the last time a few feet
from the dais. The room seemed deserted, but he
knew that many weapons were trained on him. His
two guards remained outside the room. It would
have been instant death for them to have set foot
inside. The man before whom he bowed was Tuli
VII, Khakhan of Bahadur. He was a tall, handsome man, somewhat portly in contrast to the
thinness common to his family. He was of middle
years and had succeeded to the Khanate some
thirty years previously, after a little intrafamily
violence over the succession. Once on the throne,
in accordance with the Law, he had had his broth-
ers murdered, thus averting the likelihood of further civil war. It was a brutal law, but it suited a
brutal people and had worked well for centuries, to
the greater good of all.

The woman who sat across from him, intent on

her next move, was the Second Lady, his favorite daughter, Bourtai. The First Lady, her mother, had been dead for many years. Like most of her line, she was tall and willowy, with the freakish silver eyes that showed up with some frequency in that family. She had a calm beauty and an air of serenity which masked the savage ferocity so necessary for survival among the royalty of Bahadur. She lifted a pawn and moved it one square.

The Khakhan sighed in appreciation of his daughter's shrewd move, then turned his attention to Timur Khan. "Join us, Noyon," he said.

Timur Khan rose and pulled up a cushion. He did not join them on the dais, of course. That would have been unthinkable. He sat cross-legged on the cushion and waited to be told the reason for his summons.

"We hear good things of your Black Tuman," Tuli said.

"They exist only to serve you," Timur Khan answered.

"Excellent. I have heard especially good reports of the new regiment you have raised on Gobi."

Not by so much as the flicker of an eyelid did Timur Khan show his dismay. He had not wished for the Khakhan to know about that regiment. "They are recruited from the best families, Khan," he said, "all young men of the true blood. Your Serenity will have no soldiers more loyal."

"See that it is so," Tuli said. "Perhaps a tour of tough duty will harden them a little. Young men should be tested to give them confidence. What is that place that is all jungle and mountain and hideous desert? The world where the catalytic crystals are found?''

"Chamuka, Father," Lady Bourtai murmured. Now Timur Khan knew who to thank for this predicament.

"Ah, yes. Chamuka. The people there grow rebellious, Timur. I would sterilize the place but I am told that production of the crystals requires a delicate balance of atmospheric, floral, and mineral action, and it would be destroyed by such a move. They are an intransigent, stiff-necked people who must be taught the error of their ways. I think a five-year tour on Chamuka will test the mettle of your new regiment, don't you, Noyon?"

It would do that. After five years on that hellhole, the twenty or so percent who survived would be tough, indeed. "They will not fail you, Khan."

"Best they do not." Tuli made a slight hand signal and a tray drifted by bearing three goblets. He and his daughter each took one and the tray drifted to Timur Khan. As the others drank, he took his goblet and drank without hesitation. The slightest reluctance would have been a sign of disloyalty, and there were far worse ways of dying than by poison. He assumed that the business for which he had been summoned was over and that he would now be executed or released to go about his duties, but he was wrong.

"Noyon," Lady Bourtai said, "do you recall, during the recent war, a supposedly secret project being carried out by our esteemed allies of the Syndicate, the Mughali? A project known only by the code name Precious Pearl?"

"I recall it," Timur Khan said cautiously. Was this something he should have been working on himself? His intelligence network was so vast that he could not attend to every activity personally, but any breakthrough of real importance was to be brought to his attention immediately. If something had been withheld from him by his subordinates, either deliberately or through negligence, there would be some slow deaths transpiring soon.

"We have learned," she continued, "that the project is at or near completion. It involves a device which, it is claimed, may be able to foretell the future."

Timur Khan was not sure that he had heard correctly. It was his good fortune that he was not a man accustomed to frequent laughter. "Foretell the future? Is it possible that Your Serenities have been victims of a hoax? The whole concept of prescience, prophecy, precognition, and such were demonstrated to be nonsense ages ago. They have been banished to the realm of pseudoscience and mysticism where they belong. I can scarcely conceive of a reputable scientist wasting time on such a project. Even the Mughali cannot be such fools."

"Nevertheless," Tuli said, "our esteemed former colleague on the Syndicate Board, Baibars of the Holy Cloak, was a man noted for his interest in, shall we say, bizarre concepts." A polite way of saying that old Baibars was a bit of a lunatic. "This Precious Pearl thing was one of his pets. It seems that, unlike most of his father's projects, young Baibars the Lion kept this one in operation. Its alternative and somewhat more descriptive name is the Limited Prescience Apprehension Device. Like your sagacious self, I have some difficulty in placing any credence in this marvel. However, if there is anything at all to it, there is only one power which by rights should have such a thing.''

"Can Your Serenity not simply demand that it be turned over to you? By treaty, they have no right to withhold technology or data which might be of military significance.''

"Ah, but is this thing in the realm of technology,'' asked the Second Lady, "or is it wizardry? Does it involve data or spells? Our treaty does not cover such things.''

"Treaties are made to be broken,'' Timur Khan said, daring to show impatience for the first time. "Only power has any importance.''

"Just now,'' Tuli said, "it is our pleasure to deal gently with Mughal. There are delicate matters in negotiation; a royal marriage, many trade agreements, other things.''

Timur Khan hid his disgust. The Royal House of Bahadur turned merchants and marriage-brokers. How could the bones of the ancestors rest easy in the grass of the steppe by the Lake, beneath the everlasting sky?

"Besides,'' Tuli continued, "if they have such a device, and if it works, is there any guarantee that we *could* win a contest with the Mughali?'' He smiled gently at the Noyon.

Timur Khan was genuinely shocked. Was the Khakhan really suggesting that the People of the Steppe could be beaten? The Mughali would need more than a gadget of prophecy to do that. An army of angels with flaming swords would not help them.

"If Your Serenities truly think this matter worthy of deeper study, I will of course send in a team to fetch this magical wonder and lay it at your feet. The Mughali are an idle and pleasure-loving people. My people should have no difficulty in prying this thing loose."

The Second Lady did not miss this gently-veiled barb directed at the luxurious habits of the Royal House. "The Mughali enjoy living well, but they held their place in the battle lines well enough during the war."

"As who would not, with Bahadur backing them," Timur Khan said. His contempt for lesser peoples was as notorious as his cruelty and his ambition.

"Bahadur must not be implicated in any such activity, of course," Tuli said.

"I have several teams of non-Bahadurans under my control. They are picked specimens from among the inferior peoples. All are capable. I shall dispatch one such team."

"Do so, and carry out our will," Tuli said by way of dismissal. "Fear me and obey with trembling." At the close of the ancient formula Timur Khan rose and backed the whole length of the room, prostrating himself three times in his retrograde progress.

The two on the dais watched his exit. When he was gone, Lady Bourtai turned to her father. "When will you get rid of him?"

"When it suits me, child. He is useful, yet.

Men of such capability are rare. Such a man is a
wonderful hedge against assassination, as well.
Who would dare attack the Royal House when it
might mean that Timur Khan Bey could become
the head of Bahadur?''

"No matter. He is too dangerous. He plots against
us.''

"And what of that? You have survived the plots
of your mother and your sisters, how can you
know fear now?''

"Just the same, Father, I fear him. He wants
some day to sit on the throne.'' She was still
looking at the door through which Timur Khan had
just left. If she could not have him killed, perhaps
it would soon be time to league herself with Timur
Khan. It would bear thinking about. She turned
back to the board between them. "Your move,
Father.''

On the flight back, Timur Khan was deep in
thought. He devoted little of that thought to the
Precious Pearl business, which had to be nonsense.
What annoyed him was the discovery of his new
regiment. He wondered who the traitor in his ranks
might be. That one's death would be a salutary
lesson to all. He wondered as well whether any of
his other secret forces had been discovered. The
Black Tumans had been organized originally as his
bodyguard, but he had quickly built them into a
private army owing allegiance to him, personally.

Despite the Second Lady's fears, he had no
intention of ever becoming Khakhan. He was a
man of action and plots, and he had no interest in
becoming bogged down in the many ceremonial

duties of the Khakhan. What he wanted was control of a Prince of the Blood, to raise from childhood in the true, austere way of the Steppe People, to make him a fit Khakhan, respected and feared. During the prince's minority, Timur Khan would be Regent, and when the prince was ready to take up the standard of nine white yak's tails, Timur Khan would hand over to him an empire restored to its former glory, its people purged of their centuries of decadence and weakness. Timur Khan would then retire to the post of Vizier, to guide the new Khakhan until he was able to steer his empire alone.

When he returned to his office he punched a search into his desk console. Which of his non-Bahadur teams was immediately available to undertake a mission? The answer came within seconds: The *Eurynome* crew were on-planet. This was ideal: they were tough, capable, and eminently expendable. Like all such teams working for Timur Khan, they were under suspended death sentence, with explosive devices buried in their skulls. They lived only at his continued pleasure.

He called in the duty captain of his guard. "Subadar." He heard heels clicking down the hallway outside the office, then the man came into the room. Timur Khan recognized him at a glance. Like all his officers, the Subadar was a young man of excellent family, heir to a prestigious title, but in the Tuman he went only by a single name, as was customary. Since he was duty captain he did not prostrate himself, but he removed his helmet, placed it beneath his left arm, and saluted. "Your pleasure, Noyon?"

"Subadar Hulagu, I have a task for you. When your relief arrives, you are to summon these persons personally." He tore a readout from his console and handed it to the guardsman. The Subadar glanced at the names and the locater frequency printed on the sheet. "They are here in Baikal somewhere," Timur Khan went on, "probably in the foreigner's quarter of the lower city, near the spaceport. When you find them, bring them to me. If I have retired by that time, hold them here until I resume my duties in the morning."

"As you command, Noyon." The Subadar combined a salute with a stiff bow and left the room. Timur Khan dismissed the matter from his mind for the nonce. There were weightier things to think about. He took a practice bow from the wall and slipped on a thumb-ring. The discipline of the bow always helped him to meditate. The practice bow had a draw even more powerful than that of his shooting bow. Slowly, he raised the bow and repeatedly drew the string to his ear. He could almost feel the wind off the steppe.

TWO

Subadar Hulagu had never been in the lower city before. This area had been built early in the colonization of the planet. The buildings were ancient, ramshackle structures in sharp contrast to the clean, shining edifices of the upper city. He had descended from his shuttle at the edge of the lower city. The modern craft could not negotiate the narrow, odd-angled passages of the lower city.

The people were different as well. Almost all were foreigners, peoples of many races, both human and semihuman. There were even a few aliens, mostly of types that breathed the same oxygen-nitrogen mixture as humans: Pirians, Ganthi, a few others. He found himself suppressing an urge to draw away as members of these lesser breeds neared him. Their very nearness gave him a sense of defilement. There were many spacers about, this near port. Most of them showed signs of excessive recreation and a taste for low amusements. Police observation 'bots floated overhead to keep things orderly, but Hulagu could see from their antiquated design and obvious decrepitude that most of them were probably nonoperational.

To one side of a thoroughfare wide enough to qualify as a street, he saw the red-and-white sign of a police station. He entered and endured the loveless stares of the red-uniformed policemen. At least these were Bahadurans, although they were short men, with the round faces characteristic of commoners. He pushed past abject groups of arrestees and stepped over the inert forms of drunks. The place stank from its burden of human detritus. A massive, scarred man in a slovenly uniform lounged behind a desk at the back of the room. He looked up at Hulagu's approach.

"Now, what business favors us with a visit from the lordly BT's?" the man inquired.

Hulagu tossed the readout sheet on the man's desk. "I've come for these persons. My locater shows them to be somewhere in this part of the city. Do you know them?" He knew this man's type: veteran of the wars, probably regular Army, Spacer Marine or some such front-line service. One and all, they hated the Black Tumans. Hulagu was too young to have fought in the wars and resented the patronizing contempt of the veterans.

"Big gods and little devils, you want *that* crew?" The man barked out a short, high-pitched laugh, then called out to the others: "Anybody know where Haakon and Rama the Felid and that bunch hang out now?"

"I saw them last night in Star Hell," said one.

"Have one of your 'bots summon them," Hulagu said.

"Every 'bot that's been sent into that district got sold as scrap within minutes," the policeman said. "There aren't three working police 'bots in all of the lower city. You think the authorities really care what these foreigners do to one another? Our main job is to keep them out of the upper city and grab them when they come back from there with stolen goods."

"Then show me where this place is," Hulagu said impatiently. "I'll go get them myself."

"Better let us give you an escort," the policeman said, not unkindly.

"To protect me from this mongrel rabble?"

"Let me tell you what you're going after, Subadar: Haakon's an ex-con who spent years in the pits busting rocks. He's captain of his own ship now, though I hate to think where he might have come by it. He's as hard as they come. His sidekick is the one listed here as Jemal. He used to make his living as a prizefighter. With powerblades. I never knew a man to survive a month of that. He must've done it for three years. As for Rama the Felid—I don't even like to think about that one. She used to boss a gang around here a few years back. I'd say she's the deadliest animal in the whole lower city, and you've no idea how dangerous that makes her. There are others in the crew, but those three are the worst."

"Just show me where they are," Hulagu demanded.

"They eat boys like you for breakfast down there," the policeman said.

Hulagu restrained himself. The man's insolence was intolerable. If he had belonged to the nobly-born class, Hulagu would have challenged him. "Your low birth protects you, policeman," he said at last. "Do you know what would happen if the scum here were responsible for the death of a single member of the Black Tumans? This entire sector of the city would be sterilized. Everything from bacteria on up would die. Police included."

The policeman watched him for a moment. "Yes, I suppose the bastard would do that. All right, on your head be it." He took a small device from his desk. It was a globe of transparent substance about ten centimeters in diameter. He set it in a hollow in the top of his desk and keyed in a set of coordinates. The ball began to pulsate with a red light, then rose to eye level and began to float toward the entrance. "Follow that," the policeman said. "It'll help you see a little, anyway. It gets dark down there."

Hulagu turned and followed the guide globe. He thought he heard a spitting sound behind him.

The globe turned down the street outside, then went into an alley which suddenly became a ramp descending below ground level. The darkness closed in, broken only by the flickering illumination of ancient walkway panels. Shadowy figures lurked in the dimness. Most of the establishments down here featured entertainments of the lowest sorts. He could smell drug smokes drifting from doorways and windows. The strains of many alien musics rode on the artificial breeze. Dim-lit windows displayed what were undoubtedly stolen or smuggled goods. Gambling establishments abounded, from casinos to impromptu games played on one of the rare still-glowing walkway panels. From time to time he stepped over a body, drunk, drugged or dead. The globe blinked on ahead of him. Naked or near-naked whores, male, female, and hermaphrodite wandered about.

Nobody molested him as he passed by. Whores drifted his way, then faded at the sight of his uniform. Juvenile gangs showed a similar circumspection.

People were dressed in rags, in rich garments, or in armor. Spacers wore their coveralls and led or carried exotic pets. Some humans were standard, some were gene-manipulated for the specialized needs of scores of worlds, others were one-of-a-kind sports. Still others were fabricated from human genes grafted with animal genes. To him, these were even worse than the true aliens.

The globe stopped outside an unmarked door and ceased its pulsating. He opened the door and went in. The quiet of the passageway outside left him unprepared for the blast of noise that greeted him from within. Noise, smoke, and glaring lights assaulted him as he stepped inside. The doorkeeper—a huge, scaly Pirian—came toward him and then stopped. Hulagu brushed past the hulking creature and found himself standing on a balcony overlooking an immense pit. The sides were lined with tiers of balconies crowded with tables for eating, drinking, and gaming. A multitude of doors opened off the balconies where visitors could indulge themselves with drugs, prostitutes, or less reputable amusements. In the pit there was a huge, circular bar, gaming tables, and fighting platforms. Someone was dancing on the bar, where the loudest music and cheering were coming from. On the platforms, two pairs were having it out with powerblades. The whole pit was packed with a shouting, sweating crowd. The idea of going down there filled him with distaste, but he had done worse things for the sake of duty.

A man was coming along the balcony toward him. He looked again. It might be a herm. He was small and blond, with long hair and expensive clothes and a great deal of jewelry. Hulagu wrinkled his nose at the scent the creature wore.

"May I serve you, Lord?" At least the voice was a man's. The blue eyes were rimmed with kohl and blinking sequins.

"I am here to find the crew of a ship called *Eurynome*. A captain Haakon, Rama the Felid, others. They were last seen here."

"*Eurynome*? Ah, sir, there are so many ships, so many spacers. As you will see, most of the customers I scrve are spacers looking for an agreeable way to spend their money, which I provide in great variety." He gestured with a beringed hand toward the balconies and the pits. Spacer's garb seemed to predominate.

"Nevertheless, I must find these people. If I do not, I will have everyone in this building killed immediately." This somewhat exceeded Hulagu's authority, but not by much.

The little man's hand swept out again. His sleeve was almost floor-length, and bright with embroidery. He pointed down to the bar. "That's Rama dancing. The others will be nearby. I will take you to them. I want no trouble with the BT's." That made sense. Nobody wanted trouble with the BT's.

He was conducted down stairs and ramps. A pool of silence widened where the black uniform passed. A passageway opened in the dense throng as if by magic. Hulagu stopped for a moment and looked up at the woman dancing on the bar. He had never seen a Felid before and had not expected her to be so big. She was nearly two meters tall, with a rangy, sinewy body that was at the same time intensely feminine. Her hair was a leonine mane striped silver and black, she had long whiskers flanking her nose, and her eyes were slit-pupiled. Otherwise she was rather human-looking, except for her fingers and toes, which had retractile claws. She waved a pair of meter-long power-blades with alarming abandon. She wore bands of long monkey fur below elbows and knees, magnifying every motion of her limbs. Apparently, she wore nothing else except paint and glowing silver gems stuck directly to her skin. The music was something primitive and loud, with lots of drums and wailing flutes. The dance was wild and athletic and ferociously sexual, but the reaction she was getting from her male spectators at the bar seemed out of proportion to her dancing skill.

"She has scent glands you wouldn't believe," the small man said, as if in answer to his thought. "She can spray sexual pheromones like a fountain.

The whores give her a rakeoff for charging up the male customers. It only works on males. Haakon's over here somewhere.'' They went wandering among the tables.

At one of the gaming tables a man looked up. He was a small Han, and his already-narrow eyes narrowed further at the sight of the BT. The Han reached into a pouch and took out a hideous, red-scaled crustacean that was all jointed legs and waving claws and placed it on the table before him. Other gamblers placed other ugly creatures on the table. ''Place your bets,'' the Han said in a quiet voice as the beasts began fighting. His eyes, however, continued to follow the BT.

They stopped at a table where two men were arm wrestling. One was completely hairless, dressed in nondescript trousers and boots and a vest of reptile hide. He wore no shirt. The man who sat across from him had black skin and wore the uniform of a passenger-line officer. The black man was grimacing with effort, exposing steel teeth. Both men streamed with sweat. The bald man wore broad steel bracelets on both wrists.

On the back of the bald man's chair crouched a boy who had feet like hands. He wore only an embroidered vest and shorts from which a long, prehensile tail protruded. Fingers, toes, and tail sported jeweled gold rings. Gold hoops dangled from his jug-handle ears. He was first to spot the BT. ''Trouble, Boss,'' the monkey-boy said.

''Just a minute,'' the bald man wheezed. The prominent muscles of arm and shoulder bunched with effort, but neither man's arm moved. Hulagu

was fascinated despite himself. He had been trained
to worship power and strength, and had never seen
such a display as these two motionless arms. He
could actually hear the tendons of one of them
creaking.

A couple wandered purposefully to the table.
One was an elegantly-dressed dark man who moved
with a lithe, dancer's grace. He wore a finely
crafted powerblade at his belt. The woman with
him was small, brown-haired, and stunningly beautiful. The man answered the description of Jemal,
the former prizefighter. The woman had to be
Mirabelle, the technothief.

With an agonized groan, the black spacer gave
in. His arm slammed to the table, smashing the
vial of acid that lay there as incentive not to lose.
He howled and poured an iced drink over the back
of his hand amid much laughter and shouting. The
victor held his arm out and a voluptuous but muscular herm began to massage it with great skill.
Only then did the bald man look up at Hulagu.

"One of Timur Khan's errand boys, is it?" he
said, the patches of skin where he once had eyebrows going up in inquiry.

"Captain Haakon?" Hulagu said.

"The very same. What's the old man want?"
He leaned back in his chair, sighing with contentment as the herm soothed the cramping muscles of
his arm. His nose and cheekbones and jaw had
been broken at some time. His fingers and knuckles had been broken as well. Everything about him
appeared to have been broken and healed stronger
than before.

"Come with me," Hulagu said.

"Why?"

Hulagu was stunned. Nobody ever defied a BT order. It was in defiance of nature. "This is a direct order from the Chief of Security himself. If you do not come with me, I shall execute you summarily."

"Then what'll you do?" said the man called Jemal. "Tell your boss you killed us?" He looked at his companion. "Where's old Timur recruiting these dummies?"

"Keep your pants on, sonny," Haakon said. "We'll come along when we're ready. Sit down. Have a drink or something." Haakon signaled and a chilled glass was delivered by one of the hovering servobots.

"You waste my time, convict," Hulagu said in a cold rage. He was reaching for his pistol when the towering Felid appeared silently at his side.

"Haakon!" she exclaimed. "Where did this lovely and utterly sexy young man come from?" She wrapped an arm about his shoulder and hit him with a blast of pheromone that should have had him writhing helplessly with lust. Fortunately, he had undergone surgery and hypnotic training to counter any such attack. "Tell me, you ravishing creature," she went on, "how did you know that I yearned to bed a BT tonight? I have spent all day devising new and unheard of perversions possible only with a man in a black uniform!"

He tried to draw his pistol but her hand was at his wrist and try as he might he couldn't move his hand an inch. His mortification surpassed in intensity anything he had ever felt. Then, the arm around his shoulder inexorably forced him into a chair. A drink was placed in front of him. He noticed that the hand that set the glass down was actually a foot. The monkey-boy leaned close and spoke confidentially. "You know, you'd end up looking a whole lot less like an idiot if you'd just have a little patience. You see, my friends here know they gotta talk to your boss when he calls them, but they don't like to be rushed, you know what I mean? So why don't you just sit here and enjoy your drink, or they'll eat your goddamn lungs."

Hulagu picked up the glass and sipped, trying to look nonchalant, as if he did this kind of thing every day, as if he were humoring these madmen. What kind of people did not tremble at the name of Timur Khan Bey? He comforted himself with the thought that they would doubtless be writhing in torture before the night was much older.

"No trouble with the BT's, Haakon," said the small blond man.

"Don't worry," the hairless man said. "He's just an errand boy. It looks like we've got some business with the government. Probably something about that last smuggling run."

The man looked at him dubiously. "I've always valued you people as customers," he said. "Now I'm not so sure, with the kind of company you keep." He walked away and gradually the local noise level resumed. Haakon turned furiously to Hulagu.

"Why couldn't Timur Khan have just left a

message at the ship? Once noise of this gets around, we won't be able to show our faces in any respectable dive in the lower city! Do you know what it means around here, being seen with a BT? We'll be disgraced forever.''

Rama sat on Hulagu's lap, pinning him firmly to the chair. ''You are lucky I like your handsome young face, you beautiful man,'' she said. ''Otherwise I would bite it off.'' She smiled, revealing sharp white teeth. Hulagu decided that this was all a dream. The small Han gambler came to the table.

''Is it a summons?'' the Han asked.

''Looks like it,'' Haakon said. ''Rama, better go get some clothes on.''

''It's a warm night,'' the Felid said. ''I think not. Besides, Timur Khan has never seen me in all my glory. Perhaps he'll think of some better employment for my talents than knocking about the worlds with you objectionable people.''

''They'll arrest you in the upper city looking like that,'' Jemal said.

''Ah, but who would dare arrest me when I have the escort of this intensely marvelous specimen of young manhood in his fearsome black uniform?'' She tore his helmet off and stuck her tongue in his ear, causing him to wince. Her tongue was like a file. He refused to be distracted from his duty.

''Where is the one called Rand?''

''Rand's with the ship,'' Jemal told him. ''Poor old Rand's pleasures don't run much to the eat, drink, and be merry variety these days.''

"We'd better be going," Mirabelle said. "If Timur Khan's in the sack by the time we get there it'll mean sitting around the Black Obelisk all night, and I can do without that."

"I guess you're right," Haakon said. "I lose track of the time down here. How long have we been here, anyway?"

"Three days, six hours, fourteen minutes," Mirabelle said. The technothief had a built-in clock.

"No wonder I'm a little sleepy," Haakon said. "Okay, you snot-nosed punk, let's go talk to your boss." They got up and walked out of the pit and up the ramps and stairways. As soon as they were out in the corridors again, Hulagu began to talk.

"I'll have you all skinned for this! No civilian may so insult a member of the Black Tumans. I shall—"

Haakon stepped in and slapped him, hard. Even through the helmet, it made his ears ring. "Learn something, punk," said Haakon in a passionless voice. "There are certain advantages to being Timur Khan's slaves. We're all under death sentence, but only Timur Khan pulls the switch. If we're summoned, that means your boss has some nasty job for us. It's likely to be something important. Do you think he values some green Subadar above his mission he has for us?" He spun Hulagu around and shoved him forward with a broad palm between his shoulder blades.

Hulagu spun and reached for his pistol but it was gone. He heard a click and a hum and he saw the faint glow of a powerblade in the hand of Jemal. Hulagu had his own knife out with creditable speed and he thumbed its switch, causing the blade to hum and crackle with static discharge. He lunged at Jemal but the man glided around the blow. Hulagu felt the weapon burn along the angle of his jaw. Another touch of the blade burned his wrist between glove and sleeve, where the armor-cloth did not protect him. He gasped, dropped the knife and clutched his injured wrist. Then the glowing blade was right before his eyes, backing him against the dirty wall of the alley.

"You shouldn't've done it." It was the rueful voice of the monkey-boy. "These people would really like to carve the tripes out of you, and they ain't at all scared of your pretty black suit." Hulagu closed his eyes and prepared to die. His only regret was that it was to come in this filthy alley, at the hands of these subhumans, instead of gloriously, on the field of battle.

"That's enough." Suddenly, the alley was flooded with light. Hulagu opened his eyes. There were men all around them and bright globes floated overhead. A man in a red uniform came from the encircling ring. It was the policeman he had last seen behind the desk.

"Put up your weapons," the cop said. "Haakon, you can't kill any BT's in my precinct."

"We weren't going to kill him," Haakon said. "But it's not often we get a BT all to ourselves. The temptation to have some fun was just too strong."

"I knew he'd get into trouble," the policeman said. "That's why I decided to follow him down here. Give him back his gun." Rama rammed the weapon back into its holster.

"Come on," the policeman ordered, "let's get you out of the lower city without any more trouble." They walked on, the much-chastened Hulagu in the lead.

As they were about to board the BT craft at the edge of the upper city, the policeman turned to the hairless spacer. "Tell me, Haakon. Would you have killed him?"

The ex-convict grinned. "I'd like to kill them all."

Timur Khan Bey entered his office to find six subhumans kneeling on his floor. Behind them stood a line of BT guards, each guard holding a pistol leveled at the head of one of the six. As always, this particular group managed to make their abasement seem to be a mockery. Especially the curious little Singeur, the monkey-human. He was on his knees, hands and face to the floor, but his tail stuck straight up in an insulting manner. No matter. If these petty gestures of defiance improved their morale, so much the better. Beside them stood a somewhat disheveled-looking Subadar.

"Here are the persons you summoned, Noyon. Their engineer is still aboard their ship."

Timur Khan glanced at the guards. "Do they represent so great a threat, Subadar?" he asked mildly.

"They are irrationally violent and defiant, Noyon. I thought it best not to take chances." Timur Khan looked at him sharply. Something had happened. Something had infected his Subadar with fear. That was not good. Perhaps a tour of duty with the new Gobi regiment on Chamuka would have a salutary effect on this one.

"You may all go," he told the BT's. Reluctantly, Subadar Hulagu holstered his weapon and exited with the others.

"Rise." The prostrated crew got to their feet.

He studied them. Three of his convict-servants had been officers in the service of nation-worlds crushed by Bahadur. Haakon and Jemal had served Delius, Soong had served Han. All had distinguished wartime records. All had done time as POWs. With the war over and all legitimate employment closed to them, they had drifted to the fringes of the underworld that flourished even under the severe rule of Bahadur.

The woman Mirabelle was a technothief. She was trained to penetrate computers and retrieve essential data, carrying it out in her own mind, to be fed back into other computers in the form of a specialized language known only to members of her profession. She was too young to have been involved in the wars, but she had been caught at her work. Technothieves had quasilegal status, but meddling with Bahaduran computers always carried a penalty.

Rama was a Felid, a member of an artificially created race which had cat genes grafted onto human genes. Felids were rare and solitary, and they seemed to live by no law comprehensible to ordinary humans. Almost everywhere, they were classed as hereditary criminals.

This crew had been given a simple choice: they could serve Timur Khan, or they could die. They had made the sensible decision. Somewhere, they had acquired the monkey-boy, who seemed to be a sort of mascot.

"I have a task for you."

Haakon and the rest listened to Timur Khan's brief recitation at first with resignation, then with incredulity, finally with alarm. "A *what*?" Haakon demanded.

"You heard me, convict," Timur Khan said coldly. "A 'Limited Prescience Apprehension Device.' At least, that is the name I was given. Whether this thing functions or not, I wish to have it."

"Cracking a top-secret Mughali scientific facility won't prove easy," Haakon said.

"Use a little ingenuity. You are noted for it, are you not? You will find that prospective execution provides a marvelous inducement to creative thought. Most of you have certain social graces and professional skills. Your ship is certainly fit to pass muster among the yachting crowd. You should be able to worm your way into the affections of such soft-headed sybarites as the Mughali. I am told that anyone with some decadent new diversion to offer is always welcome there among the highest social circles. Use your imagination." His gaze swept the crew before him. "You certainly have the raw material to work with."

The shuttle took them from the orbiting dock to their ship, *Eurynome*. Rama, still in paint and jewels, stretched in her catlike way. "Home again.

The little worlds and their diversions are pleasant, but only here do I feel free.''

Haakon hit a pressure plate beneath a ship's intercom. ''Rand. Come to the dock.'' He, too, seemed to move with a new freedom. In the dismal alleys of the lower city he was a dangerous man, but those alleys were full of dangerous men. Here, he was a true aristocrat; captain of a free trader.

''What is it?''

The man who stood in the doorway was human by little more than courtesy. At first glance he appeared to be dressed in a suit of battle armor. It was a jointed, shiny carapace of gray alloy. In place of eyes, nose, and mouth he had visual receptors and a voice-grill in a metal mask. What he wore was a therapeutic suit of Galen manufacture. A ship's engineer, Rand had been standing too close to a Tesla generator some years before when the touchy thing blew. He had been burned down to little more than a skeleton and a brain, but his life was saved. He was gradually regenerating inside the suit, with servomotors acting in place of muscles. Unlike the others, Rand had no criminal record. As with his temperamental Tesla, he just happened to be standing in the wrong spot when Timur Khan needed a ship's engineer. Haakon told him of their new mission.

''What about it, Hack?'' Jemal said. ''You think Timur Khan's finally flipped out completely? A fortune-telling machine, of all things! Why doesn't he just go to one of the gyppo booths down in the lower city? Plenty of fortune-tellers there.''

"You heard how he gave us this one," Haakon said. "I don't think he believes in this thing either. This is something he's been handed from higher up. He's passed it on to us."

"Higher up than Timur Khan," Soong said, "leaves only the Royal House."

"That's the way I read it," Haakon confirmed. "That family's produced some notable loonies before now. I guess we had to expect something like this sooner or later."

"It could have been worse," Mirabelle said. "It might've been the fountain of youth or something."

"Maybe we'll be lucky," Jemal said wishfully. "Maybe they'll forget all about it before we get back."

"Dream on," Haakon said. "While you're doing it, remember what those people are like with those who fail them."

Rama was admiring her painted, bejeweled self in a mirror. "He didn't even notice my magnificence," she sulked. "I think there's something wrong with him."

THREE

Haakon sat in a chair in the ship's little infirmary while Mirabelle altered his appearance to let him pass among respectable people. She was working from a likeness of Haakon as a young man. The likeness had been made when he was a cadet at the Space Service Acadamy of Delius. It showed a youth with fine, aristocratic features and shoulder-length blond hair.

"God, you were a good-looking boy back then," Mirabelle said. "I'll bet the girls back on Delius fought over you."

"Something women have never ceased to do since," Haakon said.

Mirabelle was sculpting plastiflesh to straighten and raise the bridge of his frequently broken nose. She had already fitted him with a blond wig set in the short, tight-fitting curls currently fashionable among the smart set. He now had eyebrows as

well. She had also built up his smashed cheekbones a little, to give them what might have been
their original contour.

"Close your eyes," Mirabelle ordered. She
sprayed his face with a fixative and coloring agent
to stabilize the plastiflesh and give real skin and
false the same coloration. "Go look at yourself."

He got out of the chair and went to a full-length
mirror. The change was amazing. The alterations
she had made had been minimal, and he still looked
like himself, recognizable to any friend or enemy
who saw him. But he was a different Haakon. The
boy in the likeness might have grown into the man
he saw in the mirror, had there been no war, no
capture and no convict pits. The man in the mirror
might have been a career officer of the aristocracy
of Delius. There was a slight enlarging and coars-
ening of the features, the inevitable result of the
plastiflesh buildup, but years of hard living and
dissipation might have had the same result.

"I'll pass," he said, satisfied with the impression. "My manners may need work, though. Your
social graces tend to suffer from too much time in
the pits, and the ports, and the lower cities. I guess
it'll come back to me. I was raised in it. Did I ever
tell you that my father was a duke?"

"Yes," she said.

"Well, I was lying. Actually, he was a viscount. That's not quite as high up as a duke, but it
was high enough for him to get me into the
Academy."

"How did Jemal get in?" she asked. "He's no
aristocrat."

"His family lacked high birth but they had the next best thing. They had money. One or the other will get you just about anything on Delius. Anywhere else, for that matter."

"You ought to get some hair implanted," she said. "And facial surgery. Those looks suit you. You should make it permanent."

"Not a chance," he said. He had stubbornly kept his convict's depilation and his battered physiognomy because he did not want to forget the years of degradation and brutality. He knew he was still a slave and was not going to fool himself that it was otherwise.

"I can't do much about your hands," she said. "It's a good thing gloves are back in fashion."

Haakon walked to an intercom. "Everybody gather in the main salon. We're going to have a brainstorming session."

Eurynome had been built as a personal vessel for a Prince-Admiral, although the war had ended before it could be commissioned. It combined incomparable elegance and luxury with the armament of a light cruiser. The main salon had divans of exotic woods and silk and leather, tapestried hangings, fur carpeting, robot servitors, and all other appurtenances fit for those who prefer to endure the hardships of war with a certain comfort and style, and who can pay for it.

Haakon and Mirabelle found their shipmates lounging about on divans, being served drinks by the 'bots. The Singeur was on the floor shooting marbles. He was equally adept with hands and feet. His name was unpronounceable by the ordinary human larynx, and for some reason he had chosen to be called Alexander.

They looked up in mock amazement when Haakon came in sporting his new face. He ignored their murmurs of admiration and came straight to the point. "We have to plan our strategy. We'll be in Mughal-controlled space soon. Soong, what have you been able to find for us on Mughal? I'll confess I don't know much about them. I never fought them and I've never been in territory they control."

"I neutralized a few of their strategists during the war," Soong said. *Neutralize* was a Han euphemism for *assassinate*. "They are a lesser member of the Syndicate. They control only the Mughal system and three others, but those four are all very wealthy systems, so their influence is greater than might seem likely at first sight. Government is plutocratic, and the social system is headed by a hereditary aristocracy on top of a complicated caste system. The aristocracy is ethnically related to that of Bahadur, though the Bahadurans do not care to admit it. The language is much the same. The Mughali aristocracy does not have the Bahaduran fanaticism about pure bloodlines, and marriages with other peoples are frequent among them, usually for political or commercial advantage. The laboring classes, incidentally, are mostly Hindi-speaking, and the merchant class are largely Arabic-speaking. These ethnic differences help keep the caste system rigid.

"The Mughali aristocracy are wealthy beyond belief and they enjoy their wealth. High living is an art form among them. As is usual with such people, they become bored and jaded quite easily. They are always looking for some new diversion. They are not utterly decadent, however, despite the opinion of Timur Khan. Military service is considered to be an obligation of the highborn, and many of them rendered distinguished service in wartime. They have a touchy sense of honor and practice a code duello. Outdoor recreations requiring considerable athletic prowess are most popular.''

"How do they duel?" Jemal asked.

"Most often in single combat with steel blades of varying form. It is up to the principals and their seconds, however. The more ostentatious have been known to duel from cruisers in space.''

"What are their favorite amusements?" Rama asked. She was sitting cross-legged on a settee and exuding a lilac scent of contentment tinged with anticipation. Her every mood was signaled by a different odor.

"Anything and everything," Soong said. "Their only limitations are individual taste and certain fluctuations of fashion. There are seasons for various amusements as well. Predictably, the most prestigious sports are those that cost the most— yacht racing, both sail and space, big-game hunting, that sort of thing. A few people keep stables of prizefighters. There has been a revival of polo. The transport and upkeep of the animals is fabulously expensive.

"Besides these active diversions there are many less strenuous but equally prestigious activities. Some of the aristocrats collect art, for instance, or

act as patrons to artists of various sorts. Some
maintain entire orchestras. Others construct elabo-
rate formal gardens. Understated taste is little esteemed among them. The merchant class tries to
ape the aristocracy and does so with considerable
success.''

"Can you profile the ruling house for us?"
Haakon asked.

"The family name is, unsurprisingly, Mughal.
It is a name from far back in Earth history, and
almost certainly was not their legal possession.
Records are scarce and confused from the early
days of settlement of this system, but it appears
that the Mughals were officers, or perhaps owners,
of immigrant ships carrying Hindu peasants and
laborers. They were the first entrepreneurs of the
system and came to be the great landowners. The
family has been noted for eccentric members. The
former emperor was called Baibars of the Holy
Cloak, a very peculiar personage, by all accounts.
His son, Baibars the Lion, apparently has some
martial pretensions.''

"Are these real emperors, like the khakhans of
Bahadur?" Haakon asked him.

"Not really. They are actually spokesmen for a
board of family regents. A few have been deposed
peacefully when the board decided they were too
disgracefully inept. Apparently, Baibars of the Holy
Cloak narrowly escaped that fate. About half the
men of the dynasty, incidentally, are named
Baibars.''

"We need an approach and a cover story,"
Haakon said.

"They like prizefighting, don't they?" Rama said. "Let's tout Jemal as a champion. He can challenge all comers with powerblades. You can pose as his manager."

"Forget it!" Jemal protested. "I'm not going back in the ring again. It's a miracle I lived as long as I did. I got cut up so much the docs told me I might have reached the end of my regenerative potential. Find some other scheme."

"That's that, then," Haakon said. "Jem, your Arabic's pretty good, isn't it?"

"I was raised with it. Spoke almost nothing else until I was fourteen."

"Good. It won't hurt to make some contacts among the merchant class. People with money usually are worth knowing." He turned and looked at Rama critically. "You're pretty bizarre, Rama. Maybe we could build you into something that would attract the jaded Mughali."

She hissed and shed one of her more disagreeable scents of annoyance. "I am beautiful and clever and strong and fierce," she said. "That is the proper way to be, unlike you ugly, stupid, weak, and cowardly people. But I am not bizarre. Of course, these Mughali may find me desirable. That is only to be expected, since they pride themselves on possessing only the best. However, if their taste runs to the exotic, I daresay they have made the acquaintance of Felids before. I fear that some of my species-mates are not immune to the seductions of wealth."

Haakon turned his attention to Soong. "I don't suppose you could revive your old skills and hire

out as an assassin, could you? I never heard of a
society that didn't have plenty of work for such. If
you set your fee high enough, your services would
be available only to the top percentage of the
population.''

"I must decline," Soong said. "What I did in
wartime to serve my people is repugnant to me in
any other context. In a great war, a few judicious
eliminations saved many thousands of lives and
was a virtuous alternative to mass slaughter. I
always tried to be discriminating and to exercise a
certain elegance in the performance of my duties.
To do the same thing for pay would be unseemly.
I prefer to remain a gambler.

"In any case, the idea is impracticable on several grounds. The aristocracy here do not seem to
lack for personal courage, and prefer to fight their
enemies face-to-face. The most likely employers
of assassins would be the merchant caste and the
inevitable criminal element. These would not give
us an entree into the highest levels of society.
Finally, no employer who hires an assassin wishes
more than the minimal contact with his employee.
Usually, negotiations are carried on through a third
party.''

"No assassins, then," Haakon mused. "We need
something to attract attention. Something that'll
appeal to jaded and pleasure-loving people." He
eyed Mirabelle's supernaturally curvaceous form.
"No," he said, "you're spectacular, but people
that rich can afford good surgeons too." Mirabelle
made a gesture toward him that was not only

insulting, but punishable with fines and imprisonments on many worlds.

For the first time, Alexander spoke up. "You know, I really look up to you people and idolize you and hero-worship and all that, but sometimes I can't figure out why, because you're really dense." He deftly flicked a marble with the opposable big toe of his left foot. The taw, an especially splendid specimen of white alley, clicked solidly against an aggie that lay five meters away on the priceless carpet.

"Okay," Jemal said. "I'll bite if nobody else will. Tell us, apeling: What obvious point are we missing here?"

Alexander preened himself, happy as always to be the center of attention. He preened with caution, though, knowing that he had a tail-kicking coming if his friends were not suitably impressed with his reasoning and explication. "Look, these people are yacht-happy, right? They like to race 'em and live in 'em and party on 'em, right? Now, who has the damnedest yacht that ever spaced?"

"Out of the mouths of apes," Rama said. "We have it. *Eurynome.*"

"Right," Alexander said, now really getting into his role as brainstormer par excellence. "Now, let's go one step farther."

"Further," Mirabelle corrected.

"Whose show is this, anyway?" Alexander demanded.

"Go on, Alex," Haakon told him.

"Okay. Let's go one step further. This prince or

whatever he is, Baibars the Lion, figures himself
for a hot military type, right?''

"That is correct,'' Soong affirmed.

"Well,'' Alexander swelled triumphantly, "what's
not only the swankiest yacht in the universe, but
also one of the slickest light cruisers that ever
packed enough armament to wipe out a small
fleet?''

"*Eurynome* again,'' Haakon agreed. "Alex, I
knew you'd justify your rations someday, if we
just kept you around long enough.''

"Aw, hell, Boss,'' Alexander said, blushing
under the praise, "you could do it, too, if you was
a genius.''

"Soong, Mirabelle, Jemal,'' Haakon snapped,
"find us the biggest, most luxurious orbiting resort
these people have. This bucket's not designed to
land on a planet except under emergency conditions, and she'd bust a few seams then. If you can
find one on a natural satellite with a low enough
gravity, that's all right too. The specs are in the
computer. Get on it immediately.''

"What'll you be doing in the meantime?'' Jemal
asked.

"I'm going to have another drink.'' Haakon
took a frosted, salt-rimmed glass from a servobot's
tray. "That's the great thing about being captain.
You don't have to do anything, you just give
orders and accept responsibility.''

"Responsibility, my tail,'' Alexander said. "If
old Timur Khan gets mad at any of you, he kills
everybody.''

"What are you worrying about?'' Haakon said.

"You're the only one here who doesn't have one of those little bombs in his skull."

"Big comfort," Alexander answered. "What do you think's going to happen to me when all your skulls explode and we're in deep space?"

"Nobody twisted your arm to get you to sign on," Jemal said. "Just give us the word, and we'll set you ashore on the first planetfall we reach."

"Naw," Alexander said, "I'll stick around. You people are kind of habit-forming. Risky as it is, I just gotta see what happens next."

"See it you will, then," Haakon said. He looked at Jemal, Soong, and Mirabelle. "What are you three standing around for? I need information. Get to it!"

The customs man smoothed his white tunic and made sure that his turban was in order. Beside his desk stretched a transparent wall a hundred meters long. It displayed a spectacular starscape which never failed to awe visitors. Nearer the station were several ships drifting at space anchor. The latest arrival was the most fabulous ship he had ever seen, and he was used to genuinely stunning craft of the kind owned by the very wealthy. It actually appeared to be lacquered from nose to tail. The inspectors who had gone ahead and boarded had sent back reports of its luxury that were scarcely to be believed.

He saw the owner of the new ship approaching down the long, bare room designed to intimidate new arrivals. Neither the owner nor his entourage seemed the least intimidated. The man in front wore hose of fine material, with a tight doublet and long, trailing sleeves. The hose displayed legs perhaps a bit too muscular to be fashionable. The man was probably an athlete. The face was refined but a bit battered. Possibly, he was one of those who had been involved in the revival of pugilism a few years back. The tight blond curls were in the latest style, and one not originating on the Mughal worlds. Behind him trailed the usual motley crew, a Han and a lovely woman who looked like a graduate of one of the mistress schools, another man who moved with the grace of a powerblade prizefighter, even a Singeur and a Felid.

Krishna Murthi flicked an imaginary speck of lint from his spotless white sleeve. When the man was at exactly the right distance, he put his hands together and bowed. "Welcome, honored sir! It has been many years since we have received a visitor of your distinction. It pains us that these trifling but necessary ceremonies must take place. Have you anything to declare, O sahib?"

"I don't believe so," Haakon said. He turned and looked at Soong. "Did we have anything to declare?"

"Nothing, my lord," the Han said.

Krishna Murthi caught the address instantly. "Ah, sir, of course these things are of trifling importance in our enlightened age, but if you could furnish proofs of entitlement, some things could be considerably simplified, from a bureaucratic standpoint."

Haakon turned and snapped his fingers. From inside his tunic, Soong produced several genuine parchments with dangling seals of wax and lead. "Letters-patent from the princes of Delius," the Han said. The customs officer took them.

"Ah. Delius. Yes, well, despite the late unpleasantness between our systems, my masters believe that matters of birth transcend those of mere politics."

"I should hope so," Haakon grumbled.

"If you would care to take your ease in our lounge for distinguished guests, I will be honored to take care of the tedious details of government personally."

The lounge opened off the customs hall and proved to be a terrace covered with a transparent bubble which displayed a fabulous view of the planet Mughal. It was one of the rare Earth-type worlds that had the perfect balance of land, water, and atmosphere, coupled with the proper distance from its primary, yearly orbit and daily rotation, which made for an ideal habitat for humanity. It was a near twin for Earth in all these qualities, and terraforming had been minimal. Like Earth, the viewer's first impression was of dazzling blueness overlaid with a cottony tracing of white cloud, beneath which could be seen stretches of green and brown land. Gaps in the cloud cover revealed stark stretches of dryland and desert, and the poles were covered with gleaming icecaps. Wars had been fought for planets as perfect as this. The Mughali had fought several to keep possession of theirs.

The terrace was laid out as an exotic garden, with trees and shrubs in which birds of brilliant plumage sang melodiously, and small, agreeable animals wandered about through winding pathways amid the plantings. Elegant servobots floated at a convenient altitude, bearing trays of refreshments quietly and efficiently. From time to time, discreet voices announced the arrival or departure times of vessels and ground shuttles.

"Jeez," Alexander said admiringly, "this sure beats the hell out of the lower cities." He grabbed a frosted mug of beer from a passing tray. The others selected more elegant liquids, in keeping with their personae.

"What's our next move?" Rama asked. She searched a proffered tray of canapes for something featuring raw meat.

"We wait," Haakon said. "Before long somebody important is sure to take an interest in us."

A quiet female voice from nowhere announced: "The management of Kashmir Three are pleased to announce the arrival of the yacht *Eurynome* and her captain-owner, Haakon, ninth Viscount of Tring on Delius. Kashmir welcomes the viscount and his entourage and wishes them a happy sojourn amid the pleasures of our resort."

"They sure treat you right around here," Alexander said. "I wonder what they'd think if they knew how many worlds we'd been booted off of."

"They wouldn't be shocked," Haakon said, sipping white wine from a crystal goblet. "When you're wellborn, you don't have to be respectable. They'll read me as a raffish gentleman-adventurer. People just love that type, for some reason. Something should be happening soon, now."

It happened before they could finish their first

drinks or fully explore the lounge. A small, dark woman in a white sari approached them and bowed gracefully, palms together, her fingers almost touching her forehead. "My lord, I am the servant of Raj Jehan of the Jahnsi. My master requests the pleasure of your company while you await your clearances. His party await nearby."

"I would be most pleased and honored to join your master," Haakon said.

"If you will follow me, then." She turned and wound her way through the garden, her swaying walk as graceful as her bow had been. Each step displayed henna-stained soles. Haakon noted that Rama and Mirabelle had their heads together. It was an unusual circumstance, because ordinarily the two women were barely on speaking terms. Plotting against me, no doubt, he thought.

They came to a sunken area where several people lounged on cushions around low tables. They arose when Haakon and his entourage arrived, and Haakon watched them carefully. He knew that the last to rise would be the Raj. The man who stood last did so by only a fraction of a second, showing fine manners. "Viscount Haakon? You must be, I am sure. Welcome to Mughal. You honor us with your visit."

"The honor is mine," Haakon said, taking the outstretched hand and studying the man. He had half expected a bloated, bearded, bejeweled prince in a huge turban with plumes and pearls. Instead he saw a slender man of middle years with short, graying hair and a military-type mustache. He wore a severely plain coverall, black with some kind of armorial design embroidered on its breast. It was the kind of dress Haakon might expect from a sportsman or a retired military man. He was willing to bet that the Raj was both, or at least pretending to be. He introduced his crewmates and was in turn introduced to the Raj's party, none of whom seemed to bear exalted titles but who appeared to be active sorts of an adventurous bent.

At Raj Jehan's gesture, they seated themselves. "So you are of a Delian family?" Jehan said. "Since you are the ninth to hold your title, I take it that you are of the old line?"

"I am," Haakon said. The man was obviously feeling him out, clarifying his social standing. "I have not been on Delius for many years, though." It was a graceful way of admitting he was in exile.

"You have not made your peace with Bahadur, then?"

"I fear not. Some upstart is probably holding the family lands now. I have only my ship and my followers now. In a way it's a good trade. Unlike my lands, I hold my ship in fief to no man."

"Spoken like a true gentleman. Perhaps you'll have your estate back someday as well. The Bahadurans are savages, to be sure. I never supported the alliance with them. We fought on their side in the last war, but you need have no anxiety on that account. We do not recognize the titles bestowed by them in the conquered territories. We still value lineage. Here, you shall always receive the honor due your station."

"That is good to know. I—" He felt a nudge in

his ribs. Rama was trying to attract his attention. "Yes?"

"Please pardon us for interrupting," Rama said. "May we ask the Raj a question?"

"Please, my dear," Jehan said, "I am at your service."

"My friend and I," Mirabelle chimed in, "were just discussing the garment your servant was wearing. It's lovely. I hope it isn't worn only by the serving class."

"The sari? By no means, it is one of the classic designs, unchanged over the centuries. It is worn here by all classes. Servants and civil functionaries always wear white, that is the only distinction. Please allow me to send my family dressmaker to your yacht or your quarters here. Her talents are formidable. She will design saris to suit you ladies to absolute perfection."

"My lord," Rama said, lowering her eyes, "you are too kind." Haakon stared at her. Rama being coy and flirtatious? This was something new. Usually, when she wanted to attract a man's attention, she just hit him in the face with a blast of high-powered pheromone. Mirabelle, of course, had the skills of a trained courtesan. But subtlety from Rama? It boggled the mind.

"Not at all," Jehan protested. "It shall give me the greatest joy to gratify you in any way. I trust you will all be my guests at my estate in the Jahnsi sometime soon."

"It will give me great pleasure," said Haakon, to whom the invitation had been addressed. "I hope as well that you will join us for some modest entertainment aboard my yacht."

"Wonderful. Next to good land, I love ships more than anything. Yours is called *Eurynome*, is it not? Of what class is she?"

"Actually," Haakon said, with a vague wave of the hand, "she fits into no standard class. You'd have to see her. Perhaps later we could go down to the dock and view her in the ports."

"No need," Jehan said. He gestured and a 'bot floated near. He punched a combination in its side. "Jussuf bin Ali?" he said.

"Yes, Lord?" said a voice from the 'bot.

"Please be so good as to rotate the station so we may view the yacht *Eurynome* from the VIP lounge."

"Hearkening and obedience," said the voice. In the bubble, the planet seemed to set. The starscape swept by and a large segment of the bubble opaqued to prevent the viewers from being blinded by the glare of the primary. A parking area came into view, lighters, shuttles, and yachts drifting by at varying distances. A splendid racing craft came into view.

"That is my yacht, *Koh-I-Noor*," Jehan said proudly.

"A lovely craft," Haakon said. Then *Eurynome* rose into view. Fortuitously, she was parked less than a hundred meters from the station, her sleek lines and lacquered surface gleaming like a jewel. "That's *Eurynome*."

"My God!" said one of the men in Raj Jehan's party. "That's a private yacht?"

Jehan was silent for a moment. "I've never seen anything so magnificent. You are the most fortunate of men, to have such a ship."

"She is my pride and joy. Would you and your party honor me by coming aboard tomorrow? I love to show her off."

"Military action could not keep me away. May I invite some friends? This will be the event of the season, and I'll get all the credit for discovering you."

"Please, invite as many as you like. I have facilities for entertaining fairly large parties, and I can think of no better introduction to the most interesting people of Mughal."

"Your pardon, Lord," said a swarthy, bearded man, "but I notice that controller lines have been attached to your ship. Is she undergoing emergency repairs to the guidance system?" Obviously, the man knew his way around ships. Haakon remembered his being introduced as Jehan's pilot.

"Not at all. The authorities were a little alarmed at the armament she carries and insisted that those overrides be attached while she's in orbit here."

"Yes, that is Admiralty policy," Jehan said. "What does she carry, explorer-scout armament?"

"No, she was built on a light cruiser frame and carries a full complement of arms."

"This is amazing," Jehan said. "I've never heard of such a craft."

"She is unique," Haakon agreed.

"There were rumors," the Raj said delicately, "toward the end of the last war, I believe it was, of one or more ships somewhat resembling this one, being built for some members of the Bahadur royalty. Is it possible that this is one such?"

"When one has the opportunity to possess such

a ship, one does not inquire too closely into its history. I certainly did not."

"Nor would I," Jehan agreed.

They returned to *Eurynome* after a brief tour of the resort station for a council meeting. "What we need is intelligence, fast," Haakon said. "So we'd better spread out for a while. Rama, Mirabelle, I know you two are itching to get back out there among the filthy rich, so go be decorative and ask a lot of questions."

"Do you want me to hit the computers here?" Mirabelle asked.

Haakon considered it. "No, you probably wouldn't find anything worthwhile. Save your talents until we reach some critical location. Just keep your ears open. Soong, you circulate among the sporting crowd. I don't know many gamblers who don't talk too much when they're nervous. See what you can pick up." The Han nodded wordlessly.

"What about me and Jemal, boss?" Alexander asked. "I bet there's lots of attractive ladies out there looking for handsome and personable escorts like us." He grinned encouragingly.

"I'm afraid they'll have to nurse their loneliness for a while longer," Haakon said. "You two are really better at alley-crawling than rubbing elbows with the glittering crowd. I'd hate to waste your talents. I want you to catch a shuttle down to a major port and test the atmosphere. Don't stick just to spacer's dives, go out among the native population. I want to know what we're getting into. See if they're rebellious or pretty well content with their lot, that kind of thing. It won't hurt to establish some contacts with the local rough crowd. You never know when some emergency might come up and we might need to go underground.''

"Why always us?" Jemal said, scowling.

"Because you're the best," Haakon said. "Rand, you going to stick with the ship?''

"Might as well," said the engineer with a metallic shrug. "Places like this, people always take me for a 'bot and tell me to bring them drinks. It'll be a few years before places like this hold much appeal for me anyway.''

"So be it, then," Haakon said. "As for me, it's my duty to show myself for the benefit of my adoring public.'' He leaned back and stretched his massive arms, ignoring the obscene gestures he was receiving from his shipmates. "*Noblesse oblige,* you know.''

FOUR

The port city was smaller than they had expected, but the local almanac confirmed that it was the largest city on the planet. Jemal sniffed the air. It smelled clean, and he could see no obvious facilities for atmosphere purification. Apparently whatever local industries there were did not involve much chemical waste.

"What a dump," Alexander said, surveying the vast slum surrounding the port. They stood outside the port-authority building, where they had undergone a customs search which had apparently been aimed at keeping the more dangerous weapons out of the city. They had been given a recorded lecture from a police 'bot admonishing them to keep their noses clean and stay out of trouble. It had also given them the addresses of a few establishments guaranteed to be pleasant and noninfectious.

"You ever see a port town that wasn't a dump

this near the docks?'' Jemal asked. He was dressed in typical spacer's on-the-town garb, a combination of functional good sense and garish bad taste. His powerblade was in a leg-sheath on the green-spangled right leg of his trousers. The weapon search had ignored it. Apparently, city dwellers could carve one another up as much as they liked.

"Yeah, but where do the rich people live?'' Alexander scanned the cityscape for mansions, penthouses, luxury hotels or floating villas. All the taller buildings had a commercial or institutional look.

"At a guess, I'd say that the rich live on country estates and congregate in luxury resorts. They'll leave the cities to the destitute."

"Sounds kinda dull," Alexander complained. He wore his usual shorts and vest and was unarmed. He was a great believer in the run-and-hide theory of survival. "Wonder what passes for public transportation around here?" His handlike feet were fine for climbing but he hated to walk.

They asked a few questions in the all but universal spacer's patois and received directions. Jemal didn't want to reveal his fluent Arabic just yet. Beneath the port building they found a speed-chair station where they fed their credit chips to a 'bot. Two ancient, cracked, dingy bucket-chairs came floating unsteadily up to them and they sat down, causing the chairs to rock and wobble. "Keep your hands or other appendages inside," droned the 'bot. "The management and the city accept no responsibility for loss of bodily members due to carelessness."

"I thought everyone had stopped using these things a hundred years ago," Jemal said as the chairs lurched toward one of the many narrow tunnels opening off the station.

"Maybe they're for nostalgia," Alexander said. "You know, like those rickshaws we took on—" The rest of his words were jerked from his mouth as the chairs shot into the tunnel at terrifying speed. They swayed alarmingly, occasionally knocking into the tunnel walls and spinning like tops. A few minutes later they emerged at their destination: a chair station identical to the one they had left. It seemed to have the same collection of derelicts and human refuse idling about. Jemal and Alexander climbed from their chairs looking decidedly green. Other travelers, more accustomed to the eccentric mode of travel, seemed to be none the worse for the journey.

"Well, I guess it's cheap, at least," Jemal said, waiting for his stomach to settle.

"Yeah," Alexander said. "I knew there had to be something good about it." He looked around at the dismal station. Beggars with the traditional baksheesh bowl sat leaning against the white ceramic wall. Many were blind, others displayed the stumps of amputated limbs. "Jeez! You ever seen so many crips? Why don't they get fixed instead of sitting around begging?"

"Too poor, most likely," Jemal said.

"I thought this was supposed to be a rich system."

"Some people are rich," Jemal agreed. "Maybe they don't want to be repaired."

"Why would anybody want to stay like that?" Alexander asked.

Jemal shrugged. "Religious reasons, maybe. Anyway, we were sent down here to find out things like that, not just to speculate on them. Come on, let's get out of this hole."

They climbed a stair into daylight. The street teemed with a dense throng of people who seemed to be doing little but who kept in continual motion doing it. They seemed to be homogeneous at first, but as one became accustomed to the sight, individual aspects emerged. The majority of men wore white trousers and smocks, women wore saris. Most men wore loosely-wound turbans. Different colors of turban, differing beard styles, seemed to denote distinct social or religious groups. Face-paint in various colors and markings had some significance. Most were barefoot or wore sandals. While Hindus constituted a majority, many other types were represented; Sikhs with beards and swords, Buddhist monks with saffron robes and begging bowls, New Prophecy devotees in blue kilts and scarlet berets, and a host of others.

There were spacers in fairly large numbers, wearing ship or Line uniform or on-the-town clothes, people of other worlds and cultures on some obscure business, even a few non-humans. There were some locals who seemed to fit none of the expected categories. There were the usual juvenile gangs, some of them very oddly dressed. Police were Sikhs, equipped with power prods instead of the traditional swords, and walking in teams of four.

"I've been in some backward places before," Jemal said, "but this is something out of another century." He could hear the strains of dozens of differing styles of music drifting from doorways and windows, and the air here was full of spicy smells. Vendors towed anti-grav sleds behind them, crying their wares.

"That don't look good," Alexander said, nodding toward one of the police teams that stalked by, eyes moving warily. "Them's tough-looking boys. They don't travel in fours like that unless they got to."

Jemal nodded agreement. "Come on," he said, "let's go poke around and see what we can find out."

They strolled into the depths of the city. The day was getting hot and awnings were unrolling automatically, transforming the sunlight into colorful stripes and patterns on the sides of the closely-placed buildings. "No air or temp control," Alexander noted. "This place is downright primitive."

Much of the local commerce seemed to be semi-official at best, and a great deal was plainly black market, which the ubiquitous police teams studiously ignored. Alexander and Jemal wandered from shop to stall to vendor's mat, pretending to be pricing items for sale. In actuality, they were testing the air, looking for signs of discontent, despair, rebelliousness, or what have you. As expected, their job was not easy. Confronted by outsiders, the locals adopted an air of geniality, willing to talk but always steering the conversation back to commerce. By late afternoon they had worked their way the length of several streets and bazaars, and had gotten nowhere.

They made a fueling stop in an awning-roofed alley, the back end of which was occupied by charcoal braziers filling the air with fragrant smoke and smells of grilling meat. It was one of the establishments catering to the non-vegetarian crowd.

Alexander shoveled in a mouthful of something curried and quickly washed it down with cold beer. "Jeez," he said, when his respiration was working again, "if this is what their major port's like, it kinda makes you wonder what it's like out in the sticks."

"I was thinking the same thing myself," Jemal said. He deftly rolled a mixture of meat and vegetables in a ball of rice and popped it into his mouth, immediately wiping his fingers on a napkin. "I hate eating like this," he muttered. "Haven't done it since I left home."

"How come?" Alexander asked around a mouthful of flat, tough bread.

"In cultures like this you don't use utensils and you eat only with the right hand. I hate to get my knife hand greasy."

Alexander looked up sharply. "You think you're gonna be needing it anytime soon?"

"You never can tell," Jemal said. "There's been some people watching us."

Alexander looked around quickly. "You mean we got a tail?"

Jemal grinned. "Half of us."

"No kidding," Alexander said with a disgusted glare. "Now quit jerking me around. This is serious. How can you tell we been attracting unwanted attention? There's ten jillion people around here.''

''It's some of those kids in the funny leather clothes,'' Jemal said. ''There's been a bunch of them trailing us for the last hour or so.''

''Probably looking for a handout, like about half the damn population around here,'' Alexander said, shifting uneasily on his seat. ''I never seen so many bowls before. This place looks like soup heaven.''

''Not this bunch.'' He signaled a waiter and the man came to their table, wiping his hands on his apron.

He was a Sikh in beard and turban and he wore a small, ceremonial dagger in deference to his religion's requirement that adult males be armed. ''You wish something else, sirs?'' he asked.

Jemal pointed with his chin toward a group of young people who lounged on the steps of a small temple across a little square. The temple was devoted to a monkey-god who bore a striking resemblance to Alexander.

''Those are the Mongrels,'' the waiter said, looking at the loungers with contempt. ''Degenerates of mixed blood. No caste like the Hindus, no Book like the Sikh or Muslim. They are worthless. Very dangerous, sir. Have nothing to do with them. They are criminals.''

''Sounds like our kind of people,'' Alexander commented when the waiter had left. ''Wonder how come they're interested in us?''

''I don't know,'' Jemal said, finishing the last of his food. ''But maybe now we'll find something out. They aren't pretty, but I'm getting kind of tired of shopkeepers and beggars."

They paid their bill and walked nonchalantly out into the square. The light was beginning to fade, and signs began to flicker on; garish, flat-image plates set above doorways, advertising goods or entertainment. The streets were clearing a little, but the music was getting louder. Jemal picked a street at random and they walked into it. Unobtrusively, the kids in the odd leather clothes got off the temple steps and followed. Other pedestrians gave them a wide berth.

"Let's give them time to catch up," Jemal said, stopping at an open stall and watching with great interest as an artisan chased intricate designs into a brass tray. The small gang of Mongrels stopped about ten paces away, now not bothering to mask their interest.

"Where'd all those cops go?" Alexander muttered.

"Home, where it's safe," Jemal said. "It's getting dark, after all. Hell, I'm getting tired of waiting around for them to do something. What do you say we ask them?"

"Suits me," Alexander said doubtfully. They approached the lounging Mongrels, who looked distinctly surprised at their action.

"I realize," Jemal began, "that we're astoundingly handsome specimens, exciting admiration wherever we go, and that you're only human, but is all this attention really justified?" His right hand did not quite touch the powerblade in its leg-sheath. The Mongrels wore knives openly, apparently of the plain steel variety. Some had short clubs thonged to their complicated belts as well.

One stepped forward, a thumb hooked into one of the many harness rings that held his outfit together. He wore bizarre face-paint, either for ritual or vanity. "Sweetly, now, spacers. No unpleasantness, for true. We just been told to keep the eye on you. Some important people want a word with, is all."

"Any reason why we should want to speak with these important people?" Jemal asked.

"For them to say," the tough answered. "Like I say, no unpleasantness. But, you want unpleasant, we can supply." The boy spoke a form of spacer patois debased into street dialect.

"I'm the one you want to talk to." The voice came from a darkened doorway to one side, and Jemal turned to face it, pivoting on the balls of his feet, upper body maintaining the same relation with hips, not letting the larger group escape his peripheral vision.

The man who stepped from the doorway was older than the others, perhaps thirty standard, his long, shaggy hair going a little gray already. He was big and lithe, with sharp, heavy features in a mahogany face. He grinned, showing big, white teeth. "Powerblade man, eh?" He turned to the others. "Jojo, you lucky he don't want unpleasant. This one carve you and your friends like dogmeat. The untouchables have to sweep you up in the morning." His big left hand rested on a hip, not far from the ornate grip of an old-fashioned powerblade.

The one called Jojo looked doubtful. "You say so, jefe."

The big man turned toward the two spacers. "You got questions, you talk to me."

"I got one," Alexander said.

"Say it, little Hanuman."

"How come you wear all that leather in this heat? You must be sweating like a pig in there."

The man laughed, not just chuckling but throwing his head back for a rich, full roar. Jemal noted the exposed throat and filed it away for future reference. He didn't think there would be trouble just yet. These people wanted something from them.

The man looked down at Alexander. "One suffers for fashion. You wouldn't want to mistake us for Hindus or Sikhs or the Mecca-merchants, now would you?" The street tinge was fading from his speech.

"You talk pretty good spacer," Jemal observed.

"And why not? We're all part spacer, though we've never been off-world." He waved a hand toward his companions, who glared at the two crewmen. "After all, spacers in port got to have their fun, and poor women got to feed their families, so accommodations are reached. The results you see around you."

Jemal and Alexander were thinking the same thing, though they did not voice it. Women spawning packs of unwanted brats? Just how primitive *was* this place? "What's the nature of your business with us?" Jemal asked.

"What are you drinking?" the big man asked.

"You offering?" Jemal asked.

"Sure. Come along with me." They walked a short distance, turning down a few alleys, finally passing through a bead-curtained entrance into a small, cramped room stuffed with the members of several gangs. Some of them wore the odd leathers of the Mongrels, but there were a number of others. At the rear of the room was a bar with a live bartender. Not a single 'bot in sight. They took a table whose residents vacated their seats at the approach of the little band.

"I'm Steiner," the big man said as he sat, propping his booted feet against the wall and pushing his chair back on its two rear legs. Even in the relaxed sprawl, he looked dangerous and ready and his hand never got too far from his blade handle. "At least, that's what my mother told me my father's name was, and I took it. Everyone around here is named Krishna or Ali or something like that. I think the name has a good sound, don't you? Kind of hard-edged and emphatic."

"Fine name," Jemal said impatiently. "Now, you had something to talk to us about?"

"Sweetly, spacer, sweetly," Steiner said holding forth a palm in a placating manner. "Let's get you a drink first."

The delay made Jemal uneasy. If a hardcase like this was nervous it meant he was scared of them, which was damned unlikely, or else he had some truly delicate and dangerous subject to broach. That could be tricky. The wrong reaction to whatever Steiner was about to say might mean that he and Alex might not make it out of this place alive.

Their drinks arrived and Jemal took the frosted

beaker with his left hand. To hell with local custom.

Steiner caught the gesture and smiled faintly. A big beaker, sweating with condensation, was set in front of Steiner. Ostentatiously, he picked it up with his right hand, the knife hand. "To your good health, sir."

With a smile of grudging admiration, Jemal raised his own beaker. "To yours." They set the beakers down to be refilled, and Jemal leaned slightly forward to hear what Steiner had to say. The preliminary sparring and chest-thumping were out of the way and now they could get down to business.

"You boyos just down today from orbit, right?" Steiner opened.

"That's right," Jemal answered.

"We—that's to say, me and my associates, we're looking for spacers who maybe got a little cargo space to spare and no close ties with our beloved but not always agreeable authorities."

Smuggling. Jemal was disappointed. He had been hoping for something less banal. "Look, Steiner," he began, "we've been on-planet for most of the day. We've seen maybe a thousand spacers wandering around just in this little quarter of the city. Why did you settle on us?"

Steiner snorted with contempt. "Spacers? Insystem merch' spacers and Navy, maybe, that's all. We don't see many deep-space people around here." He leaned forward a little, difficult as that was in his position. "Mostly, we don't get people off of big, flashy yachts like your *Eurynome*."

Alexander jerked slightly, about to express his

surprise, but Jemal grabbed his tail under the table and gave it a twist.

"*Eurynome*?" Jemal said. "She's just a typical tub, nothing special. Not much cargo space either." This last, at least, was true.

Steiner grinned. "Give us a break, boyo. You think I don't know all about your ship? We had images and readouts before you got off the ship. She's got Teslas more advanced than any ever seen in this sector. She's fitted up like a raj's palace inside too. And we don't need a lot of cargo space."

"That's enough," Jemal said. "I don't want to hear any more. Thanks for the drink." He got up and headed for the door with Alexander close behind, but the Mongrels stood before them, blocking the exit.

"Why in such a rush, spacers?" Steiner asked. The bar was suddenly very quiet, although everybody else was ostentatiously paying no attention to the doings of the Mongrels and their guests.

"I'm not interested, Steiner," Jemal said. "Nobody's been aboard our ship so far except for government people. If you know so much about *Eurynome*, you got it from someone who works for the authorities. I want nothing to do with it."

Steiner grinned. "So we got friends who work in high places. Is that so unusual?"

"Not a bit. But I never knew anybody to play a double game like that who wouldn't sell you out the minute it looked like the wind was blowing the wrong way. You think I'm going to chance my freedom and my ship and my shipmates on a proposition like that?"

Steiner looked uncomfortable. "All right, you got cause to be cautious. But you haven't heard the proposition yet."

"It can't be that good."

"You think not? You know what the Gilgamesh Treatment is?"

"Sure," Jemal replied, "it's the treatment that keeps people from aging, if they can afford it. Galen has a monopoly on it, and they save it for the big rich."

"You know what makes it work?" Steiner queried.

"Are you kidding me? If I knew the answer to that one I'd be richer than the Khakhan. It's the most closely guarded trade secret in existence. Now, why are you asking all this?"

"Be patient," Steiner said, hands out placatingly. "I got to explain a few things first. The Gilgamesh business is a whole series of treatments, very complex. But, it all hinges on one thing: a drug called Chelaya."

"Never heard of it," Jemal said.

"I have," Alexander said, unexpectedly.

"Where?" Jemal asked him.

"Remember how I told you I stowed away in that ship to get away from home?"

"Sure," Jemal said. "Hold Six. How could I forget?"

Alexander's sojourn in Hold Six had been the golden period of his life before joining *Eurynome*. Before being caught, he had made a mint out of selling luxury items to ground crews.

"Well," Alexander said, "I don't remember

what planet it was, but I saw some rousters loading a crate into Hold Two. The crate was maybe as big as this table, and it was going into that hold all by itself. You could've put a small cruiser into that hold. I heard 'em say that it was this Chelaya stuff, and they put that hold under maximum seal. It had to be plenty valuable. I couldn't get into that hold no matter how hard I tried.''

"That's the stuff, all right," Steiner said. "Chelaya. When they need it on Galen, they've been known to charter a whole ship just to pick up a flask of it you could stick in your pocket. It just wouldn't do to let the richest and most powerful people of half a galaxy get old, now would it?''

"So what's this got to do with us?" Jemal demanded.

"Chelaya is made right here, on Mughal. The whole damned economy is geared to it. Everyone who isn't in one of the support or food-producing trades works to make the stuff.''

"Can't it be turned out artificially?" Jemal asked.

"No. It's peculiar stuff. It takes hand labor. Lots of it. That's why most of the population here lives out in the villages and on the plantations. I guess you noticed a lot of beggars around?''

"They're hard to miss," Jemal confirmed. "We were wondering about that.''

"Villagers and plantation workers who tried to run," Steiner said. "You see, it's not pleasant work they do out there. Run once, and you're flogged. Run twice, they take off a leg. Persist, and they take off the other leg. Steal from the master, and you lose a hand. Complain, and they cut out your tongue. Look back like you're resentful, and they take your eyes.''

"So all these crips are like an example, huh?" Alexander said, looking a little queasy.

"A real object lesson, boyo," Steiner said. "Well taken, too, you better believe."

"And you and your friends have some of this Chelaya, and you want to move it, right?" Jemal asked.

"Something like that," Steiner responded.

Jemal thought awhile. "I'll have to talk it over with my captain."

"You mean His Lordship Whatever-it-is? Why bother? You can handle this yourself."

"No deal. You talk to my boss and settle this. You want to set up a meet, or you want to forget the whole thing?"

"I don't know," Steiner said. "You, I can deal with. I'm not used to talking to no blue-blooded aristocrat."

"Oh, you'll hit it off real good with him," Alexander chimed in. "He's not what you'd call your typical blue blood."

"All right. Tomorrow night?"

"I think he's laying on a party for tomorrow. The night after. Where? I don't think I could find this place again."

"Someone'll meet you at the port. Tell your boss not to dress too upper-class, if you take my meaning. Might attract some unwanted attention."

"Don't worry," Jemal told him. "He likes to go slumming with us lowlife types. Now, if you don't mind, we'd better be heading back to the ship."

*   *   *

Their guide left them at the entrance to the port area.

"How come you're going along with them?" Alexander demanded. "You know the captain's not gonna touch a setup like this, no matter how valuable this Chelaya stuff is."

"I had a number of reasons," Jemal said reasonably. "Foremost among which was, I wanted to get out of that place alive."

"Yeah, I guess that was a consideration," Alexander agreed.

"Also, I think Hack's going to want to hear about this. I don't think Steiner was giving us the whole story by a wide margin. And, if his gang's got contacts within the government, that's another avenue for accomplishing our mission for Timur Khan."

"That fortune-telling gadget. You really believe in that?"

"Not for a minute," Jemal said. "But I know we sure as hell have to look into it. Timur Khan has a short way with people who lie down on the job."

"Amen," Alexander said.

FIVE

Haakon was inspecting *Eurynome* prior to the arrival of his guests when Alexander and Jemal arrived. "Boss, we gotta talk," Alexander announced.

"We may have run into something important down there," Jemal confirmed.

"It'll have to wait," Haakon said. "Jem, go get out of those sleazy togs and put on something elegant. Alex—" He looked the monkey-boy over critically. "God, I don't know what could ever make you look presentable. At least take a bath or something."

"Right, Boss." Alexander scampered off on all fours.

"Kind of taking this socializing business seriously aren't you, Hack?"

"I damn well have to. We've got a job to accomplish, or have you forgotten? We'll suck up to these aristos first, then we'll see what's to be accomplished among the great unwashed.''

"Whatever you say. Just keep this in mind: They may be pretty and have refined manners, but I'm finding out that it's all built on something pretty ugly.''

"Did you ever hear of a ruling oligarchy that didn't grow out of some kind of cesspool?'' Haakon asked, eyebrows arched mock-quizzically.

" 'Every great fortune began with a crime,' '' said Soong as he emerged through the portal separating *Eurynome*'s lounge from the companionway leading to the crew's quarters.

"Is that from one of those Chinese poets you're always quoting?'' Jemal asked.

"Balzac. Not Chinese, I fear. He was perceptive for a barbarian, though.'' He turned to Haakon. "Any rules in dealing with these grand people? They are fond of gaming, we know that.''

"You mean how much do you dare take them for?'' Haakon asked.

"It would be good to know ahead of time if there are boundaries we dare not approach.''

"As far as I can see, there's nothing to be gained by soft-pedaling these people. They prize style, so let's give it to them. Just don't bet the ship,'' Haakon warned.

"Suppose he should lose?'' Jemal protested.

"Such lack of faith,'' Soong chided.

"Where are the ladies?'' Jemal asked. All about the lounge and other areas of the ship, servobots were readying the craft for the kind of lavish hospitality *Eurynome* had been designed for.

"They won't show until all the big shots have arrived," Haakon said. "You know they'll want to make an entrance. They were closeted half the day with that designer Raj Jehan sent over."

"I can't believe this," Jemal said. "Mirabelle, sure, but Rama? Did the Raj's designer survive the experience?"

"She charmed her," Soong said. "Rama has been very much on her best behavior since we arrived here. I suspect that she loves Timur Khan's pain transmitter as little as the rest of us, and wishes to accomplish our mission with efficiency and dispatch."

"Well, I'm glad somebody's showing a spirit of businesslike forthrightness," Haakon grumbled.

"You're getting old, Hack," Jemal told him.

"Aren't we all?" Haakon said.

The first guests to arrive were greeted at the lock by Alexander. Somewhere, the monkey-boy had located a tuxedo and had it cut down to his singular dimensions. The trousers had been transformed into shorts with an aperture for his tail provided. The coat, dickey, and studs looked so incongruous that they seemed almost natural. He looked over the arrivals critically. Being first to arrive, they were of course somewhat lower ranking on the guest list. The most prestigious guests would arrive fashionably late.

A small 'bot floated before the party and announced in a quiet voice: "His Radiance the Dey of Algecar and his party, Lady Govinda, Raj Malik, the Rani of—" Alexander batted the 'bot aside and grinned up at the little group. He grinned especially at the Lady Govinda, a Junoesque woman who was almost as tall as Rama, putting her most outstanding attributes just above Alex's eye level.

"Welcome to *Eurynome*, folks," Alexander said. "Step right on in and loosen your belts, they really got a spread laid on in there. Plenty of guest rooms to pass out in too."

Lady Govinda looked down at him with an uncertain smile. "What a—a quaint creature. Are you a pet?"

"Shit no, lady. I run this ship. I just let Haakon run the navigation and the parties." He grinned up admiringly. "Jeez! Did anybody ever tell you what big—"

"Sirs, ladies," Jemal said, clamping a hand over Alexander's mouth, "how good of you to come. I'm sorry to arrive so tardily. It looks as if our mascot has decided to be majordomo for the evening." He patted Alexander on the head and smiled down at him murderously.

"I think he's charming," Lady Govinda said, running a hand through Alexander's rust-colored mop of hair. His hand slid slyly behind her, out of sight of the others, and her eyes started suddenly as Jemal was greeting the new arrivals individually.

Out of his on-the-town rig and dressed in elegant finery, Jemal could pass muster in the most fashionable company. His one-piece suit and half-cape were of mood-sensitive fabric whose colors rippled in changing patterns according to the wearer's passing emotions. It had, of course, been rigged always to display a joyful serenity rather than what Jemal might really be feeling.

He conducted them to the main lounge, where Haakon and Soong stood ready to receive them. True to Haakon's prediction, Mirabelle and Rama had not yet made an appearance. More guests arrived every few minutes, all of them exclaiming at the luxurious appointments and refined elegance of the ship. It was not that they were unused to such things, but that they had never expected to encounter such richness in a space vessel. Most royal yachts looked shabby by comparison. Small servobots bustled about serving drinks and the mild drugs deemed appropriate to a genteel reception for the high-living set.

Finally, Raj Jehan arrived with his entourage. "You are more than fortunate, Captain," he said to Haakon. "I never dreamed of such a vessel." He leaned down to study a small bronze sculpture that stood on a low pedestal. "That's Old Earth work, is it not?"

"Somebody named Rodin," Haakon confirmed. "Nineteenth or twentieth century, I don't recall which. Would you care to see the bridge? I know a ship fancier like you will be interested.

"I would love to," Jehan said. Haakon guided them into the control section, which was lighted only by subdued glowplates. One of Jehan's retinue ran a hand over a fretted control panel, admiring its green-black sheen.

"*Shakudo*," the admirer exclaimed. "I've only seen that finish on bronze jewelry and sword furniture."

The control room was functional, almost Spartan in comparison with the rest of the ship, but all its materials were the finest, finished with the most exquisite workmanship. Where other ships used various artificial substances for durability and easy molding capabilities, *Eurynome*'s bridge was fitted with exotic woods, precious metals and minerals, pure crystals, and rare organic substances.

Raj Jehan reached out and lightly touched a control rod. It was perfectly plain and functional, just a knob on a stick, but the stick was of pattern-welded steel acid-etched into beautiful patterns and subtle colors. The plain, spherical knob was of red sea-ivory from Hovahness. "It is perfect," Raj Jehan said at last. "I think, if I had such a ship, I would abandon my estates and live on it for the rest of my life."

"In essence, that's what we've done," Haakon told him as they returned to the lounge.

"Captain Haakon, I must inform you that there will be another guest arriving soon," Jehan said.

"The more the merrier. A friend of yours?"

"A kinsman. I took the liberty of contacting our glorious monarch, Baibars the Lion. His enthusiasm for yachting matches my own, and he is itching to see *Eurynome*. I hope you don't mind."

Haakon hid his exultation by scanning the now-crowded room with concern. He had never hoped to reach the top of Mughal society so quickly. "The monarch? We didn't set up to receive royalty. Will his entourage be large?"

"Have no fear," Raj Jehan said, laying a calming hand on Haakon's shoulder. He almost started at the coiled lump of muscle he felt beneath the extravagant cloth. "We have a protocol for such things. The Lion is a sportsman, and likes to socialize. He would enjoy little of these diversions if he had to endure ritual honors everywhere he went. He will wear no regalia and he will be accompanied only by a single bodyguard. We will address him as Raj Baibars, and he will be introduced as the Raj of Purna. It is one of his minor titles, in prestige about equal to my own. Of course, he will receive the courtesies due to royalty traveling semi-incognito."

Haakon knew the drill. The pretense would be maintained that Baibars was just another nobleman, but he would receive slightly lower bows and everyone else would hasten to stand as soon as he showed an inclination to do so. Nobody would interrupt when he was speaking, and everyone would laugh loudly at his jokes. It took the deft touch of a courtier to keep this behavior from appearing to be toadying.

Haakon circulated among the other guests. "Have you heard?" he asked Jemal as the two came briefly together.

"About our guest? Yes, I heard. I can't believe such luck. We're going to have to do something about Alexander, though. Lock him up or something."

"What's he been doing?" Haakon asked.

"He just goosed the Rani of Khajuraho."

"She take offense?"

"No," Jemal said, "that's just it. She winked at him. It's her husband I'm worrying about."

"Leave him," Haakon said. "They think he's some kind of court jester."

At that moment, Mirabelle and Rama appeared at the top of the short stairway leading down into the lounge from the crew quarters. The two appeared at the same instant, almost in lockstep. There was a hush and a faint, flowery scent flooded the room. Rama was broadcasting one of her more subtle scents, laced with an almost subliminal aphrodisiac.

Mirabelle was stunning in a gold sari which set her skin, hair, and eyes off to perfection, but Rama was, as always, overpowering. Her sari was striped silver and black to match her hair, and artfully draped to leave her midriff bare while covering the supernumerary nipples on her flanks. She descended the stair as if she smelled blood out there on the floor somewhere. She stalked toward Haakon, and Jehan rejoined him.

"She is a stunning, ah, acquisition," Jehan said.

"Nobody acquires Rama," Haakon told him. "She's wished on you, or she decides to move in, but you don't acquire her."

The crowd parted to let Rama pass, and Mirabelle, knowing herself outpointed, followed at a more sedate pace.

"Haakon," Rama said, "I see you've been keeping our guest to yourself. Now run off and let him enjoy my company. How do you like my ship, you ravishing prince?"

"I, ah, well . . ." Raj Jehan was edging back from her, intimidated by her size and sheer presence.

Alexander came scampering across the lounge,

pinching a sari-clad buttock as he passed. "Boss, we got another guest. Two of them, and wait'll you see—"

"Raj Baibars?" Haakon asked.

"Yeah, that's what he said, but—"

"Baibars?" Rama said, whirling away from Jehan and shutting off her pheromone spray as easily as someone hitting a switch. "We are to receive royalty?" She glared at Haakon. "Why was I not told, you tactless lout? If I had known he was coming to see me, I would have delayed my entrance!" She radiated a decidedly unpleasant scent.

"Don't mind her," Mirabelle told Jehan. "She just has a strong nose for the alpha male."

Jehan smiled at her. After Rama's fearsome presence, Mirabelle's extravagant beauty seemed positively wholesome.

"My own taste, I fear, runs to the less exotic." He linked an arm through hers and they turned to face the portal through which a small 'bot was leading their latest guest. All fell silent and bowed as it announced: "The Raj of Purna."

The man who followed the 'bot was of medium height, in appearance a man in his mid-thirties. His hair was dark, his face showed a slight chubbiness, his eyes a bored restlessness. His clothing was severely plain, with no jewelry. Jehan stepped forward to make introductions while Baibars studied the lavish interior with interest.

"Most pleased to meet you, Captain Haakon," Baibars said, "and very good of you to invite me to your fabulous yacht." Haakon forebore to mention that he had issued no such invitation. Baibars turned slightly. "And this is my bodyguard. I only require one, as you will see. Numa, come here."

Rama was about to launch herself at Baibars, but she froze, an odd, wailing sound coming from deep within her larynx. The man who appeared in the portal was over two meters high. The armorcloth singlet he wore fitted his rocklike physique like a coat of oil. A tawny mane of coarse hair covered his shoulders and upper back and came to a peak above his yellow, slit-pupiled eyes.

"See, boss? That's what I was trying to tell you," Alex hissed.

"Oh, my God," Haakon said in a whispering groan. "A *male* Felid!" He was genuinely appalled for the first time in years.

"I see that Numa and this lady have something in common," Baibars said. Mirabelle came up to him and touched him on the shoulder.

"Raj Baibars, I think you should move from between them. I don't know what's going to happen next, but it might not be pleasant."

Gradually, the whole crowd backed away, leaving the cat couple plenty of room for their greeting. The two stood there, seemingly oblivious of their surroundings and neighbors, making strange sounds and exuding stranger scents.

"Do you think they'll fight?" Lady Govinda asked. "I do hope so. It would just make the occasion."

"It would be interesting," Baibars said, taking a drink from the tray of a passing 'bot. "Which would you place your bet on, Captain Haakon?"

Haakon pondered for a moment. "It's hard to

figure. I've never seen anything remotely human that's a match for Rama. But then, she's the only Felid I've ever known. The males may be stronger. He's even bigger than she is.''

Soong came up to them. ''Make no bets, Captain. There are too many unknown factors here. Besides, he is wearing armorcloth. It can stop even her claws.''

''Hey, why are you all talking like they was gonna kill one another?'' Alexander demanded.

Rama's tiger-striped hair was fanned out over her shoulders now, and all twenty claws were out. Her screeching whine had almost reached supersonic level. Her lips writhed back from her teeth and she exuded a smell that was devastating. Numa's back was arched forward, his claws were likewise out, and a rumble from somewhere in his massive chest was reaching for the subsonic. His ears flattened back against his head.

''It's just this feeling we've got,'' Jemal answered Alexander.

The ship's ventilation kicked into overdrive in an effort to clear the smell from the room. The room buzzed with anticipation and bets were already being laid.

Mirabelle came to Haakon's side. ''Maybe you should put a stop to this, chief.''

He leaned close and whispered so that only she could hear. ''A reprieve from Timur Khan's death sentence couldn't induce me to step between those two.''

She nodded. ''I guess you're right.''

Rama's whine turned into a bloodcurdling squall,

and she launched herself at Numa, hands and feet in blurring motion. The two formed a knot of confused limbs, and then sprang apart. They were both bloodied, and Rama's beautiful sari was now in shreds all over the room. She made an incredibly adroit dive, rolled between Numa's legs, and came up behind him with legs around his waist and one arm wrapped around his neck. As he tried fruitlessly to claw her loose, her free hand darted down his neckline and found the control behind his belt buckle. Even as he flung her over his back and across the room, his armorcloth suit was ribboning away from his body, to compact itself into a square packet topped by the buckle.

"Ooh," a lady said to her husband. "Don't you wish you were built like that?"

"Muscles aren't everything," the man sniffed.

"Who's looking at his muscles?" she retorted.

"Do you think it's part of their mating ritual?" Raj Jehan hazarded.

"My God!" Baibars said. "What must their wars be like?"

The two came together again, sending a servobot spinning across the room and spraying the guests with colorful liquors. Rama sank teeth and claws in briefly, then was knocked across the room in the wake of the 'bot, fetching up against the wall with a loud thunk.

"What if they kill each other?" Alexander said concernedly.

"No problem," Baibars answered. "Dueling is legal here."

Numa sought to follow up his advantage with a

flying leap at Rama, only to be met with a clawed foot in the belly. He managed to avoid evisceration with an inhumanly quick sidewise twist, but the wind went out of him in a whoosh. Rama squalled triumphantly and leaped for his throat, but caught a massive fist on her chin instead. She staggered back a few paces and sat ungracefully at the base of the pedestal that held the Rodin sculpture.

"Think it's going to be a tie?" Jemal said.

"Seventy thousand dinars on Numa!" said a guest.

"Taken," Raj Jehan answered. A tiny 'bot near Jehan registered the bet.

Numa lurched to his feet and stalked over to Rama, who had curled herself into a ball on the floor. Even though he moved with caution, she managed to catch him by surprise. A leg swept out and caught his ankle, toppling him to the ground as Rama jerked the pedestal out from under the sculpture, sending it bouncing along the floor. She raised the pedestal—a rod of light metal a meter long and thick as a leg—above her head, bringing it down in the center of Numa's mane. He slumped back, clearly out for the count.

"Damn!" Haakon said. "I should've bet on her."

Ignoring all present, Rama bent and grasped Numa by an arm and a thigh. She hoisted the hundred-and-forty-or-so kilos of male Felid over her shoulder without visible effort and began to carry him to her quarters, exuding an aphrodisiac pheromone so powerful that some of the male guests took tranquilizers. The women paled at what was to them a dreadful stench. The few herms present looked puzzled.

"Do you suppose he'll ever come out of there alive?" Baibars injected into the silence as the Felids left the room.

"I don't know," Haakon said, "but I strongly recommend that we not pry too closely."

"I agree," Baibars said. "Captain, let me congratulate you. I haven't been here ten minutes and already this has been the most memorable and enjoyable party I've attended this season. And I haven't really seen the ship yet."

"Then by all means let me give you the tour," Haakon said. Baibars now appeared animated and excited, in contrast to his lackadaisical look upon entry. Another coup. Haakon felt he was making real progress, despite a certain uneasiness about what might be going on in Rama's quarters. Not that he was jealous, of course, but still . . .

Haakon, Jehan, and Baibars sat in Haakon's private quarters, where Haakon was introducing the other two to a drink he had acquired a taste for on Aztlan. It consisted of tequila, lime juice, and orange liqueur served over ice in a glass whose rim was rubbed with salt.

"Very robust," Baibars pronounced. "Best new drink I've come across in years."

Below, in the lounge, Soong and Jemal were keeping the guests entertained with various wager-oriented pastimes and making a handsome profit at it. Some of the guests were already past any such amusements, and space had been allotted for them to recover. Inevitably, speculation was rife on the ultimate outcome of the epic combat of earlier that evening. Some held that the two combatants were even now ascending heights of Felid bliss in exotic sexual rapport, others that Rama was gnawing the last scraps of flesh from Numa's short ribs and was about to start on the long.

"I envy you, Captain," Baibars said. He was beginning to get a little tight. "You have this magnificent ship, and no worries."

"I am aware of my blessings, Raj," Haakon said, thinking of the tiny bomb implanted in his skull.

"It's not easy being an emperor," Baibars informed him. "Protocol, ritual, family tradition"—he waved a hand airily, taking another salty swig—"it all mounts up on a man. Sometimes I wish I could just chuck it all and go roistering and adventuring about the stars like you."

"It has its compensations," Haakon said.

The old gentleman-adventurer image still worked like a charm. Even the emperor of an unbelievably rich system envied him. If the bastard only knew. The guests below were staying largely because they could not leave until Baibars left. Then Jehan could leave, then the rest. It was the protocol of centuries.

Haakon wondered if Baibars would really consider the life of an adventurer adequate compensation for losing that kind of deference. Probably not. The man was just not experienced enough in the ways of the real world to realize what life meant when lived on the terms of Haakon and his crew.

"It must be a good life," Baibars said, unaware that he had been tried in Haakon's balance and found wanting. "Not like what I've lived with. My father was a man so strange that many of my most learned advisers must spend much of their time just trying to figure out what he was up to during his reign. Most of the family thought he was a crackpot, but the old bastard was sharp. He had some things up his sleeve that would amaze you."

"O Monument of Wisdom," Jehan said gently, "I am sure that the good captain would love to hear about your polo stable, the wonder of five systems. Could you not tell us of their recent victories?"

"Your father, Baibars of the Holy Cloak, was a wonder to us," Haakon said, taking his cue from Baibars. "Even though I was on the other side during the late unpleasantness, the wiles and stratagems of your learned father set us all in terror." Actually, he had never heard the name before being handed this assignment, but young Baibars seemed anxious to hear vindication of his father's peculiar beliefs.

"You see, Jehan," Baibars said. "Father was right."

"Blessed be his memory," Jehan intoned.

"You probably do not know this, Haakon," Baibars said, "but the Bahadurans treated my father as a contemptible dotard."

"Highness—" Jehan began with some heat, but Baibars silenced him with a glare.

"The fools of Bahadur we held in the greatest distaste," Haakon said. "They are mighty warriors but they have no art, no refinement, and no imagination. You people of Mughal, on the other hand, were not only brave and skillful, but gallant and chivalrous as well."

Baibars beamed. There is no flattery as gratifying as the unqualified praise of an enemy. "It was likewise with us. The exigencies of interstellar diplomacy required that we side with Bahadur, but we always regretted having to go to war with Delius and many of the other allied powers."

"How many mere humans stand against the awesome cycles of history?" Haakon said, thinking: You weak-spined bastards, you didn't have the courage to face up to the Bahadurans and tell them to fuck off the way we did.

"It is true, so true," Baibars said. Jehan looked at him patiently.

"Among us," Haakon expanded, "rumors of the plots and devices of your father would spread from no apparent source and sweep the fleet, spreading panic." He paused and took a drink, waiting to be prodded.

"And of what fashion were these rumors?" prodded Baibars.

"Oh, they were many and varied. Those of us belonging to the officer class discounted them as mere fantasy, but they spread like wildfire among the common soldiery. There was the one that said Baibars had devised a way to transmit living matter, so that soldiers could be materialized among our ranks without warning, for instance."

"We heard that one," Jehan said, "only among our soldiers, it was Han who supposedly developed the device."

"It must be so among all soldiers since wars began," Haakon said. "There was the cloak of invisibility that Baibars was supposed to have developed, as well."

Baibars laughed. "I think that one goes far back into early Earth mythology."

"And there was the device that was supposed to be able to predict the future. What use to fight an enemy, they said, who could predict the outcome of every battle?"

"The idle speculations of uneducated soldiers are the bane of a commander," Jehan said sourly. Baibars seemed to be on the verge of saying something, but Jehan silenced him with a glance. The Emperor took a small pill from his belt and swallowed it, clearing his head of the drink he had taken aboard.

"Raj Baibars," Jehan said. "I urge you to return with my party this evening. Numa is indisposed and you must not travel about without a bodyguard. Besides myself, several of my company are skilled in the violent arts."

"Thank you, Raj Jehan," Baibars said. "I accept your offer. Captain Haakon, I thank you for a most memorable and enjoyable evening. I shall treasure it."

"The honor was mine," Haakon said, taking

his hand. "Sorry about your bodyguard. I'll send him back to you, if he survives."

Baibars waved a hand airily. "You needn't bother. These Felids are not easy to live with, but I suppose you know that."

"Indeed I do," Haakon said with fervent sincerity.

"Well, if the fellow would rather stay with your Rama, let him. I'll never find a single guard as good, but ten mediocre humans are easier to put up with than one Felid."

"They are a recalcitrant breed, to be sure," Haakon said.

As Baibars was being seen off at the ship's dock, he turned to Haakon and said: "You are a fascinating man, Captain Haakon, with a fascinating ship and crew. Promise me you will visit me at the royal palace in Newest Delhi. There is much there that you will find to be of interest."

"I look forward to it with greatest eagerness, Raj," Haakon said with perfect truth.

Jehan turned to him after Baibars was safely aboard.

"Captain Haakon. You must have realized that our Lord was a bit incapacitated by drink tonight. He tends to talk a bit too much when in such a state."

"I thought the Raj spoke quite lucidly and interestingly," Haakon said.

"There were times when he spoke of things that might sound foolish coming from a man with all his wits about him," Jehan persisted gently.

"Well," Haakon said, uncharacteristically self-effacing, "there was all that stuff about his father. I'm sure you understand, though. When one is speaking with royalty, it does no harm to throw in a bit of flattery now and then. Men always like to hear a father praised, especially by an enemy." Haakon smiled at Jehan, one courtier to another.

"Just so," Jehan said, seemingly reassured.

SIX

While the crew had breakfast the next morning, Jemal filled Haakon in on his doings at the port.

"Chelaya, huh?" Haakon said. "I've heard something about it. I knew the economy here had to be built on something pretty rare and valuable. There's damn sure no industry down there."

"What makes it so horrendous to raise?" Mirabelle asked. "Or to mine, or whatever?"

"I don't know," Jemal said. "Steiner mentioned plantations, so I guess it's some kind of agricultural product. Maybe it just takes intensive hand-labor to gather, like saffron."

"That kind of work don't make people want to run so bad they'd risk losing a leg," Alexander said.

"No use speculating about it," Haakon said. "We don't have sufficient data, and in any case, Timur Khan didn't send us here to find out about

Chelaya. He sent us to find this future-reading device. We've already got a line on that."

"From what you have told us," Soong interjected, "the Raj Jehan does not want anyone bringing up that subject with Baibars."

"At least that means there's something to the story," Haakon said. "What we've got to do is get Baibars alone, away from Jehan."

"Not always easy to do with a monarch," Soong pointed out.

"We've got our entree, though. We're so close now that I'm wondering if it's worthwhile to pursue a street-level course of action."

"I think we should keep at it," Jemal said. "You said yourself that it wouldn't hurt to have a back door available. Besides, you can't count on the favor of princes. It's one of the oldest rules of human behavior. I recommend we follow up on the Mongrel business."

"All right. I can't see that it could do any harm, if we're discreet." He looked up to see a new arrival standing in the portal of the dining area. "Well, look who's here. Pull up a stump, Numa. You look like you could use some sustenance."

The enormous Felid stepped into the room. He was wearing only a strip of some silken cloth around his waist, apparently scavenged from Rama's sizable collection of luxurious fabrics. Every square centimeter of his body seemed to be covered with scratches. His eyes were bleary and bloodshot, and sizable chunks of his beautiful mane had been torn out by the roots. He winced as he sat.

"Good to see you alive," Jemal said. "We were beginning to worry."

"Don't get your hopes up," Numa said. "It's not over yet."

"I'm going to summon a medical 'bot to patch up those wounds," Mirabelle told him. She next addressed the sensor plate on the table: "Breakfast for a Felid, and double the liquids." She turned back to Numa. "You look like you've sweated and bled yourself just about dry. Should we check on Rama? If she's in worse shape than you, she may need emergency treatment."

"She sent for some therapeutic aids when I left," Numa said. "Don't worry about her, she's getting ready for round two."

"I guess you and Rama really hit it off good, huh?" Alexander said brightly.

" 'Hit' is the operational word, all right." He winced as the medical 'bot floated around him, spraying him with disinfectant and anesthetic preparatory to stitching his worst slashes. The table served up a platter of meat chunks swimming in blood. He speared ten chunks on his claws and nibbled them off in sequence. The whiskers flanking his nose were broken and drooping. He was a sad travesty of the gorgeous creature who had entered the lounge.

"That was quite a show you two put on last night," Haakon said. "Is that business genetically programmed, or did you just not like each other's looks?"

"When a male and a female Felid meet, we're kind of taken over by our genes and glands. It's our reproductive setup. Females can't ovulate unless you beat the hell out of them. Males need a life-or-death shot of adrenaline to raise our sperm count up to reproductive level. Then the pheromones we put out really put an edge on us. The fighting's designed to improve the species too. If I hadn't put up a strong enough fight, she'd have killed me.''

"I don't think your boss is too happy with you," Jemal said.

"Tough. I'm tired of protecting his royal butt anyway. He only hired me because he likes to be called 'the Lion' and he thought I'd make a good pet.''

"Little did he know, eh?" Haakon said.

"How often do you encounter a female Felid?" Soong asked.

"She's the first I've seen since my mother kicked me out," Numa answered.

"You mean you're a virgin?" Mirabelle said incredulously.

He looked at her with disgust. "I said she's the first *Felid* female I've run across. The other kind have everything except the claws and the pheromones, and to tell you the truth, I prefer it that way. I don't think I could survive too many encounters with the likes of her.'' He finished the meat and washed it down with several liters of water and fruit juices spiked with vitamin supplements.

"So the old lady booted you out, huh?" Alexander said. "Family life just didn't work out?"

"Mama Felids are like that," Numa said.

"They're ferociously protective until you're about half grown, then they start attacking you every time you show up. Eventually, you just have to take off."

"Sounds rough," Alexander said.

Numa just shrugged. He finished the liquids, stood up and stretched his sore muscles. "Well, time to get back to work. See you." He staggered sorely out of the room.

"Think we've got another crewman?" Jemal said.

"I sure hope not," Haakon said. "One Felid is too many already."

"I don't think you need to worry," Mirabelle said. "Felids are solitary by nature. Eventually, she'll kick him out just as his mother did."

"When do you want to head down?" Jemal asked.

"No need to leave for a few hours," Haakon said. "From your description, the port doesn't sound too enticing. If we arrive a little late to suit them, that's all right. Let them wait. We don't want to look eager."

"Who goes?" Jemal asked.

"Just you and I. The rest of you wander about the resort. Be visible. Spend liberally. Timur Khan's picking up the tab, after all. We've made a good start and I want to follow it up. You know the kind of people to cultivate. Keep in with the big rich, but dumb playboys will get us nowhere. Be on the lookout for high government officials, especially those involved in military, intelligence, and scientific areas. There should be plenty of them vacationing and living it up here.''

"Hot damn," Alexander said, clapping his feet together. "I'm gonna have a ball!"

"Try to restrain yourself, Al," Haakon told him. "After last night I ought to confine you to ship. Hell, I ought to lock you up."

"The ladies love me, boss," Alexander said. "I got the kind of style and class they all go for."

"That's a terrible thing to say about women," Mirabelle protested.

"I can't help it if I'm irresistible," Alexander said.

"Clamp a lid on it," Haakon ordered.

The Mongrel who met them outside the port was a girl of no more than fifteen, wearing an outfit of tight green leather that exposed a lot of bare skin. Hollow cheeks and short-cut hair reduced her face to little more than a pair of enormous brown eyes.

"Steiner tells me to meet you," she said. She was not one of those Jemal had seen earlier. She looked over Haakon, who had resumed his hairless and battered appearance, his steel bracelets, vest, spacer's pants and boots. She turned back to Jemal. "You the off-world raj?"

"I'm the captain of *Eurynome*," Haakon told her.

"*You're* a raj?" she said, laughing incredulously.

"That's right," Haakon said. "What do you want? I should cut myself to show you my blue blood?"

"I just want to see Steiner's face, is all. I'm Lorah. Come on."

She led them into the warren of streets surrounding the port buildings. The two did not attract a glance from the milling throngs. Spacers were a common sight so near the port and there was nothing to distinguish these two. The grubby Mongrel girl attracted a few scowls, which she ignored.

The girl led them through alleyways and past markets selling black-market goods openly. Abruptly, she turned down a set of steps which led into the unlighted bowels of the city. Before they had descended ten steps, Haakon grabbed her shoulder and halted her.

"Where are we going?" he demanded.

"They going to meet you down here," she said. "This is an old city transport system, not used a hundred, maybe two hundred years. Used to be magnetic trains run down here. We get all over the city in these tubes."

"Don't get too far ahead," Haakon ordered. "I see you making a fast move, I'll know you're setting us up. You can't move fast enough to keep me from breaking your neck."

"Easy, spacer. We going to a lot of trouble to roll two men, don't you think? Easier ways to do that."

"I'm chronically cautious," Haakon told her. "Call it a psych problem if you like, but stick close and move slow."

They reached the bottom of the steps and went down a long corridor. Glow panels flickered halfheartedly to life as they approached and winked out as they passed. It was better than no lighting at all, but just barely. It seemed to go on forever. They turned down several side corridors, finally stopping at a door set almost invisibly into the curving wall. Lorah knocked in a distinct pattern and the door opened.

Haakon put a hand in the middle of Lorah's back and shoved her through, kicking the door hard as he whirled to the left, powerblade in hand. The door slammed against the wall hard enough to stun anyone hiding behind it. Jemal jumped through and past him, turning to guard Haakon's back. Four astonished faces turned to them.

Steiner was first to break the silence. "You boyos don't take no chances, do you?"

"Wouldn't be alive to talk to you if we did," Haakon said.

"You didn't have to do that," Lorah said, rubbing a knee that had cracked into a table on her precipitate entry.

"I know that now," Haakon said. "I didn't before."

"So you're His Lordship, eh?" Steiner said. "You don't look much like a raj."

"You don't look much like the boss of this outfit," Haakon said. "Introduce me to him."

"What makes you think I don't run things, spacer?" Steiner asked, his grin fading a fraction.

"Because you're a punk. You look like one, you talk like one, and you act like one. If somebody's running a big operation around here, it's not you."

Steiner stood, his chair going over backward. "I don't take that kind of stuff. You got a blade. Use it." His own left hand was poised less than an inch from the handle of his own.

"Oh, sit down, Steiner," said one of the others in the room. They sat near the walls, their features unclear in the dim light of the flickering overhead glow-plate. Haakon turned to face them while Jemal kept an eye on Steiner. In the dimness, Jemal's powerblade glowed faintly.

"You're pretty hard on poor Steiner," said the one who had spoken. The voice sounded cultivated.

"Overaged juvenile delinquents don't inspire my confidence. I hope you're more impressive, but it's kind of hard to tell in this light."

"You aren't exactly an advertisement for the quiet, lawful life yourself, Captain," one of the others pointed out. Haakon noted that these two, at least, seemed to be free to talk without waiting for permission.

"Do you have names?" Haakon asked.

"Naturally," said the first speaker. "But we're not here to socialize. We're here to do business. For that we can bypass introductions. How would you like to be very rich, Captain?"

"I'm already rich."

"I said *very* rich. Rich beyond your dreams."

"I've heard that one before."

"Then why did you come here," asked another, "if you thought we had nothing to offer?"

"I didn't say I didn't want anything from you. I'm just telling you I'm not interested in money."

They mulled that for a few moments. "What are you interested in, Captain?"

"First let's hear your proposition. Then I'll decide whether I should make mine."

The others hesitated, then the one who had not yet spoken said: "Captain, you arrived here with documents proving you to be a nobleman and former officer of Delius, formerly at war with us and our allies."

"What of it?"

"We thought you might be interested in an opportunity to deal a crippling blow to the Mughal system, and thereby to Bahadur."

"By pulling a little smuggling run for you? I don't think this Chelaya stuff is all that valuable."

"It's more than a little smuggling run, Captain," said the first speaker. "What we propose to do will break the Mughal monopoly on Chelaya. The economy, social structure, and strategic importance of the system depend on the Chelaya monopoly. Without it . . ." the speaker spread his hands, "we are just a collection of beautiful worlds with pleasant climates, best suited for agriculture."

"And why are you so interested in bringing about this transformation?"

"Aren't you being a little inquisitive, Captain?" said one.

"Nothing piques my curiosity like putting my life and my ship on the line for perfect strangers. There's nothing more dangerous than amateurs."

"We're pretty experienced, Captain," the first speaker said. "The fact we're still alive and whole says a lot. You'd know that if you'd lived here long."

"I'd know a lot if I'd lived here for long. Experienced at what?"

"At subversion," the first speaker said. "Insurrection, plotting, and organizing and setting up cells."

"So you're rebels. Now we're getting somewhere. What is it? Agrarian reform, that sort of thing?"

"Quit trying to bait us, Captain," the first speaker said. "You know it's far more serious than that. We're seeking to overthrow a centuries-old power structure based on virtual slavery."

"I've seen some of that power structure," Haakon told them. "They live pretty well. I don't think they'll take kindly to having the status quo overturned."

"That's precisely why we're meeting in these tunnels," the second speaker said. "Now, are you ready to discuss this seriously?"

"Just a minute," the first speaker interrupted. "The Captain has said he's not interested in money payment. Let's hear his price before we commit ourselves further."

Haakon said nothing for several seconds. What he had to say next could put him in the power of these men. Instinct told him, though, that they were serious people: tight-lipped revolutionaries who meant business. They might kill him and Jemal before they left this room, but it was unlikely that they would betray them to the authorities. "Are any of you familiar with a government project begun during the last war and code-named Precious Pearl?''

They sat silently for a moment, almost visibly gathering their wits. Then the first speaker said: "So you're not a smuggler, and you're not a visiting playboy. You're a spy."

"A little of all three. Are you going to answer my question?"

"Yes, we are aware of it."

"Now we're making real progress," Haakon said. "I need to know all about it."

"When I say we are aware of Precious Pearl," the first speaker said, "I do not mean to imply that we have detailed knowledge of it, nor that we can acquire such knowledge and deliver it to you. We can make no promises."

"Well, I'm damn sure not making any promises, either. It's time for you to talk a little now."

"Who are you spying for, skinhead?" said Steiner, breaking his sullen silence.

"Does it matter?"

"It does," the first speaker said. "Who is it?"

"The Cingulum," Haakon said, lying through his teeth.

That silenced them for a moment. The famed refuge for governments and peoples broken by the wars had gained quasimythical status.

"The Cingulum is a legend," the first speaker said.

"Far from it. We've pulled missions for them before." This part was true.

"Could you put us in contact with the Cingulum?" asked the second speaker.

"Maybe. If I decide you're worth it. They don't care for people to be handing out their coordinates to anybody who asks."

"That's understandable. I think we're all ready to talk," the first speaker said. "Will you put that powerblade away, now?"

Haakon and Jemal switched their weapons off and put them away. They pulled up chairs and sat. Steiner tossed Haakon a bottle, and he took a drink before passing it to Jemal. "Maybe you're not such a punk after all, Steiner," he said.

"Don't forget it, boyo." Steiner grinned.

"My name is Yussuf," the first speaker said. He indicated the second speaker. "This is Krishna, and this," he indicated the laconic third man, "is Gopal." Haakon doubted that these were their real names, but any name was better than none at all. "We three are part of the guiding committee of the Free Mughal Party. The Party has been operating underground for more than a hundred years, gaining power very slowly. The recent wars brought about a great increase in activity, for obvious reasons. Nobody likes to fight a costly war, allied with objectionable people, for the purpose of keeping an obscenely rich and privileged aristocracy in power."

"The way I heard it," Jemal put in, "it wasn't that kind of war for you. Mughal's contribution was mainly in warships officered and largely manned by members of the landowning-military caste. There was no conscription of mass peasant armies for beam fodder."

"But it had to be paid for, boyo," Steiner said.

The Mongrel sat in a reversed chair, chin resting on crossed forearms. "And you know the local rajahs don't want to suffer a drop in their high living just because there's a war on. Quotas were doubled. So were work hours. And it was man-killing work to begin with."

"Tell me about that," Haakon said.

"Chelaya," Yussuf said, "is extracted from the reproductive system of a plant native to Mughal, the Chelis. The Chelis is a semicarnivorous plant that is dangerous even to be near, much less to work with every day. It has poisonous thorns, it ejects deadly corrosive gas, and its limbs can crush an unwary human in an instant."

"Why aren't the workers given protective clothing?" Haakon asked. "The things you've described are easy to deal with."

"The problem," Yussuf went on, "is the value of the plant itself. You see, the Chelis has developed all these protective systems because it is really a rather delicate organism. The interior of the plant, past the defensive systems, must be handled very gently or the plant dies. It is deadly allergic to any off-world minerals of the sort that go into protective clothing. Even too firm a touch can kill it with a combination of pressure and salt. The penalty for damaging a plant is instant execution by an overseer."

"Can't protective clothing be developed from native materials?" Jemal asked.

"Probably," Yussuf said. "But that would render Chelaya production easier, less costly, therefore less profitable. Any such development has been discouraged.

"Each mature plant produces about ten grams of the Chelaya base per planet year. The year's harvest is then taken to processing stations where a bioengineered bacterium is injected into it. Within a few months, the whole mass has been processed. The pure Chelaya is skimmed from the top. The rest is dross."

"What's the ratio of the pure stuff to the dross?" Haakon asked.

"Twenty metric tons of base will yield approximately six grams of pure Chelaya," Gopal said.

"No wonder it's expensive," Haakon said. "How many die harvesting the stuff?"

"Official figures are not kept, of course," Yussuf said. "However, we keep a tally compiled from figures gathered by our various cells. Consistently, losses seem to run about five million per year planetwide."

"Not to seem hard-hearted or anything," Haakon said, "but I have a hard time working up much sympathy for people who put up with that kind of treatment without rebelling. If they're sheep by nature, why should I try to better their lot?"

"Come now, Captain," Yussuf said, "you know better than that. You're an educated man, you know your history. The population of this world is large, but the people live in isolated villages or on plantations. Education is severely restricted and few are literate. Even such primitive long-distance communication as radio and telephone are forbidden outside the cities. You know how effective that kind of control is in preventing rebellion. Without communication, there can be no organization. For all the average villager knows, his village is the whole world. He has never been more than ten kilometers from the hut where he was born. Unable to organize, the only alternative is a desperate attempt at flight, doomed to futility because the same system prevails over the whole planet. Even so, some try. You've seen the cripples.''

"All right," Haakon said. "But what's your place in all this? You aren't villagers. The way I read it, you're professional people, right? Academic, medical, administrative, that sort of thing?''

"Correct," Gopal said. "Except for Steiner and young Lorah here, we are all classic bourgeois. If you've read your history, you know that it is among this class that most real revolutions evolve, as opposed to mere rebellions and coups d'état. We are the ones with enough education to understand the situation, and unlike the aristocracy, our social conscience has not been stunted by an immovable stake in the status quo. We are not reactionary concerning change.''

"I've seen lots of revolutions," Haakon persisted. "Often as not, you socially-conscious people end up on top, and the situation is as bad as before, if not worse. At least a ruling aristocracy has certain traditions to keep it under control. I was part of one once myself, remember.''

"Assuredly," Yussuf said. "But the Delian aristocracy have for centuries been but one body within a parliamentary system of government, with their powers and privileges closely defined by a planetwide constitution. What we have on Mughal is a throwback to an earlier age. Just like Bahadur.

"Besides, the mission we wish to entrust you with will destroy the very basis of tyrannical power on Mughal. Even should we become as corrupted as you imply we might, there would be no foundation for such power."

Haakon still looked dubious. Jemal leaned forward and asked: "What's Bahadur's stake in this? I can't believe that Mughal's been in possession of anything this lucrative for so long without being a target for conquest."

"The production of the drug is a vast commercial operation," Yussuf said. "You know how the Bahadurans dislike taking over such an enterprise. They fear that it will be weakening to their warrior aristocracy. They much prefer to let subject peoples deal with such matters, and collect tribute. And that is what the Mughal system is, despite the talk of alliance. The lords of Mughal are mere subject princes, and the annual tribute to Bahadur is staggering: a full half of each year's production."

Haakon's eyes lit up at the figure. "So, you figure that a break in the Chelaya monopoly would be a real blow to Bahadur, eh?"

"A very severe blow, we think," Gopal said. "Wherever the Bahadur Empire spreads its tentacles, production falls off, industry and research stagnate. Medieval empires are not sympathetic to such things. Mughal is the one exception. The value of the Chelaya remains incalculable, as it must. What could reduce the value of a substance that prolongs life and youth?"

"Only a glut of it," Jemal answered.

"That is just what we intend to bring about," Yussuf said. "If not immediately, then within a span of years."

"How?" demanded Haakon.

"We have scientists who have been working for many, many years in underground laboratories. From spores and cuttings they have developed a strain of dwarf Chelis plants, hardier than the wild ones, relatively harmless, and with a higher yield of the Chelaya base. Many died getting those spores and cuttings into our hands. We need to smuggle several thousand cloned plants off-world, along with a culture of the refining bacteria and a soil sample. It's possible that, with a great deal of effort, a duplicate soil or hydroponic liquid could be developed that, under controlled conditions, would allow the production of relatively cheap Chelaya. It would not only break the Chelaya monopoly and significantly reduce Bahadur's income, but it would bring the Gilgamesh Treatment within the means of a far greater number of people."

"Pressure would have to be brought to bear on Galen for that last part," Haakon pointed out.

"The medics of Galen are amenable to pressure," Krishna said. "Especially the economic kind."

"But," Yussuf said, "we must do this soon. The authorities have suspected the existence of our project for years. They are getting closer to discovering our identities and the locations of our labs. We have to get the fruits of our research off-world soon, or many years and lives will have been wasted."

Haakon sat back and pondered for a few minutes. Jemal passed him the bottle and he took another swig. "All right," he said at last. "You have a deal, but I need to have this Precious Pearl thing. Whether it's a device or a set of computer figures or a mutant human, I have to have it. If it's in a computer, just get me the location. I have a technothief in my crew who'll have the figures out of it faster than you'd believe. Do that, and you've got yourself a ship."

"That concludes our business for now, then," Yussuf said. "We must return to our occupations, and I know you have other irons in the fire yourself. When we have some concrete information concerning Precious Pearl we shall be in contact with you. Steiner, guide them back to the port."

As they returned through the winding streets toward the port, Haakon turned to Steiner: "What's your stake in this?"

"I don't like the system, spacer."

"Why? You don't live in a village. You don't work on a plantation. I'll bet you've never seen one of those plants."

"That's right," Steiner admitted, "but us Mongrels is born with a curse on us. There's no place for us in their caste setup. That means no trades, no work except the kind untouchables do, and we won't accept that. The only reason there's a caste system at all is to keep people organized for the Chelaya production. I hear it's about died out everywhere else."

"And you think these people will change things? Make it better for you and the other Mongrels?"

Steiner shrugged. "I don't know. I hope so. I guess we'll always be trash to the pure-bloods here, but with a new government, maybe we can get off-world. I'd like to get into space." He looked up into the narrow strip of starry sky between the flanking tenements, then looked back at Haakon and grinned. "Besides, I just like to raise hell."

SEVEN

Soong watched with interest as two gentlemen settled an affair of honor with tulwars: relatively short, curved swords of antique design. Both were already bloodied from minor wounds, circling cautiously, then leaping close for a brief flurry of blocks and cuts before leaping back out of range again. He caught sight of Mirabelle strolling toward him. She had a short, well-dressed man in tow. She watched the duelists for a few moments.

"Will they fight to the death?" she asked.

"Unlikely," Soong said. "I've seen at least three possibly fatal blows pulled at the last second. I believe they are just trying to impress their friends."

"Most incorrect," said the man with Mirabelle. "Posturing like that, I mean. It's an insult to an ancient and honorable tradition. Duelists should be serious. Foolishness of this sort, it gives dueling a bad name.''

"A sad fate for a time-honored practice," Soong commented.

"Yes. Ought to be a reform movement, some kind of regulation to prevent this sort of degeneration.''

"Soong," Mirabelle said, "this is His Excellency Mir Jafar. His Excellency is currently on leave from his post as minister of defense intelligence.''

"An honor, sir," Soong said, bowing. "Kashmir Three seems to specialize in guests of distinction.''

"It's an exclusive place," Mir Jafar confirmed. "After all, why fly into space to rub elbows with the hoi polloi? One can do that in the cities. And the nouveau riche are such a bore.''

"Decidedly," Soong said.

"I've invited His Excellency to dine with us aboard *Eurynome* this evening," Mirabelle told him, smiling radiantly at the official and contriving to look much shorter than she was.

"How splendid! It shall be an honor for us all.''

"Oh, the honor's mine, I assure you." Mir Jafar leaned forward and said confidentially: "It's all over the resort who was on your guest list last night. Raj Jehan and the Lion himself, indeed! Do you think the cat-people will put on another performance?''

"Alas, they are rugged specimens, but I think that would be asking too much of them," Soong said.

"Pity. Ah, well, who else is likely to be there?''

"Only guests of the highest distinction, I assure you," Soong said.

"Wonderful. Well, sir, my dear, I shall arrive at the time appointed." He made a courtly bow over Mirabelle's hand and walked away. She favored him with her most fetching smile as he turned and waved.

"All right, so he's an insufferable snob," she said, without losing the fetching smile. "He's just the type we've been trying to find. Have you had any luck?"

"I met a director of a national psychological testing laboratory that specializes in government and military work. I enticed him into a game of Planet Siege at which I allowed him to win heavily. I asked for a chance to win my money back tonight after dinner at the ship's games tank. Of course, he was delighted to give me the chance."

"It's a start," she said.

Haakon punched the greeting plate on the door to Rama's quarters. "What do you want, beastly man?" she said after an interval.

"Just checking to see if you're still alive. Can I come in?"

The door slid open. "Come on in. You might as well see what a ghastly wreckage the beautiful Rama has become." As the door opened, Haakon was hit by a wave of smell that rendered human speech inadequate as a means of description. Hastily, he donned a respirator he had prudently brought along.

Rama's quarters were the most splendid on the

ship, the suite of rooms originally intended for the Prince-Admiral. Haakon had opted for the cruising master's rooms opening off the bridge, and the rest had drawn lots for this one. Rama had won the draw. Ordinarily, its beauty and good taste were astonishing, despite Rama's gaudy embellishments. Just now, it looked as if *Eurynome* had come out second best in a ship-to-ship action. The furnishings were toppled, torn up, broken, or otherwise savaged. Rama's paints and cosmetics were all over the floor, walls, and ceiling. Numa lay rolled up in a corner, partly covered by a carpet and some uprooted plants.

Rama sat amid the ruins of her lavish bed, licking a long gash that ran from elbow to wrist. Her eyes were blackened, she was covered with scratches and bruises, and her claws looked blunted from overuse. Her striped hair hung bedraggled. "You see?" she said, glaring at him. "You see what I've become? I'll never be beautiful again. I, who was so magnificent, reduced to this condition of plainness."

"Oh, knock it off," Haakon said, his voice a little muffled by the respirator. "I've seen you recover in a week from injuries that would kill most people. You'll be like new in a couple of days."

"Even so, a couple of days of unbeauty are unbearable for one such as I." She ran a hand through her mane and looked at herself in the self-viewing screen across the room. "I'll be at least three days in attaining my accustomed superbness.'' She looked back at him. ''Glands are terrible things.''

''How about this evening? We've lured some marks aboard and we have to pump them for information.''

''Oh, if I'm really needed, I suppose I could work some minor miracles and make myself presentable. Even in this condition I'm more striking than that insipid little technothief.''

''How'd the honeymoon work out? You manage to get impregnated?''

''Gah! I suppose I must be. What an awful thought. I'll grow bloated and distorted. Then I'll give birth to some mewling little beast and have to care for it no matter how much I hate it.''

''There's always abortion,'' he suggested helpfully.

''Unfortunately, we have a built-in psychological block against it, and against infanticide, too, worse luck!''

''It's hard to picture you as a mama. This is going to be fun.''

She pointed a taloned finger at the door. ''Get out! You are heartless. And take that lout with you.'' She pointed at Numa's huddled hulk.

''You brought him here. You carry him out.''

''I was about to kill him when you arrived. I still might.''

Sighing, Haakon crossed the room, grabbed Numa by the ankles, and began lugging him to the door. ''Hell of a job for a ship's master to be doing.'' Numa's arms dragged limply above his lolling head. ''You want me to toss him off the ship?''

"Yes. Put him out the airlock without a suit. No, I might need him later. Lock him up someplace. Maybe one of the maintenance lockers. I'll be ready by dinner. My curse on all glands and gene programmers. On you, too, you ugly person. Get out." But the door had already closed behind Haakon and his burden.

The planet was a white-and-blue ball, floating in nothingness against a neutral background. The green rods and spheres of Defense ships and orbital battle stations surrounded the orb. Closing in were the red rods of Offense attack ships.

"Range," Soong said softly.

"Accepted," said Mohammed Sheffi. The blue blips of neutron torpedoes left the Offense fleet, headed for the planetary surface and the battle stations. Immediately, the globe was enveloped in the delicate latticework of a laser net. Most of the torpedoes winked out like insects striking a sanitation screen. A few made it through the net to strike the planetary surface.

"That was a major power plant," said one of the spectators, reading the damage report on the monitor. "Your net is down by five percent."

"A trifle," said Mohammed Sheffi. "I'll pull his fangs now." He ran his fingers swiftly over the controls, and a mass of multiwarhead missiles and drones left the Defense fleet, closely followed by small, ship-launched battle stations firing close-range lasers. Offense replied with a blanket fire of small missiles. Many of the Defense weapons were destroyed but much of the fire was wasted on the drones, which were indistinguishable from the real missiles. Several Offense ships were destroyed or damaged. Offense began to pull back and the fleet assumed retreat formation.

"Withdrawal action to gravitational lee of principal moon," Soong said.

"Pursuit action on flotilla scale," Mohammed Sheffi said with satisfaction. "When shall we resume?"

"Eighty-seven ship-hours hence," Soong said. Images in the tank wavered and flashed, then coalesced with the Offense fleet near the moon, taking advantage of its nearby mass and gravitation to confuse and hamper Defense targeting.

"Hmm," Mohammed Sheffi said. "This is going to be interesting."

"A few fleet burners would come in handy, wouldn't they?" said one of the kibitzers.

"We agreed on twenty-second century weaponry," Soong said. "It's much better for this type of gaming."

"Who's winning?" Haakon asked. Once again, he was rigged in his finest.

"Too soon to predict," Soong said. "However, although I have Offense this game, I am currently on the defensive."

Mohammed Sheffi allowed himself a slight, complacent smile. "It has been a long time since anyone has given me such a masterful game." It cost nothing to be magnanimous in victory, and increased one's reputation as a gentleman. Sheffi set his frosted glass on the polished mahogany railing surrounding the tank and pondered his next move.

Haakon allowed himself a smile of his own. He knew that Soong had not been beaten at this game in many years, unless he allowed it. Whether Mughal aristocrat or petty street crook, a mark was a mark. If there was any information to be had from this mark concerning Precious Pearl, Soong would have it out of him. He went on to see how Mirabelle was doing.

He found her in one of the ship's viewing bubbles. This was a sunken pit lined with cushions which in *Eurynome*'s case were upholstered in hand-knotted carpets from Turkestan. The pit was faced with a crystal bubble so thin that it was almost a force-screen. It was as if the loungers were sprawled in the vacuum without life-support systems. She had chosen a bubble with a spectacular view of the incomparably beautiful planet below.

"Is all to your liking, Excellency?" Haakon called down into the bubble. Mir Jafar looked up, his turban slightly askew.

"Superlative hospitality, Captain. Seen nothing like it since I was last at the Lion's great hunting lodge in Rajnapur. And Lady Mirabelle is the most charming of hostesses."

Mirabelle looked up from her calculatedly casual sprawl amid the priceless cushions. "His Excellency has been telling me about his adventures in the intelligence service during the wars. He's had some thrilling experiences."

"And just the man to deal with them, I'm sure," Haakon contributed.

He wondered whether she was putting it on a little thick, but he trusted Mirabelle's judgment concerning men. If this dodo liked heavy flattery, that's what she would give him. It never ceased to amaze Haakon how much information men were willing to part with in order to impress Mirabelle. Truly astounding. Rama, on the other hand, could scare it out of them. Thinking of that, he went to look her up.

He found her seated cross-legged amid a circle of spellbound men and women in one of the silk-upholstered socializing rooms. She had solved the cosmetic problem by painting herself glossy black from hairline to toes. Her claws were resharpened and silver gilt. She exuded an exciting, enthralling scent which was both flowery and spicy. She was regaling her audience with bloodthirsty stories of her past, some of them true.

"With the bag of firegems still in my hand," she was saying, "I threw the door open. The pursuit was close behind me. I shut the door and locked it, turned, and what did I see? A Jemadar of the BT's, standing there gawking at me."

"Disconcerting, I would think," said one of her audience.

"More so for him than for me. The fool was so confident that he left his helmet off when they came after me. He went for his gun. I struck!" Faster than sight, before the man who had spoken could draw back, her hand flashed out, fingers spread and silvered talons out, their points just indenting the skin of his forehead, cheeks, and the underside of his chin. "I ripped his face off and continued on my way."

"The BT's are supposed to be the best-trained fighters in existence," protested a young woman in an unusual, brocaded sari.

"I've licked the blood of many BT's from my claws."

"Lady Rama," said a man with extravagant, graying whiskers, "your tales reveal a certain disdain for legality on your part."

"The little laws of little worlds do not apply to me," she said haughtily, adding: "Of course, I have the highest regard for the laws of Mughal, which are of a wisdom and justice unmatched anywhere."

"Have you studied the legal code of Mughal, Lady Rama?" asked the bewhiskered gentleman dubiously.

"No. But I am sure people of such refinement and beauty would never accept anything not the best."

Everything in good hands in that room, Haakon thought, wondering where Alexander had gotten to. He had last seen him walking hand-in-hand with a bejeweled lady of some raj's court, his tail wrapped around her waist. Maybe the little ape really did have something.

He heard the signal for a new arrival at the lock. A late guest? He tried to remember whether any of the invited personages had not shown yet, but they all seemed to be here. He turned his steps to investigate the arrival.

At the lock he readied himself to repel crashers. The lock irised open and the lady who stepped through stopped the words dead in his larynx. Her sari, something sheer that left a shoulder bare, was a startling midnight black, a black with tiny, almost subliminal silver highlights that gave it the depth of a starscape. Her skin was perfectly white, her face a delicate, heart-shaped perfection with eyes of the purest black Haakon had ever seen in a human being. In her exposed navel was set a spectacular black diamond. A tiny, matching black diamond was set above the flare of her left nostril. Palms together, she bowed above her fingertips. Her nails were lacquered black. "Captain Haakon?"

He gave his best, courtliest bow. It was a little rusty from disuse, but good enough to pass muster. "The same. I don't believe we have met, my lady. I surely would have remembered."

"I am Maya."

"No surname? No titles? Just Maya?"

"Just Maya."

"How refreshing. Lately, all of my guests have come equipped with more titles than a library. How does it come about that we are honored with your presence?"

"Purely because I wished to meet you and see your ship. Nobody invited me."

Haakon reached back into his past training and experience for the kind of devastating gallantry he knew was called for in a situation like this. "Lady, beauty such as yours serves as invitation and passport. Who but a fool would refuse you admittance?" By God, that was pretty good, he thought. I'll have to remember that one.

She gave the very slightest but most gracious inclination of her head. "You are too kind, Captain. Or do you prefer Lord Haakon? Or is a viscount a sir?"

"I prefer Haakon. Confiscated estates form a poor basis for a title. I won't resume it until the family lands are restored and Delius is free of Bahaduran domination."

A very faint smile played at the corners of her lips. Damned shapely lips, too, he thought.

"Come now. You weren't shy about making your status known when you arrived here, Captain."

"Well, there's no point in being fanatic about this humility business, is there?"

"None at all. Now, am I going to get to see the famous *Eurynome*?"

"By all means. If you will come with me." He led her into the main lounge.

Many heads turned to see her enter. He wondered if those were looks of recognition. A refreshment 'bot floated to her, and she made a low-voiced request. From its innards the 'bot produced a sphere of something that looked like thick, gray smoke. A thin tube extruded from the side of the sphere. She took a sip, and Haakon couldn't tell whether she was swallowing the stuff or inhaling it.

By now, the ship tour was becoming routine, but Haakon took a special delight in displaying his ship to Maya. She made little comment, neither gushing like most nor seeking mightily to remain unimpressed like others. Yet, she seemed to understand perfectly everything she was shown or told. Haakon was intrigued by her. They finished the tour on *Eurynome*'s upper deck, a small, terraced garden covered by an invisible dome that gave one the impression of being outdoors in space. To one side loomed the space station, to another hung the spectacular globe of Mughal. All around drifted ships.

"*Eurynome*," she said at last. "What a perfect name for a ship."

"Really?" Haakon said. "I must confess I don't know what it means. She had that title when I came into possession of her."

"It's from one of the Greek creation myths," Maya said, her enormous black eyes utterly unrevealing. "Eurynome was a nymph, and the first-created of all living things. The name, as I recall, means 'far-traveler.' "

"Fitting, indeed. Is myth your forte?"

"Far more than that. It's my being."

Before Haakon could question this enigmatic statement, Jemal arrived on the deck with a few prosperous guests in tow. "Captain," Jemal said, "the Raj of Peshawar maintains that you could not possibly defeat his bodyguard in an arm wrestle." From behind the little group a gigantic Sikh stepped forward.

Haakon sighed. "Well, Maya, it seems as if I must uphold the honor of *Eurynome*. I trust you'll—" He turned to her but she was gone.

Nonplussed, he led his guests down to a lounge where, for the next half hour, he strove against the

Sikh who was, indeed, very nearly as strong as Haakon himself. But not quite. Haakon was victorious, to much applause.

When the match was over, he looked for Maya, but she was nowhere aboard. He checked the lock's data, but she had not left. The ship's locater confirmed that she was nowhere in *Eurynome*. It was not only a puzzle, it was alarming. The ship was supposed to have the tightest possible security. The woman seemed able to come and go at will, without recourse to the usual laws of physics.

Besides, she haunted him. There was something in her face, or her bearing, or her voice. He needed to see her again. It was of utmost importance. His shipmates were not sympathetic.

"What do you want with the hussy?" Rama demanded. "And what right had she to wear black, on an evening when I was wearing black? Are you intending to betray me with that diamond-umbilicused slut?"

"What do you mean, betray you?" Haakon said. "Did you have some claim on me?"

"We have been rather intimate."

"So what? When did that ever slow you down? Besides, you've been screwing the brains out of poor old Numa."

"I can't help that," Rama said huffily. "That's my genes and my hormones. You're supposed to show a little restraint."

"Restraint? What are you talking about? The woman came walking onto my ship without invitation—"

"Because you allowed her to," Soong pointed out mildly.

"And then she left, presumably by some means unknown to whoever designed this ship and its security systems, and I want to know why."

"Don't give us that," Mirabelle said. "That woman sunk her hook into you. You're caught now. You'll go mooning about trying to find out who she is, where she lives—"

"Beauty and the beast, huh?" Alexander said helpfully.

"Exactly," Jemal commented. "You've never seen anything really pathetic until you've seen a hardass like Haakon crack up over a woman."

"Cool your overheated imaginations, people," Haakon said dangerously. "Forget my possibly romantic bias and concentrate on the cogent point here. The woman got off the ship without being detected. How did it happen?"

"If she's a technothief," Mirabelle said, "or has had the kind of training I had, she may be skilled in evading detection systems."

"Could you beat *Eurynome*'s systems?" Haakon asked.

"Yes, but that's because I've had plenty of time to study them. Just having come aboard, and walking around for a while as she did, I don't know. It's hard to believe she's that good. You'll have to take into account that I'm feeling professional jealousy."

"When the local port people came aboard to inspect, and they attached those defense systems overrides," Jemal said, "could they have gotten readouts on all of the ship's systems?"

"They tried," Haakon said. "*Eurynome*'s equipped for that. She snowed them with irrelevant data, hid the good stuff, all the usual tactics. They couldn't have gotten much that was useful. All research indicates that Mughal technology is well behind the Bahaduran. *Eurynome* should be well up to protecting herself against their incursions, just as she's capable of nullifying their overrides."

"It wouldn't be the first time somebody's underestimated an enemy," Rand pointed out. The engineer rested his armored elbows on the council table and leaned forward, resting the chin of his mask on his metallic knuckles. "It also might not be the first time somebody's deliberately cultivated a reputation for backwardness in order to mask the development of new hardware or technology. Even Bahadur's pulled that one, and they're not very subtle as a general thing."

"You're right there," Haakon admitted.

"I think you are all missing a vital point," Soong said.

"Tell us," Haakon directed.

"Why did she do it?" The Han gambler looked about from face to face, meeting only blank gazes. "Why didn't she just walk off the ship like the rest of the guests? Why draw attention to herself in such a fashion?"

"She did something, maybe took something, and could not risk detection," Rama said.

"If she's a technothief," Mirabelle said, "she

would carry it in her head and walk off looking perfectly innocent. Nothing noticeable has turned up missing, has it?''

''Nothing,'' Haakon said.

''Could she be a lure, a decoy?'' Jemal speculated. ''She's sure occupying our thoughts and our time. Maybe it's a distraction to keep us from noticing some more subtle assault against us.''

''What kind of assault?'' Haakon asked.

''Good question,'' Jemal replied.

EIGHT

"Where are you going?" Haakon asked.

Mirabelle was dressed in an understated safari outfit that was more utilitarian and less decorative than it appeared at first glance.

"Mir Jafar has invited me to spend a day or two at his hunting lodge in the wild country. It'll be a sizable and fashionable gathering, I'm told."

"Do you think it's worth cultivating him?" Haakon asked. "I'd hate to have you down there taking unnecessary risks if he's just a functionary who's never been let in on any of the real work."

"Why Haakon," she said, "I'm touched. You're really worrying about me. Don't fret. I can take care of myself, as you well know. And yes, I think he's worth pumping for information. He's a fool, but fools are often put in charge of important government work. More often than not, now that I think of it."

"Well, all right, but don't hang around if you sense any danger. We're here to keep Timur Khan from killing us, not to let the Mughali do it instead." She left.

Haakon was sitting in a lounge, sipping at a cold glass of something or other and fuming. He had arrived nowhere in his attempts to locate Maya. The Free Mughal people had not contacted them yet. He had to let the others do the tedious work of ferreting out information concerning Precious Pearl, if indeed the damned thing existed at all. He was bored. He'd been a convict or a hunted man living in the underworld for so long that he had forgotten how deadly dull the life of the idle rich could be. No wonder so many of them took up pointless but exciting sports and diversions.

Jemal came through and spotted him in the embrace of the relaxation chair. "You're going to turn into a sot sitting around and boozing like that, letting your brain turn to porridge over that woman."

Haakon glared at him bleakly. "Isn't a day and a half kind of a short time to be predicting my decline into drunkenness and lovesick idiocy?"

"All the signs are there."

"What the hell do you know about it? Next, Rama's going to come in and tell me—"

"Forget it. She's been running herself through some basic Felid fecundity tests."

"Uh-oh, how did they turn out?"

"Positive."

"Oh, no." Haakon buried his battered face in his even more battered hands. "She's unbearable at the best of times. What's she going to be like pregnant? Or nursing? Are we going to have to put up with a little Felid brat? Don't we have enough troubles already?''

Jemal shrugged. "What's the difference? This ship's never been anything but a madhouse. Maybe it'll quiet old Rama down, make her a little more domestic.''

"Dream on,'' Haakon said. "If anything can make her harder to live with, this is it. Hell, Mirabelle will probably want to get knocked up now just to compete.''

The room was a reproduction of a jungle on the world of Prospero. Prospero's main claim to fame was its luminescent flora and fauna. Every living organism on the planet had some degree of bioluminescence. It made for unbelievably gorgeous nights in what was otherwise a rather drab and dismal swamp. Of course, in the jungle lounge on Kashmir III it was always night. The single, huge window was always turned so that nothing was visible beyond except starscape. No light from the primary or reflected by the planet or its satellites was ever allowed to intrude.

Haakon took a slug from his frosted glass then leaned close to a little brazier on the table to sniff its smoke. The smoke was not narcotic. Its purpose was to counteract the nausea often brought on by the potent liquor Haakon was downing. He had chosen this spot because the only light was from the various glowing organisms, and he did not want to be recognized. *Eurynome* was the great rage of the season, and everyone with pretensions to fashionable status was trying to cadge an invitation aboard. That was just what he had wanted in order to accomplish his mission, but just now he wanted nothing to do with any of the smart set of Mughal.

A large, multilegged insect equivalent, rather like an immense beetle, made its clumsy way across the table. The various animals and plants in the jungle room were authentic, brought in from Prospero at immense expense. The blue light from the creature's back lit Haakon's face and hands dimly. The rest of him, clothed in a dark coverall, reflected no light.

"Your hands are rather battered, Captain. They're really not the hands of a viscount."

He squinted across the table. He hadn't heard her arrive, hadn't heard her sit down. The form across from him was so dim that he really couldn't be sure that it was there at all, but the voice was real.

"Good to see you again, Maya. Are you going to stay, or will you disappear again?"

He heard no answer, and began to wonder whether his mind was finally going, but then a snake crawled across her shoulder. The limber reptile was lit with brilliant bands of orange and green and it revealed her unmistakably. She seemed to be favoring her basic black and white, as she had that night on the ship.

"I'll stay. For a while, anyway." She ran her fingers across the table's order plate, and it delivered something liquid in which bubbles floated to the surface and burst, releasing tiny puffs of smoke.

"Who are you?" Haakon asked.

"I told you. Maya."

"That tells me very little. Why did you come to my ship?"

"I wanted to see it."

"You had no invitation."

"You let me aboard anyway."

"Suppose it had not been I who met you. None of the others would have allowed you aboard. Rama would've taken some hide from you in giving you the bum's rush. The 'bots were programmed to keep out unwanted visitors."

"But it was you. I knew it would be." She leaned back and her chair adjusted itself to accommodate her new position. The chair was all but invisible, and he could see her silhouette against the faint glow of a feathery bush.

"How?"

"Now, Captain, do you really expect me to reveal all my secrets so soon?"

"What do you want with me?"

"You're an attractive man, in a rough-hewn sort of way. Isn't that enough?"

Haakon laughed thinly. "I won't claim to be without vanity, but I'm not that dumb. Your disappearing act got my attention, all right, but I knew it wasn't romantic attraction that brought you to me. So what is it? Who are you working for?"

"The same question occurred to me, but you have no more intention of answering it than have I." Unexpectedly, she reached across the table and took his hands in both of hers. He tensed for a moment, then relaxed. It was the first physical contact he had had with her, and he didn't want to break it, even though he knew by the way her fingertips and thumbs were moving over his hands that she was doing some kind of analysis. Because of the dim lighting, he had removed his fashionable gloves.

"These hands have seen some use," she said. Her thumbs ran gently across his palms. "Every bone broken at some time. These calluses are the result of brutal manual labor in the not-too-distant past. As I said before, odd hands for a viscount."

"There was a war, remember? In war, rough things happen, even to viscounts."

"Very rough. Did you know that constant contact with a tool handle and its repeated shocks will actually leave marks on the bones of the hands? What was it? A pick? A sledgehammer? I've heard that they break men in the convict pits of Bahadur by such means."

"Do I look like a broken man?" Could she really read all that from his hands? Or was she faking it? Had she gotten the information from somewhere else? Was she just making lucky guesses?

"No, not broken. But these marks are surgically correctable. You are rich enough to afford the best medical treatment. Why do you remain like this? You must be in continual pain."

He decided a new tangent was called for. "There are people down on the surface even worse off than I am. They don't get corrective surgery either, I'm told."

"Odd for a titled personage to notice such things.

After all, social inequity is the very basis of aristocracy."

"But I'm not an aristocrat anymore. I'm a ship's captain."

"Yes, and such a marvelous ship too. The upkeep on such a vessel must be immense. Since you've lost your estates, you must find it difficult to support *Eurynome*."

"I saved up my allowance when I was young." She was beginning to talk like a cop. But she was still holding his hands.

"Did you know that your crewmen have been associating with some undesirable people?"

"They do that a lot when they're in port." His mind raced. How much did she know?

"You, too, I hear." A comment that could be interpreted at least two ways, if not more.

"Now where did you hear that? I only associate with the best, remember?"

She leaned forward over the table, still holding his hands. A creature that looked like a land-going jellyfish oozed across the table, and in its violet luminescence he saw her face half-clearly for the first time since she had been on the ship. Her features were as perfect as he remembered, but the low-level lighting gave her a sinister cast. But then, he realized, it must make him look positively evil. "You could come to great harm by following your present course."

"I've followed a lot of courses that promised great harm."

"You are involving yourself in something beyond

your comprehension, and you are dealing with people who should not be trusted.''

"What makes you think I trust anybody? And why should I trust you? On the contrary, you've been behaving in a very suspicious fashion; crashing my party, then disappearing like you did. You aroused my suspicions very efficiently.''

"And more than your suspicions?'' She smiled faintly, but the black discs of her eyes were unreadable.

"Sure of yourself, aren't you?''

"Yes. And I can read every tremor of your hands, every variation in your pulse rate.''

"Hell,'' Haakon said, "I thought you were holding my hands because you'd fallen for my ruggedly handsome features and my boyish charm.''

"Be serious,'' she urged. "I'm through fencing with you.''

"Don't give me that,'' he cut her short. "You were the one who started the game playing, now you talk in hints and innuendos. I don't think you know anything, Maya. I think you're just guessing. If you think I'm going to incriminate myself by making some kind of admission based on your supposed knowledge of my alleged nefarious activities, you're mistaken. I've had a certain amount of experience with police and intelligence procedures. Besides—I admit it—I'm smart. Until you can back your play, I'm going to assume you're bluffing. I'd be a fool to do otherwise.''

"You're stubborn, and you're a fool, and you're in over your head,'' she insisted.

"Hell, if you'll keep holding my hands like

this, I'll let you call me names all night." She
jerked her hands back and he was both disappointed at the break in contact and pleased that,
for the first time, he had been able to elicit an
emotional response from her.

"If you won't be warned," she said coldly,
"then I will not trouble you further."

"I have a counter proposal," he said.

"I'm listening."

"Come to *Eurynome* tomorrow evening. I'll give
you one more chance to convince me to stop whatever it is you think I'm doing."

"Why should I do any such thing?"

"Because it's important to you." He thought
he could see her smile slightly, but he wasn't
sure.

"I'll be here."

"Good. What would you like to—" He strained
his eyes in the dimness. There seemed to be no
form in front of the faintly glowing bush. He
reached out and swept his hand across the table.
Nothing there.

"Silly bitch," he muttered. Why couldn't she
say good-bye and walk away like any ordinary
human being? Well, maybe she wasn't an ordinary
human being.

One of the staff came to his table. The woman
was too dusky for him to see well but her white
sari shone plainly.

"Is everything satisfactory, Raj?" she asked,
bowing over folded hands.

"Excellent," he told her. "The lady who was
just here, did you see her leave?"

"Lady, Raj? Which Lady? There have been quite a number in the Prospero Room this evening."

"The dark-haired lady in the black sari. She left just a moment ago."

The woman thought for a moment. "There have been many black-haired ladies here this evening, but I've seen no black saris. It is a very rare color in clothing for women here. I am sure I would have noticed. I have been on the door all evening and I have seen no such lady enter or leave."

"Hmm. Well, never mind. I'm probably just imagining things."

"Will there be anything else, Raj?"

"Nothing, thank you."

"Very well. Steiner says to meet him tomorrow at the port entrance, 0930 local." The woman walked away, and even in his variously shocked and bemused condition, Haakon found leisure to admire the graceful sway of her backside. The prison years had taught him always to take time for the finer things.

Haakon and Jemal were at the port entrance by 0915. The captain looked around. Nothing much seemed to have changed in the last couple of days. In fact, he figured that nothing much had changed around here in the last couple of centuries. The same throngs of people, the same crippled beggars. It looked different, though. He realized that it was probably due to his new knowledge of the social realities. Things always looked different when you knew what was behind them.

"No sign of Steiner," Jemal said. "But in this

mob he could be three meters away before we could spot him.''

"He's probably watching us, though," Haakon said. "Him or one of his Mongrels. He'll want to make sure we're not being tailed. It's what I'd do in his place. It's a pretty serious game we're playing.''

"Your friend Maya knows something. I still think you're crazy to let her back on the ship.''

"I'd rather have her where I can see her. Besides, I'm not sure we could keep her off the ship if she really wants to be there. That woman gets around.''

They were both in common spacer's clothes, armed only with powerblades and a lifetime of hard-won skills and attitudes. They scanned their surroundings with the easy assurance of men who had stood on a great many worlds and had encountered and survived the worst from nature, aliens, and their fellow men. Mostly from their fellow men. They also had the extra confidence of men who knew and trusted one another, knew that in a pinch his back would be protected by the other. The visible signs were almost imperceptible, but they were there. It would have to be an exceedingly strong or desperate or numerous enemy that would try to take on this particular pair of commonplace spacers.

"Come along, spacers," the girl in the green leather outfit said. It was Lorah, and she had gotten within three meters of them before they had spotted her. They had been looking for Steiner, unconsciously setting their sights above the level of the crowd. Steiner was a big man, and the girl had been able to mask her movements by taking advantage of the throng.

"We were supposed to meet Steiner here," Haakon said, "not you."

"Steiner couldn't come. There was some trouble last night. He wants me to bring you to him." She glared up at them defiantly, still angry at the way they had handled her last time.

"No deal," Haakon said. "The message I got said Steiner. Nobody else." He cocked his head at Jemal and the two turned to go back into the port.

"Come on, spacers," the girl said. "Don't give me a hard time. Look, there's been trouble, but you gotta meet with Steiner, it's important." Her cocky attitude was beginning to crack. They turned and looked at her.

"Why should we trust some grubby little street girl?" Jemal said. "How do we know you wouldn't lead us into a trap?"

"Don't think I wouldn't like to," she said, some of her toughness returning, "the way you shoved me around. But it ain't that way. Steiner's gotta see you, and I don't bring you back better I don't go back at all. Now, you gonna come?" She was holding up her facade well, but there was real fear in her voice.

Haakon looked at Jemal for a moment. "Okay, kid, let's go. But we're going to be watching you twice as close as last time."

"And that was pretty damned close," Jemal concluded.

They walked behind the Mongrel girl, all their

senses on high alert for the slightest dissonance in their surroundings, any sign that all was not as it should be. The planet was a new one, but this was familiar territory to them. Once again it was the maze of streets, but this time it seemed to be the consequence of the chaotic layout of the city rather than a calculated effort to confuse them, as before.

A Mongrel who stood leaning casually against a building caught sight of them. The boy made a slight hand signal, and Lorah replied with another.

Haakon grabbed her upper arm, squeezing hard enough for her to gasp. "I hope for your sake you and that punk were just saying hello," he said. "If you're just setting us up, I'll pull this arm off."

"Easy! We're coming into Mongrel territory. I was just telling him everything's okay. He's on watch. I'll be signing to every Mongrel we pass. I don't, they'll think I'm in trouble, then you got problems."

"We won't be alone in that respect," Haakon promised her.

Still, he felt better. The girl was visibly relaxing now that she was back on friendly turf. If she were walking them into an ambush, she would be getting more tense, not less so.

She stopped before a doorway where two Mongrels stood, trying to look as if they had nothing better to do. Haakon spotted another on the roof and two more on the opposite rooftop.

"These the ones," she told the two on guard.

The older of the two, a woman perhaps in her early twenties, rapped on the door in a rhythmic pattern. Without waiting for an answer, she opened the door and motioned them inside.

The two men went through warily, steering Lorah ahead of them but without any shoving this time. The door shut behind them, plunging the room into dimness lit only by a couple of small, high-set windows. They could see, as their eyes adjusted, that the room was dingy, nearly squalid, with rickety furniture and whitewashed walls. Except for some music reproduction equipment, it might have been from centuries past.

"This way," Lorah said. She led them into another, even smaller room, which contained only a bed.

On the bed lay Steiner, propped to half-sitting position by cushions and holding a humming powerblade. Above the waist he was wearing only a sickly grin and a lot of bandages.

Jemal stepped forward, well within range of the powerblade, and bent low to study the injuries. A deep burn on one shoulder had been made by some kind of beam weapon, and a long cut slanted from below his rib cage on the left, up and across his right pectoral, ending at the armpit. The transparent plastiflesh bandages had been well applied and allowed observation of the healing process without removal.

"Looks like you let one get a little too close to you there, friend," Jemal said.

"If the first one hadn't got my shoulder with the beamer, I'd'a gutted the one with the powerblade." He tried his grin again and it came back, although sweat dripped down his face. "Got 'im anyway, as it was. Just made me a little slow getting away, was all. One of my boys nailed the one with the beamer, put a hatchet in the back of his skull.''

"So you got away," Haakon said. "Who didn't?''

"Krishna. The one who gave you his name as Krishna, anyway. Name was really Chandrasekhar, which I can tell you seeing he's dead. Some kind of professor at the big university here in the city. Taught political economics. He'd come down to our meet place to deliver a message, and that was where they hit us.''

"It wasn't government people, was it?'' Haakon said. "Not with powerblades. Who was it? Rival gang?''

"The Garudas, from—'' His face spasmed with pain and sweat stood on his brow, then the spasm passed. "From the lower south end. No big trouble for years, but they been biding their time. We were set up.''

"I figured," Haakon said. "I've just about used up my whole store of belief in coincidence. Who set you up, and why, and how come the Garudas instead of the authorities?''

"Now, that's a bunch of questions all at once, and you haven't asked the really important one yet," Steiner said.

"I'll ask it," Jemal said. "What was Krishna's message?''

"I can tell you what he told me, which wasn't much, seeing as how he got himself killed before he could finish business. This is it: He says old Baibars—he meant the father of the one we got

now—was on to something really radical, something so important it could change the whole balance of power in all of human-occupied space. It
could put Mughal in power instead of Bahadur.
Only thing was, old Baibars was a crazy old coot
and nobody took him seriously. He had this scientist—only he was more like a wizard—named
DaSilva, from off-world somewhere. This DaSilva
character had some kind of psychic process that
could do things like transfer material from one
place to another instantly, and do tricks with time
and space, and even predict the future. The process, along with DaSilva, got clamped under the
code name Precious Pearl. They go in for these
poetical code names around here. The project, and
DaSilva, were shifted after old Baibars died near
the end of the war. They went to someplace called
the Jahnsi, over on the East Continent. Raj is
named Jehan, big man in the government. That's
as far as he got before we were hit.''

''That's a help, but I'm not sure it'll be enough,''
Haakon said.

''He did the best he could. I don't know, maybe
they'll come up with more, but I imagine they'll
be laying low after this.'' Steiner fell back on the
bed and finally, as an afterthought, switched his
powerblade off. ''That's all I got for you, spacers.
Sorry if it ain't what you wanted, but I got to rest
now.''

Haakon came forward and examined the bandages. ''Looks like a pretty good job of doctoring.''

''Yeah, we got some good people we can go to.
They don't report to the authorities. This plastiflesh

stuff, they say it's straight from Galen. They tell me it could fix me up like new in seven or eight days. I don't know. I been cut not near so bad and took a lot longer than that to recover. Ain't as young as I was then, neither."

"I think you'll come out of it okay, Steiner," Haakon said. "Just take it slow and watch your back."

"I got my people to do that, spacer." Steiner managed a good imitation of his old, cocky grin. "Till I get back on my feet anyway. You watch yours."

Haakon and Jemal walked to the doorway of the room, then Haakon turned. "Steiner, does the name Maya mean anything to you?"

Steiner looked perplexed. "Maya? Don't ring a bell. There's an old Hindi word pronounced like that, but it ain't a name."

"What's the Hindi word mean?" Haakon asked.

"It means illusion. But it don't mean hallucination or anything like that. It's something from their religion. You'd have to get one of their holy men to explain it to you, but you'd need a year to take it all in. That's what the Hindus are like. A name, you say? Maybe it's just a coincidence in sounds."

"Maybe," Haakon said. "Steiner, you say you'd like to get off this planet some day?"

"Sure," Steiner said. Then, suspiciously: "Why you asking?"

"Because maybe I'll take you with me when I leave. Can't say I'd take you far, but anyplace I dump you is better than here."

Steiner's gaze narrowed. "Why just maybe, spacer?"

Haakon for the first time grinned back at him. "Because maybe I'll be dead, Steiner. No use to you then."

"Watch yourself, spacer," Steiner said, sinking back on the bed.

NINE

"All set?" Haakon asked.

"Ready," Jemal told him.

Haakon was waiting by the lock for their guest to arrive. Jemal was in the control room setting up the monitoring systems. Rama stood by Haakon, complaining about his plan.

"You're a fool to let her on board. I object."

"Objection noted," Haakon said. "Overruled, but noted. I'd as soon have her here, where I can keep an eye on her, as out there somewhere, knowing too much and doing God knows what."

"Given what we already know about her," Mirabelle said, "what makes you think you can hold her?"

"Maybe I can't," he admitted, "but the way we've set it up, we'll learn plenty anyway. I'm sure she's got something to do with the Precious Pearl project. She's tied in with old Baibars and DaSilva."

"If she was one of old Baibars's pets," Soong observed, "then she belongs to young Baibars now. It could displease him greatly to learn that we are here, ferreting out intelligence for Bahadur."

"If she's his," Haakon persisted, "then why hasn't she reported her suspicions to him? She sure as hell has them, from the way she was talking in the Prospero Room."

"She could be playing a double game," Soong said. "I urge you not to trust her."

Haakon slammed a hand against an instrument panel, a histrionic gesture since the panel, despite its fragile appearance, was as near indestructible as any work of man. "Trust! Why the hell all of a sudden is everybody telling me not to trust anybody? I never trust anybody. Do I look like an idiot?" His crewmates just stared in stony silence. "All right," he said in disgust, "get to your stations."

The others scattered to their places, except for Alexander. "Boss, what you gotta do, you gotta turn me loose on this lady. She'll love me. I'll have that diamond out of her belly button in no time."

"Quite the lover since that Rani picked you up, aren't you?" Haakon said patiently. "What about the diamond in her nose?"

"That'll take a little time, but I got a maneuver—"

"Alexander, get the hell out of here, before I kick your tail-bedizened butt off the ship."

"Aw, Boss," Alexander complained, "there's

nothing to do here. Can't I go back over to the resort?'' He grinned ingratiatingly.

"Anywhere,'' Haakon said. "Get out of here. While you're there, try to make some discreet inquiries concerning Maya. The way people were looking at her when she was here, I'm sure some of them recognized her. But be discreet, remember.''

"Sure, Boss.'' Alexander hopped into one of the small locks opening on the little emergency shuttles and the lock irised behind him.

Haakon shook his head. It was futile to tell Alexander to be discreet about anything. A 'bot came floating by, bearing one of his tequila-and-lime concoctions on an ornate tray. He took it and sipped the cold liquid across the salt-encrusted rim.

"I figured you needed it,'' said Jemal's voice from the 'bot's speaker grill. "Romantic anticipation is hard on the nerves.''

Haakon muttered a complicated obscenity which he cut short as the lock's alerter produced a muffled bong. The lock irised, and Maya stepped through. Once again, she was in a black sari, this time of a slightly different design and color value, once again looking ravishing.

"Once again, welcome aboard,'' he said.

"Once again, I thank you.'' She studied his face for a moment. "And my compliments to your makeup artist. You really look quite presentable.''

"Be careful, you'll turn my head with praise like that. Shall we adjourn to more comfortable surroundings?'' He led her to the main lounge, where a 'bot delivered one of her favored smoke concoctions.

She arranged herself fetchingly on one of the priceless cushions, displaying an enticing length of thigh as she did so. Her feet were bare except for sandal pads clinging to her soles. She wore a circle of black diamonds around one ankle and diamond rings on several toes.

"Where are your crew?" she asked.

He shrugged. "Off somewhere, pursuing their own affairs. I don't ride close herd on them when we're in port."

"Are the two cat-people still aboard?"

"Possibly. Rama insists she's not through with poor Numa, and I think she's keeping him in storage someplace."

"Is that—well, I won't say legal, but is it really ethical?"

"With Felids terms like that just don't apply. I've tried to get Numa off the ship and he refuses to leave, although half the time he's hiding from her. It's programmed into them."

"How unromantic. I greatly prefer a less automatic response to and from the opposite sex."

"At least it's efficient. However, I'll go along with you. I prefer to respond to people on a basis of mental acuity rather than body chemistry. That's not to say that chemistry is totally absent, of course."

"And what does this mental acuity of yours tell you about me?" Her eyes were as unrevealing as ever.

"I think you're a fake. I think you make use of

hints and innuendos because you really don't know anything. You're just making guesses and trying to trick me into revealing something."

She smiled. "Just as, right now, you're trying to trick me into showing you that my powers are real?"

"Powers? Is that what they are? Tell me about them, and about Baibars of the Holy Cloak, and about a man named DaSilva."

"Your meeting today must have been informative."

"You should know all about it, shouldn't you? Unless your sources of intelligence are faulty. Of course, the term was '*limited* prescience.' "

"That's correct," she said coolly. "And I'm going to warn you again, Captain. Leave this business alone. You're interfering in something far more delicate and dangerous than you can conceive."

"Maya, I now have all means of exit from this ship blocked off."

She looked puzzled. "Are you trying to tell me that I'm a prisoner?"

"That's right."

"Do you really think you can keep me here if I do not wish it?" She was beginning to get angry now, a development Haakon found all to the good. More likelihood that she would make a mistaken move.

"That's what I'd like to find out. Rama."

A connecting door snapped open, and Rama crouched there, claws out and lips back, exposing her sharp teeth. With a demented howl and a blast of her appalling fighting-scent, she leapt the intervening distance, straight for Maya. Maya was not there when she landed.

"That was a pretty good trick," Rama said. "I wonder where she went?"

"Good question," Haakon said.

He had been watching Maya closely, and yet he couldn't exactly pinpoint the instant she had disappeared. It was as if he had glanced away for a moment, and when he had looked back, she was not there. Yet he knew that he had not looked away. And there had been no sound of displaced air. "Is she on the ship?" Haakon asked, addressing the empty air.

"According to our instruments," Jemal's voice said over the intercom, "she's not aboard. I'd hate to make any rash statements about that lady, though."

"Did you get a full record of events, though?" Haakon asked.

"Right. I don't know how much it'll tell us."

"Let's go over it and see," Haakon said.

In the ship's holo tank they reran the action, viewing it repeatedly from all sides. Each time, the event remained baffling: Rama leapt and Maya disappeared. That was all.

"That was a dramatic pounce, there, Rama," Jemal said. "Where did you learn that shriek?"

"In my exciting life I have often had to fight my way out of difficult situations," she said. "There's nothing like a good roar for paralyzing your enemy. Cats have always known that."

"Run it again," Haakon said. "This time much slower."

The images flashed on again. Halfway through Rama's leisurely leap, Maya disappeared almost instantaneously. Almost, but not quite.

"It looked to me as if she vanished from bottom to top," Jemal said. "Anybody else see that?"

"I saw it," Soong said.

"So did I," Haakon confirmed. "Run it again, this time dead slow, and magnify."

Now the image of Maya loomed enormous in the room. She appeared to be utterly motionless, but that was because of the extreme slow motion of the playback. This time when she vanished, she could be seen disappearing as tiny lines beginning at her feet and continuing upward. A thin line tracked across from left to right, the next line from right to left.

"Scanning lines," Jemal said.

"What's that?" Haakon asked.

"Scanning lines. It's an old form of image transmission. Pictures were scanned electronically and beamed to their destination, where they were reconstructed on a primitive screen a line at a time. Of course, the process was too fast for the viewer to perceive it that way."

"Are you saying that the woman was just a beamed image?" Mirabelle asked.

"She is real," Haakon insisted. "I touched her."

"She is real, all right," Jemal confirmed. "Instruments say that from the time she arrived until she disappeared, there was a genuine human being aboard the ship. I'm not saying that this is identical to that old transmitting technique, just that they seem to have something in common: the use of scan lines.''

"Blow it up larger," Haakon ordered. "I want to get a look at those lines in a size I can see." Next, the tank was filled with an image of Maya's ankle, enlarged to a hundred times its natural size.

"Pretty damned good-looking ankle, I must admit," Jemal murmured.

"I was always a man of good taste," Haakon said. "Now, what's this?"

Cranked back to its slowest speed, they watched as the lines that now appeared at least three or four millimeters in thickness scanned across the ankle. They could also see the lines were not continuous, but made up of tiny squares that winked out in sequence instead of a continuous withdrawal of the line.

"The lines are built up of squares," Mirabelle observed. "Does that agree with this old technology of yours?"

"I don't know," Jemal said. "I'll have to check. Anyway, what we know for sure is that somebody has a way of transmitting humans across space and fetching them back at will."

"The scan lines indicate some kind of electronic-mechanical device," Haakon said. "Nothing psychic or mystical."

"Oh, hell," Jemal said, the implications just dawning on him. "Forget this future-telling device. What will happen if Timur Khan ever gets his hands on *this*?"

"We were instructed to come here and bring

back the prescience device or process or whatever it is," Haakon said. "Nothing about any telekinesis gadget. I'm damned if I'm going to give it to him."

"The two may be connected," Mirabelle pointed out. "It all involves this man DaSilva and old Baibars. Suppose we can't bring back the one without the other?"

"I wish you hadn't said that," Haakon said, running a hand through his artificial hair.

"Whatever it is," Rama said, "I say we take it back to Timur Khan. I for one don't want this little device," she tapped a spot behind her ear with the claw of a forefinger, "to splatter my brains all over this lovely ship."

"Some things," Jemal said grimly, "may be more important than our lives."

"Speak for yourself," Rama said. "My life is very important to me, indeed."

"We'll worry about the possible implications when they're unavoidable," Haakon said. "Right now, our problem is to get back in touch with Maya. I don't suppose she'd accept another invitation."

"Most unlikely," Soong concurred. "Your treatment of her was most cavalier and not at all hospitable."

"To hell with that," Haakon said affably. "She was playing games with me so I played games with her. Even both ways."

"Was she playing games?" Mirabelle asked. "She was trying to warn us about something."

"She wasn't trying very damned hard," Haakon

said impatiently. "It's not all that difficult to transmit a warning. All you've got to do is say something like: 'Hey, watch out, you're stepping in a pile of brush dragon droppings.' "

"Trivial sort of warning," Rama sniffed.

"Like hell. Brush dragons live on Third Delhi. Their droppings are alive and carnivorous."

"I don't know which is worse," Rama said, "your blundering or your lying. Nothing has carnivorous droppings."

"I agree, Rama," Mirabelle said sweetly. "If that trick were possible, you'd have managed it by now." Rama glared at her. Mutiny and mayhem crackled electrically in the air.

"Ye of little faith," Haakon said disgustedly.

He wondered whether he had better flood the room with sleeping gas and let everybody sleep it off. Then he reminded himself that Rama might be pregnant and the gas might cause a spontaneous abortion. Then he'd really be in trouble.

Alexander came scampering into the room, looking pleased with himself, his pockets full of things that had probably belonged to someone else a short time before. "Hey, Boss! I found out what you wanted to know."

"Did I want to know something?" Haakon said distractedly. With his current pack of worries, he did not remember having sent Alexander after any information.

"Sure. You wanted to know who Lady Maya is." Alexander grinned all over his simian face.

"Talk," Haakon said. "I'm not in a very good

mood. What you have to say better cheer me up, Alex."

"Can't say as to that. But people around here don't like to go near her or even talk about her. I had to use all my leverage with Lady Govinda. See, she likes for me to—"

"Alex," Haakon said, "let's play a little game. Pretend you have about three seconds to live and the only way to save your life is to make your next words valuable and to the point. Can you play that game, Alex?" He glared dangerously.

"Sure, it's simple enough," Alexander said. "Lady Maya is actually Princess Maya, or something like that. She's the sister of Baibars the Lion."

"See, she's kind of the black sheep of the family," Alexander said. They had adjourned to one of the ship's lounges for the full story. Alexander was peeling a ghastly-looking mutant banana with his toes. "Anybody here know what a sheep is? I been hearing that black sheep bit all my life, but I never seen one."

"It's a fuzzy animal about your size, native to Earth," Jemal explained patiently. "White ones were good, black ones were bad. Something to do with evil spirits, I believe. Now, please continue, Alex."

"Well, anyway, old Baibars, that's to say Baibars of the Holy Cloak, whatever the hell a holy cloak is, had two children. That was young Baibars and his sister, Maya, only Maya wasn't her real name. Her real name was something I can't pronounce,

but lucky for me she picked Maya for herself
instead. Now Maya was old Baibars's favorite, as
you can imagine when you compare her with that
dumbass brother of hers, but a woman can't inherit
the throne around here, and the family council,
who really pick the heir, hated her.''

"Why was that?" Haakon asked.

"Because she's crazy. They think so, anyway.
She'd do weird things like go off by herself and
live in some crummy city for months at a time
until they tracked her down and brought her back
to the palace. There's even a rumor that she spent
a season as a harvester on one of the Chelis plantations. Daddy always took her back in, but when
her brother got to be the local bigwig, he must've
exiled her or something, because nobody's seen
her. Until the other night here on the ship, that
is." He stuffed an obscene length of off-colored
banana into his face and bit it off with the kind of
sensual abandon most people reserve for less prosaic acts.

"Wasn't Lady Govinda a little suspicious about
these questions?" Soong asked.

"Naw," Alexander said after swallowing an
enormous wad of banana. "I just told her Maya
showed up without an invite, and we was curious
about who she was. I don't think she was suspicious. Besides, she didn't want me to stop what I
was doing, which you really ought to try, Boss.
You see, I was—"

"We've heard all about it, Alex," Mirabelle
said. "You described it in great detail last time
you visited Lady Govinda. Most accomplished."

"That reminds me," Rama said. "Where is Numa?"

"Hiding in the aft starboard hold, last I saw of him," Jemal said.

"That weakling! Well, I'm not through with him yet." She stalked out, trailing a scent of mating pheromones. All the males aboard, except for Numa, had been wearing nose-filters for days.

"Next move?" Jemal queried.

"I'm at a dead end," Haakon said. "Maya's disappeared again, and our subversives on the ground are lying low for the moment." He thought for a while. "Jem, that scan line process we just saw presupposes some kind of central location of origin for the beam or whatever. Do you think we could trace that beam?"

"I don't know," Jemal answered. "We don't even know what we'd be looking for. Still, our detection systems are set up to track and pinpoint almost anything. It's a matter of working out just what questions to ask the computers."

"Get on it," Haakon told him. "Soong, help Jem." The Han gambler nodded minutely.

"I have another engagement at Mir Jafar's hunting lodge," Mirabelle said. "I've been charming the other guests, and a few of them are beginning to confide in me. I think I may be bringing home some valuable information soon." She smiled across the table at Alexander. "Want to come along? You seem to be developing a talent for intrigue."

Alexander grinned. "Sure. These people think I'm great stuff. I never seen a hunting lodge before. Pretty luxurious, huh?"

"Even better than the resort here," she assured him.

"Great!" He clapped his feet together with glee. "I never get enough luxury. Comes of spending your life in the trees when you're a kid."

"Go," Haakon said wearily. "Somebody come up with something quick. I'm getting tired of playing viscount. I wasn't cut out to be a playboy. Get out of here." With their usual disregard for his moods, Haakon's crew scattered to their activities, chattering happily.

TEN

The veranda of the hunting lodge was cantilevered over a valley so lush and green that it still had the power to take the viewer's breath away after the hundredth visit. Many-hued birds rose in flocks from the treetops, and predatory forest animals could be glimpsed prowling through the trees. So clear was the air that herds of animals could plainly be seen roaming the veldt many miles distant. Cumulus clouds piled in towering glory far to the east, their lower billows stained crimson and gold with sunset, their crests shining silver-white in the direct rays of the sun.

"Hey! Pretty slick place he's got here, huh?" Alexander observed. The Singeur was dressed in his finest, gold-embroidered velvet shorts and vest, and the rings on his fingers, toes, tail, and in his ears were among the very best he had ever stolen.

"Alex, you should have been a poet," Mirabelle said.

"Yeah, I got a way with words." He inspected a tray of drinks proffered by a passing 'bot. They were mostly exotic-looking things, many of them in self-frosting glasses, some with chemical smokes rising from side tubes or bubbling up from the bottom. "Got any beer?" The 'bot produced a tall, foaming schooner from its insides. "That's more like it." Alexander sucked the contents down in one long, lip-protruding gurgle and tossed the empty glass over his shoulder into the valley below. "Now gimme another one." His second beer arrived in a frosted mug.

Mirabelle took a glass of pale wine and sipped at it as she looked over the other guests. It seemed to be customary at this hour for people to stroll about without intruding on one another's solitude. From somewhere, she could hear the sounds of sitar and vina playing what she had learned was an evening raga. It was meditative music, relaxing and conducive to an uncluttered and incautious state of mind. Mirabelle reminded herself not to let the soothing sounds or the extravagantly beautiful scenery cause her to drop her guard.

The other guests were of the by-now-customary glittering aristocracy of the planet. Some were dressed in traditional finery, some in the dress of far-flung districts, still others in the fashionable costume of other worlds. Much of the latter, to Mirabelle's practiced eye, was out of date. She had chosen an evening dress of understated design which made no statement through material or decoration, but instead made a great presentation of her physical endowments, which were considerable.

A subtle change in the music seemed to signal a shifting of protocol, and now the guests began to gather in small groups, the composition of which changed from one moment to the next, the popular remaining the center of each group while the aspiring peripatetically wandered from one knot to another. Mirabelle quickly found herself as the decided center of an admiring clique, largely but not exclusively male in composition.

"Will you be coming with us on the hunt tomorrow, Lady Mirabelle?" asked a bejeweled dandy in a turban.

"I'm not sure. What are you hunting?"

"We never know for sure," said a man attired as an Edwardian English sportsman. "Whatever presents itself. That's what makes Mir Jafar's hunts so fascinating. His preserve is the most extensive in the system. He has all the traditional beasts, plus many exotic species brought in from other systems." He swept an arm out to take in the majestic sweep of the valley below. "Out there, in the forest, are tiger, giant serpent, even some mutant gorillas, which are very elusive."

"Hunting apes is great sport," added another. Alexander looked ready to work some mischief on the speaker, but with a subtle gesture Mirabelle signaled him to desist.

"On the plain," continued the fake Edwardian, "are lion, eland, elephant, zebra. Delphic prairie crabs, all manner of game. Do join us, please."

"How can I resist such variety of slaughter? Of

course I'll come. I do hope you aren't the kind of
hunters who get up dreadfully early, though. Are
you?"

"By no means," said another, who had been
waiting eagerly for a chance to interject something. "We let the beaters and the net carriers and
other huntsmen do all that. When the game is run
to ground we come out for the kill in flitters."

"How convenient. In that case, of course I'll
come."

"Hey, chief," Alexander said, nudging the bejeweled one with an elbow, "why bother with the
flitter? You could set up a laser-sighted beamer
right there on the rail and kill everything in sight
without ever having to shift your ass."

The pseudo-Edwardian smiled down at Alexander and patted him on the head. "But that would
mean missing all the sport, little monkey."

"Well, hell, I guess we wouldn't want to miss
that." He smiled up at the tweedy gentleman and
goosed him, causing a ripple of laughter from
Mirabelle's circle of admirers. She smiled sweetly
at him and twisted his ear, hard. He lapsed into
sulky silence.

" 'Hunting apes is great sport,' " quoted Alexander, adopting a mincing foppishness that the
original speaker had not displayed. " 'Little monkey' my butt! Did you ever see a worse collection
of degenerates?"

"Lots of them," she answered. "And much
worse."

They lounged in the suite of rooms that had

been allotted to Mirabelle. She had adroitly separated herself from the last and most tenacious of her would-be seducers and now sat in a chaise with her feet propped up and a 'bot hovering behind her waving an inefficient but luxurious-looking feather fan. She sipped from a crystal goblet while Alexander sucked up another beer, this time from a stein with a hinged top. "Besides," she continued, "you got your revenge on them."

"Huh?" Alexander said, all innocence. "What do you mean?"

"You know very well. Show me what you got."

"Well, if you insist." He fished in a pocket and drew out a string of huge pearls. "That's from the one that was dripping with all the jewels. He'll never miss 'em." He felt around his other pockets and came up with a gold pocket watch on a chain. "And this is from that guy in the funny-looking old clothes. I got it when I goosed him. Can't figure out what it is though."

"Press the catch on the side," she advised. He did so and the lid sprang open, exposing the crystal and the delicate hands of black, filigreed steel. Around the periphery of the dial ran a circle of Roman numerals with four represented as IIII instead of IV.

"What's it for?" Alexander asked after studying the dial. He held it to an oversized ear and listened to the ticking.

"It's a timepiece. The position of those little pointers show hours and minutes. The figures are numerals in an ancient numerical system."

"How do you read milliseconds? And what's the power source?"

"Back when those things were used they didn't need milliseconds. That one doesn't even have a second hand. Inside there's a whole mess of springs and gears. That's why it's so bulky. It has to be wound up every so often." She held out a hand. "Hand it over. If you think he's not going to notice that's missing, you're insane. I'll tell him I found it out on the veranda."

With poor grace Alexander surrendered the watch. "Well, it's pretty inefficient anyway. What about the pearls?"

She shrugged. "Keep them if you want, although why you want to lift things like that escapes me. You live like a king as it is."

"I just don't want to lose my touch. You gotta exercise what you're good at, you know."

"You're incorrigible," she said. "I've long since given up trying to reform you."

"Good thing too. You never know when you're gonna need a real—" He broke off and looked sharply toward a corner of the room. Mirabelle didn't look in that direction, but her hand went casually to the ornamental buckle at her waist.

"Well, looky here," Alexander said, grinning. "You been here all this time or didja just kind of materialize? I'd like to see you do that sometime. I seen the holos they made of you disappearing, see, and . . ." He was babbling on, trying to give Mirabelle time to prepare for whatever action she deemed necessary.

"Why don't you step around where I can see you?" Mirabelle said.

Maya walked into the pool of light that lay between the lounging woman and the Singeur. She placed her hands together and bowed over her fingertips. "Good evening, Lady Mirabelle," she said.

"Just Mirabelle will do. By now you know these titles are as phony as our story that we're here for our amusement."

"Except for Captain Haakon's title," Maya said.

"True. He's a real viscount, if you place any value on the titles of pretenders in exile. He doesn't. Sit. I'd offer you a drink if I'd invited you, but since you showed up as you did, what do you say we talk business?"

"As you wish." She sat on an ottoman that shaped itself to her weight and contours.

Mirabelle leaned forward, left hand upturned in the palm of the right. The thumb and fingers of her right hand idly twisted a ring on the forefinger of her left hand. It was one of her very few nervous habits and Alexander, who knew her very well, could gauge by it the tension she was feeling. Her voice betrayed no such tension. "Haakon is fond of playing games, especially games that keep good-looking women hanging around his ship. I don't play games like that. I have neither the time nor the inclination, so I'll give it to you straight. We're here for the prescience device or process that was developed under the code name 'Precious Pearl.' You can help us, or you can try to stop us, but you may as well quit trying to talk us out of it. Our

lives are at stake. I mean that in the most literal
sense. Take it from there.''

Maya studied her for a while. "I see. Since you
are being so candid, may I ask who you are working for?''

"Bahadur. Specifically, we're on Timur Khan's
leash. You must know what that means.''

"You confirm a great many things I had suspected. Your Captain Haakon carries on a good
act, but he has the marks of the Bahadur convict
pits all over him, despite your excellent camou-
flage. What's Timur Khan using these days? Slow
poison for which you need regular doses of
antidote?''

"Surgically-implanted explosives in our brains.
Maybe slow poison, too, for all I know. I wouldn't
put it past him to use a backup system. So you can
see that veiled warnings and sweet reason aren't
going to sway us. Either help us or resort to
violence.'' Once again, her hand rested idly on the
ornamental buckle. Her sprawl was so relaxed that
she almost looked limp, but Alexander knew the
signs. He was ready to jump on Maya at the first
hint of action, but he wondered how much good he
could do against a woman who could disappear at
will.

"You can both relax,'' Maya said. "I've made
my decision. I'll help you as well as I can. I'm not
certain how satisfactory you'll find my aid to be.''

"A cessation of these cryptic goings-on will be
a big help for starters. And do you have the power
to agree to help us? Somehow I don't believe
you're alone in all this.''

"No, I'm not alone, but yes, I am empowered to negotiate and use my own discretion."

"And you're not bothered by the prospect that this device or whatever could end up in the hands of Timur Khan Bey?"

For the first time, Maya laughed. It was brief, low-pitched, and had a smoky quality that caused Alexander's tail to twitch. "Bothered? Hardly. I think we can circumvent any danger posed by Bahadur. Perhaps we can make use of you and your delightful ship. After all, our aid shouldn't come cheap."

"Name your price," Mirabelle said.

"Give me time. I don't know what you have to trade, yet."

"And yet you're willing to aid us. Why?"

"Let's say I sense a certain community of interest among us." She turned to the 'bot behind Mirabelle. "Put me through to Mir Jafar."

After a few moments an irritated voice said "yes?"

"Mir Jafar, this is Maya. I've dropped by for a visit. I do hope you don't mind."

"Maya? I know nobody named—Princess Jaganmata?" A screen flashed into life on one wall, revealing the confused but rapidly composing face of Mir Jafar. A green light below the screen proclaimed that visual transmission was two-way. Maya turned to face the screen. "Ah, it is the princess, indeed! You do me too much honor, Highness. Have you come for the hunt?"

"If it isn't too much trouble to put up another guest. I do apologize for dropping by like this."

"Not at all, Highness, not at all. Let me see, you'll need a suite— I believe all the suites are taken. I'll have a bungalow flown in. It can be here within two hours."

"Nonsense, Mir Jafar," Mirabelle said. "You've given me enough room for twenty people, and I have nobody but Alexander. Allow Maya to keep me company here." She put on her most fetching smile.

"But of course, Lady Mirabelle. Is there anything else I can provide you, Princess Jagan—ah, Maya?"

"Nothing, Mir Jafar. You're a dear, a prince among men." Mir Jafar fawningly took leave and broke communication. Maya turned back to Mirabelle. "Now he'll be frantically contacting my brother and his cohorts. You've been wasting your time cultivating him. He knows nothing."

Mirabelle cocked a shapely eyebrow at her. "Jaganmata? I'd have changed my name too."

"I'll bet you did anyway. You really weren't born with a name like Mirabelle, were you?"

Mirabelle smiled ruefully. "Touché. Now, how about that drink I didn't offer you first time around?"

The flitter held a dozen ardent sportsmen, most of them in fanciful versions of the attire of hunters from earlier eras. The tweedy pseudo-Englishman was there, along with a man in lederhosen and Tryolean hat, a character in buckskins whose beam gun was disguised as a flintlock, and others even more fancifully or grotesquely dressed. All of the supposed fabrics or skins were modern synthetics equipped with temperature and humidity control for maximum comfort. Clearly, these were not among those aristocrats described by Soong whose lives were devoted to the strenuous and hazardous pursuits calculated to invest a life of ease and wealth with interest and excitement. Mirabelle asked some discreet questions concerning this.

"Oh, those fools who like to risk being eaten or bitten or gored?" Mir Jafar said in response. He was dressed as a white hunter of the nineteenth century. "You'll see some of those around here, right enough. They like to go after boar with spears, or tigers with bows and arrows, or prairie crabs with spiked clubs. Deep-seated death wish, if you ask me. No real activity for a gentleman. Now, if you want danger and adventure, the military's the place for it. Do your nation a service instead of merely indulging yourself." He sat back more comfortably and accepted a drink proffered by a hovering 'bot.

"Shall I opaque the roof a bit, Mir Jafar?" asked the man in the Tyrolean hat. "It's getting a bit hot."

"Yes, do. No sense being incinerated so early in the day."

"Jeez," said Alexander to his two lady companions, "I wonder how long this bunch'd last in lower Baikal? I bet the whole crew, beam rifles and all, would never make it through the first alley."

Mirabelle threaded her fingers through his curly hair. "They're not like us, Alex," she said so the others could not hear. "They've never had to contend with real life."

"Aristocrats!" Alexander snorted contemptuously.

"These aren't aristocrats," Maya said. "They're climbers, bloated by money. They hope to be taken for aristocrats by aping the real thing." She caught herself and looked at Alexander. "I suppose that was the wrong word to use, wasn't it?"

"Yeah, but you're better than they are. None of *them* woulda noticed." He grinned to take the edge off the rebuke.

Silently, another raftlike floating barge drew next to their own. A somewhat less lavish craft, it was black with a family device red-enameled on its sides. A hunting party more soberly dressed than Mir Jafar's waved with traditional sportsmanlike camaraderie.

"Jehan of Jahnsi," said Maya. "I was wondering when we'd see him. Mir Jafar was burning up the communication beams last night. Jehan got here ahead of my brother. It figures. Poor Baibars is never the first one to arrive anywhere."

"Is Raj Jehan a powerful influence on him?" Mirabelle asked.

"Powerful isn't the word for it. Jehan is the most powerful member of the board of regents, and that makes him the real power in the system. Baibars is only the figurehead."

The two women lounged at the rear of the barge, and to all appearances might have been discussing the latest fashions or court gossip. They had the skills of practiced conspirators and were able to speak openly without being overheard and without the appearance of hiding their conversation.

Aiding their privacy was the fact that, from the first, the other inhabitants of the barge were avoiding Maya. Most of them were crowded rather uncomfortably into the front of the craft, leaving the two women and the Singeur to themselves. Beyond the inescapable deference due to royalty, nobody seemed to want anything to do with Maya. Whatever the social climbing aspirations of these hunters, this was one member of the royal family they did not want in their midst.

"I just got a report," hailed Jehan from the other barge. "Some runners heading up Parvati Valley about six kilometers from here. What do you say, Mir Jafar? Shall we let the tigers live a day longer and go after the runners?"

Mir Jafar waved assent and gave the craft course-change instructions.

"Runners!" said one of the hunters. "That's better sport than cats or elephants."

"Oh, I don't know," said another languidly. "They're usually rather easy, unless you flush one that's really agile."

"What are runners?" Mirabelle asked.

"Runaways from the plantations," Maya told her. "They become fair game once they stray from home."

"You mean they kill people for fun out here?" Alexander said, aghast.

"They seldom shoot to kill," Maya said. "After all, the runners are somebody's valuable property. No, they just like to chase them and capture them, perhaps play games like seeing how close they can shoot without hitting the runner, or making bets on whether they can accurately beam a heel or a knee." She looked at Mirabelle appraisingly. "You don't look terribly shocked."

Mirabelle shrugged. "I'm afraid that local standards of decadence and cruelty are pretty small-scale compared to some I've encountered."

The two flitters cruised through the lush forest that was earthlike yet subtly alien. The trees were immense, far larger than any that had ever grown on Earth, and the ground below the lowest limbs was clear and parklike. Multicolored birds flew squawking through the branches and small herds of beasts on the ground fled as they sped overhead. The flitters dove beneath the branches and weaved among the vast trunks, unerringly guided by autopilot systems that could have avoided stones in a hailstorm.

"There's the game!" Mir Jafar said excitedly.

They had turned up a spectacular, steep-sided valley. Through notches in the crest of the valley wall, shimmering, ribbonlike waterfalls tumbled down the slopes. Ahead, Mirabelle caught sight of the fugitives: two emaciated men and an equally lean woman in ragged white clothes. They looked back in terror to see the pursuing craft, then began to scramble frantically up the valley in a vain attempt to escape.

"Why don't they give up?" Mirabelle said. "They can't possibly escape."

"Hell, they might as well try," Alexander said with suppressed rage. "It's all the same, they're gonna lose a leg whether they surrender or get caught. Might as well chance it.''

"It's an odd escape route," Maya said. "I'd head up one of the sides and look for cover there. It's hard to fly flitters close to the walls, and there are supposed to be hundreds of caves all through the cliffs.''

"Got them!" Mir Jafar said.

The runners were forced to slow down as they encountered a choked field of boulders through which a swift stream flowed, impeding their escape. Mir Jafar and Jehan had taken manual control of their craft and were jockeying for a superior shooting position.

"I'll take the one on the right!" said a man dressed in the cloud-camouflage costume of a Delius fur-serpent hunter. He rushed to the square bow of the craft and raised his rifle to his shoulder. The next moment he was thrown violently back into the center of the barge with a gaping rent in his chest.

"Hey! That was an old-fashioned pulse-beam!" Alexander said happily. "That's more like it! Let's see how these clowns like game that shoots back.'' Both women had dived to the bottom of the barge and grabbed projections to hang on to.

"Is he dead?" Mirabelle said, pointing with her chin at the sprawled man.

"Deader'n hell," Alexander confirmed. "Not that I'd twitch to help him if he wasn't.''

Aboard the flitter, all was confusion. Beams of some kind of weapon were sizzling overhead, and most of the hunters were huddled in the bottom, as close to the center as they could get. A few of the hardier souls poked their weapons over the rail for a quick shot, but none stayed long enough to take a careful sight. One was flung back with a hole beneath his chin, throwing his pukka sahib pith helmet across the barge with a corresponding exit hole burned in its crown.

"They're in a panic," Mirabelle said composedly. "What will happen if the raft gets upended?"

"That won't happen," Maya said. "These things have more safety systems than you'd believe possible. For some reason these people always think their lives are valuable. No, our worst risk is that it'll tilt enough to expose us to the people shooting below."

Above them, they saw Jehan's barge circling. It was clear that nobody up there was panicking. The craft was under manual control, circling just fast enough to make a difficult target, but not taking such extreme evasive action that its occupants could not shoot back.

"There's a man who knows how to deal with an ambush," Mirabelle muttered.

"Yes," Maya said. "Pity."

Alexander turned to a 'bot hovering nearby, insanely maintaining its equilibrium despite the crazy antics of the half-controlled raft. "Gimme a beer, circuithead, and better put it in a globe." The requisite globe was delivered, and Alexander sucked industriously at the tube extruded from its side. "You know, them guys down there ain't very good. I guess that first shot was a lucky one. They shoulda waited till we was down lower, maybe even on the ground. They'da played their cards right, they coulda got everybody on both rafts without losing a man. Way it is now, they gonna get their butts kicked.'' He jerked a chin up toward the raft circling overhead. ''That guy knows what he's doing.''

The firing below became sporadic, then stopped altogether. Jehan's raft came down and stopped level with Mir Jafar's, the two almost touching. Raj Jehan stepped across, bending low to avoid the almost invisible roof. Hesitantly, the hunters stood up. ''Raj Jehan!'' Mir Jafar said. ''We must call in troops at once! I have never heard of such an outrage. Who do you—''

Jehan brushed by Mir Jafar without looking at him. ''Is Princess Jaganmata safe?''

Mir Jafar looked back to the rear of his craft. ''The Princess? Why, I—''

Once again, he did not get to finish what he was saying. Jehan whirled and stepped over the two bodies on the deck like a stroller avoiding fallen logs. ''Highness, are you well?'' he asked.

''Quite well, Raj Jehan,'' she told him.

''As usual. Your brother will be happy to learn that, once again, his sister has avoided harm.'' He turned to Mirabelle. ''And you, my lady?''

''Perfectly all right, Raj Jehan. Thank you for your concern. It was all most exhilarating. I had been expecting a rather dull and pointless slaughter of helpless beasts. Those people below were much more entertaining. Who were they?''

''I expect to find out soon.'' He turned to Maya.

"You wouldn't be able to enlighten us in this matter would you, Highness?"

"I'm afraid not. I've never involved myself with hopeless causes. I'm sure you and your people will track down and destroy those pitiful bandits down there."

"We shall. But this was better planned than most such actions. The runners were acting deliberately as bait, and sucked us in neatly. That's new."

"Pretty damn ballsy, too, wouldn't you say?" Immediately, for once, Alexander wished he had kept his mouth shut. The glance Jehan shot him was brief but penetrating. This man was an entirely different proposition from the likes of Mir Jafar. Jehan returned his attention to Maya.

"Highness, your brother the Lion requests that you accept his invitation to visit him at the palace. Will you accompany me?" He said the word "requests" as if it required considerable force to eject.

"Why, of course, I'd love to visit the old place." She turned to Mirabelle. "Lady Mirabelle, would you care to come along? It's a very beautiful palace. You would find it a most rewarding visit."

Mirabelle raised an eyebrow microscopically. "Why, of course. That sounds wonderful." She turned to Mir Jafar. "Thank you for a most enjoyable hunting trip, Mir Jafar. We really must do this again sometime."

"Then if you ladies will accompany me," said Jehan over Mir Jafar's stammer, "please come aboard my flitter. We'll return to the lodge for your belongings." Graciously, the two women transferred to the other raft.

Alexander hopped across the two bodies and settled himself next to a 'bot. "Gimme a beer," he ordered. This one arrived in a silver-mounted ox horn.

ELEVEN

"They're going *where*?" Haakon demanded.

"You heard me the first time," Jemal answered. "They've been invited to the palace."

"Invited," Haakon huffed. "Ordered is more like it, I'd say."

"Somehow," Jemal answered, "I don't think anybody orders Maya anyplace. They seem to be going quite willingly. Mirabelle was in plain view through the whole communication and she didn't flash any of our signals. I could see Alex behind her, sopping up beer like he didn't have a care in the world. You know damn well he'd show it if he was scared."

"What the hell. She's grown and can take care of herself. Now, what about this?" He held up a thin slip of paper on which was written: *Meet me tomorrow. Same time, same procedure. Steiner.*

"One of the servants in a white sari handed it to

me," Soong said. "She brought it when I called for a fresh deck of cards."

"Should we chance it?" Jemal asked.

"Might as well," Haakon said. "We're not doing anything just now, and I'm bored."

"It might be unwise," Soong objected. "With two of us in Baibars's palace under unknown circumstances, and Rama besotted with her biological imperatives."

"I heard that!" Rama said through the intercom. Soong looked abashed at having made a rare diplomatic indiscretion. "You wait there," Rama went on. "I'm going down to the planet with you. I'm sick of this ship, and I'm sick of that disgusting Numa. I'm sick of you, too, but I haven't had to endure your company recently. Give me time to change."

"You'll have plenty of time to change, Rama," Haakon said patiently. "We're not going anywhere until tomorrow, if we decide to go at all."

"Good. That shall give me time to fully restore my beauty. And I am going, even if nobody else goes." Noisily, she broke transmission.

"Do you think this would be wise?" Soong said. "She is not in the best of condition, either physical or mental."

"Sick or well, she's worth about five good men in a street brawl," Haakon contended. "As for her mental condition, I've never seen her any way other than crazy. Sure, she can go with us if she wants. Soong, you and Rand hold the fort. We'll use the usual distress signals if there's trouble."

"As you order, Captain."

*   *   *

Lorah met them in the usual spot. Her eyes widened at the sight of Rama. The Felid had regained most of her looks and composure, and she wore a minimal street garb in keeping with the city's heat. "What's this?" Lorah demanded.

"A shipmate," Haakon said.

"Steiner said nothing about no cat-woman. You two I know. I could get trouble I show up with that." She jerked her chin toward Rama, who was nearly twice her height and easily three times her bulk.

"Little one," Rama purred, "you have no concept of trouble. I can teach you what real trouble is."

"Settle down," Haakon cautioned. "Take us to Steiner, Lorah. You get more bothersome all the time."

An hour later, after the usual circuitous tour of the city, they found Steiner, this time in a multi-roomed building that seemed to be a clubhouse-cum-warehouse for the Mongrels. It was stuffed with goods, all of which had that ineffable quality which distinguishes the nefariously acquired from the legitimately purchased.

"Welcome to my little kingdom, spacers," he greeted them. "I hope you'll forgive the clutter. In these unsettled times, business is slow." Steiner looked much better than when they had last seen him. He moved a little stiffly, but otherwise he looked much as when they had first met.

"Those Galen bandages work as advertised?" Jemal asked.

Steiner grinned. "Pretty much. Never thought I'd be up and around this soon."

"What have you got for us?" Haakon asked.

"Always get right to the point, eh, spacer?"

"That's right."

"Well, we got a meet coming up tonight that I think you ought to attend. It's going to be representatives from most of the city gangs, to discuss some important matters."

"Why should we be interested?" Haakon asked.

"There's going to be some matters under discussion that's of great importance to you, boyo. There's been a lot of unrest all over—little revolts, agitation, things like that. This meeting's going to concern what might be happening right here in the city. This is a chance for you. Maybe some real opportunity opening up here."

"Will the Free Mughal Party be represented?" Haakon asked.

"You may not see any of the people you met last time, but they'll have representatives there. Me, for one." He turned to Lorah. "Kid, show 'em where their clothes are. You see," he turned back to Haakon, "these are suspicious people we'll be among. You're going to go dressed as Mongrels. It's safer that way." He looked Rama up and down. "They're not used to seeing great big, stripy-haired cat-ladies, though." He shrugged. "It'll be okay. Not everybody's born here. We get spacers who get beached and can't get a ship out. They end up coming to us because they don't have any caste and can't enter a trade. She can be one of those, if anybody asks."

Lorah took them to a small room where the various components of typical Mongrel garb hung on pegs. The clothing was complex, with separate arms, legs, jerkins, and breechclouts, all held together with a multiplicity of metal rings, straps, buckles, and laces. From among the optional items, Haakon selected brown leather leggings and clout. He retained his vest, bracelets, and boots, and didn't bother with sleeves. Jemal constructed a complete red leather outfit but left his knife arm bare.

Characteristically, Rama put together the most striking rig, using white and black leather studded with decorative metal, covering her arms and long legs but little else. Hanging fringes magnified every move she made. She admired herself in a mirror for a while, then added some pieces of massive metal jewelry. At last she was satisfied with the effect.

"You're stepping right into character," Jemal commented. "That stuff looks natural on you."

"I ran gangs like this in cities like this for many years," she said. "I was not always the successful businesswoman I am now. If I were to stay here, I would be in control of this mob within days."

Lorah sat on a crate in a corner, studying Rama resentfully from under a jagged fringe of hair. "Not damn likely, cat-woman. We was born and grew up in these streets. They don't nobody here accept a new boss just because she's big and got stripy hair and claws."

Rama smiled and walked over to Lorah, taking advantage of her towering height to force the girl to look up to maintain eye contact. Instinctively, Lorah placed a hand on the grip of the curved knife sheathed on the thigh of her right legging.

"Dear one," Rama purred, "independence and loyalty to your turf are fine things, but they are nothing compared to fear. I ran my gangs without interference or opposition because my subordinates feared me. They feared me more than they feared the other gangs or the authorities. It would be no different here and you would be no exception. Now tell me"—Rama leaned forward, slit-pupiled eyes narrowed murderously, hair fanned out, whiskers and ears laid back, and exuding an acrid fighting scent—"aren't you just the tiniest bit intimidated?"

Lorah cringed back, her hand falling away from the knife, then broke away and darted out through the open door. Rama chuckled softly as her hair smoothed out.

"That was uncalled for, Rama," Jemal said, adjusting the hang of his knife belt more comfortably. "It's not all that hard to throw a scare into a half-grown kid. I could do it myself, if I wanted to."

"It's never good to let the weak ones get an erroneous idea of their power, especially the young ones. Now she is under no such misapprehension. Besides," she turned to Haakon, "I wanted her out of the room. We need to discuss this. What is the meaning of this charade? Do you believe this nonsense about our having something to gain by attending some kind of gang summit conference?"

"Not for a minute," Haakon told her. "But all

we can do is play it by ear. Obviously, *somebody* feels he has something to gain by our presence, and I'd like to find out who and why."

"There may be no conference," Jemal said. "They could be leading us into an ambush."

Haakon sighed dramatically. "Use your head, Jem. Look at where we are now: a small room with one door. If they wanted to jump us, could they have a better place in mind? If we get out of this room alive, we'll know they're not trying to jump us."

"You're rationalizing," Jemal persisted. "You're just bored and looking for some excitement."

"That's all right with me," Rama said. "I'm all for excitement. As long as I know where we stand." She flexed up and down on the balls of her feet, exposing and sheathing her claws rhythmically.

"You're coming unglued, both of you," Jemal said. "You're fed up with partying, and spoiling for a little lower-city fun. Between Numa and Maya, they've lowered your intelligence and standards of judgment about forty percent." He looked down at his oppressively heavy leathers. "Hell, I'm bored too. Let's get on with it. Maybe something interesting's about to happen."

Steiner expressed satisfaction with their appearance. "You could pass inspection on any streetcorner, boyos. There's just too many people for the police to take note of a few new faces." He turned to Rama. "What did you do to poor little Lorah? She came out of there looking like she been through an ask-and-answer session with the police information service."

"I just have a strong personality," Rama answered. "She was a little overwhelmed."

"Sweetly, now, cat-lady," Steiner cautioned. "She's one of mine, and I don't intimidate. Besides, you don't want to attract more attention than absolutely necessary, and the last thing you want to worry about is disaffection among your friends. You'll find more than enough enemies outside."

"I'll worry about my own back, if you don't mind," she told him. "You keep your underlings in line. It is not my job, and I might be rough on them."

"Back off, Rama," Haakon cautioned. "Steiner's our ally. We don't want trouble here."

"As you wish," she said, relaxing immediately. She examined the back of a hand and began licking it. It was still slightly scabbed from her reproductive exertions.

"Let's go," Steiner said.

Outside, a Mongrel escort awaited them, about thirty strong. The streets cleared as the group moved out. A sudden concentration of gang strength was always a bad sign. They saw no sign of police anywhere. Evidently, the guardians of law and order were staying clear of the streets as well.

Their destination turned out to be a large, open park, the first such that Haakon or Jemal had seen in the city. It was already crowded with other packs, some in quasi-uniform like the Mongrels, others in traditional Mughal clothing or whatever bizarre garb the individual members fancied.

"Why such a public place?" Haakon asked. "The police will have watching and listening devices all around."

"In the first place," Steiner said, "there isn't an indoor space in the whole city that could hold this crowd. Second, this is neutral territory, so everybody could agree to meet here. The police have agreed to leave us alone. We've done this a couple of times before. But just in case, we got a camp shield from the military. That took a big bribe, but it'll keep us invisible and silent from outside. Hell, it'll even protect us if it rains.

"And most of all, these people just don't like to get trapped in a closed space with limited exit. Here in the park, if the cops renege and raid us, or somebody tries to take advantage of the situation and use it to get rid of some competition, then we can scatter in all directions."

"That makes sense," Haakon said, thinking of what he'd said a few minutes before in the warehouse. Steiner's eyes narrowed as a small group of young men appeared, wearing bright red shirts and black sashes of some silky material.

"Well, well," Steiner muttered, "here comes the Garudas to pay their respects."

The spokesman for the silk-shirted men was a short man with a dark, pockmarked face. He smiled hugely when he was within conversational distance. "Peace, Steiner. You're looking well. I rejoice to see you recovering so swiftly."

"Peace, Mundra. I grieve to see that your following is shy two of its accustomed members."

Mundra smiled even wider and shrugged elaborately. "These things happen. It's the nature of business that you lose as well as gain, and that there is always sacrifice involved."

"We really must get together and discuss this at length sometime," Steiner said. "There are some things that go beyond the call of ordinary business obligations."

"Ah, but there are no—" Mundra was silenced by the approach of a man who walked without escort. Steiner turned to face the new arrival as well. The subtly altered stance of both gang leaders told Haakon that the man who now stood before them was regarded with great respect. Both men deferred to him.

He was certainly physically intimidating. He wore only a white loincloth. Otherwise he did not even bother with sandals. Even taller than Rama, he was as hairless as Haakon, although a faint stubble on his scalp showed that this was the result of daily shaving rather than depilation. His arms were like legs, and were crossed over a barrel chest above a huge, round belly. His legs were short and stumpy for his height, and he stood with them widespread, his bare toes dug into the turf, looking like a permanent feature of the landscape. He smiled at them benevolently. "Peace, Steiner, Mundra."

"Peace, Ganesha," they both answered.

"I hear of hard doings between the Garudas and the Mongrels, my good friends," Ganesha said mildly. "Things involving powerblades and beamers. People seriously injured and even killed. These things sadden me, children."

"The Mongrels never went looking for trouble," Steiner said heatedly. "We was on a peaceful business assignment when they—"

Ganesha silenced him with a gesture. "I have
no interest in causes and origins, children. These
things are passing and illusory. What I wish is to
see harmony reign among my brethren, and an end
to this petty bickering, which is profitless and
distresses the cosmic order. If that order is too
much disturbed," he looked at them in turn, "great
harm could come to you."

"We want no trouble with you," Mundra said
with his eyes lowered.

"That is easily accomplished," Ganesha told
him. "Just do nothing to arouse my displeasure."
He casually glanced at Haakon, Jemal, and Rama,
who stood slightly to one side of Steiner. "New
members, Steiner?"

"Probationary," Steiner answered. "They're
beached spacers. I might make 'em permanent
members if they work out."

"Well, I must be about my business. Peace to
you, children." Ganesha turned and walked away
with massive dignity. Mundra jerked his head at
his followers and began to walk away as well.

"Mundra," Steiner said. The short man turned.
"We still got to get together to discuss that business matter. Sometime soon, all right?" Mundra
nodded and walked off.

"Who's Ganesha?" Haakon asked.

"He's the city boss," Steiner said. "He's the
ten-percent man. You want to operate in this city,
you cut him in for ten percent. He arbitrates dis-
putes and he's the go-between who handles relations with the authorities. You want to bribe an
official for a license or something like that, you

take it to Ganesha, and ten percent always sticks to his fingers.''

"Why's he so interested in keeping peace between you and the Garudas?'' Jemal asked.

"He's not. He figures it was a setup. Somebody was paid for it, and he didn't get his ten percent. That kind of thing upsets him, and he figures anything that costs him throws the cosmic balance out of kilter.''

"He's not the kind of man I would want to upset,'' Rama said. Coming from her, it was a most meaningful statement.

Above them the clear air with its fine view of the stars grew shimmery, and the noise of the surrounding city became muffled.

"There's the shield,'' Steiner said. "From now on, we're shut off from the outside. They must be getting ready to start the meeting. Come on, let's go get near the stand.''

As he led them toward the center of the throng, Jemal asked: "How solid is this shield? Will it keep people out, or just keep them from eavesdropping?''

"It's a military protective shield,'' Steiner said. "It'll keep people out unless they've got specialized equipment.''

"Will it keep us in?'' Haakon asked.

"Only as long as the generator's going. Since we know where that is, we can always shut it off if we want to get away quick.''

In the center of the park, a low platform, apparently a permanent structure, stood beneath an immense tree, the lowest branches of which began at

least twenty meters above the ground. Most of the
trees in the park seemed to be of this type; huge,
spreading shade trees which made for an open park
with relief from the hot rays of Mughal's primary.
Haakon was uncomfortably aware that such foliage
gave little cover and no escape possibilities.

A small group of men stood on the platform,
prominent among them the ponderous bulk of
Ganesha. Behind the platform two men manipulated a small console on which readout lights blinked
and which emitted a low hum. This, Haakon assumed, must be the shield generator.

He studied the crowd around them and realized
that relatively few of them were actually members
of the organized gangs. The bulk seemed to be
made up of the ubiquitous crippled street beggars.
There were many women in the crowd besides the
obvious street-gang members like Lorah. Most were
dressed in plain white saris, but Haakon noticed
that they all wore three vertical stripes of green
paint on their brows.

He leaned close to Steiner. "Those women with
the green face-paint, are they the prostitutes?"

"Right you are, boyo. Never see those stripes
without remembering my dear old mother."

Rama's eyes darted from side to side nervously.
"I don't like that shield," she said. "This place
looks open but it isn't."

"I don't like it either," Haakon said.

"Don't look to me for sympathy," Jemal said.
"I warned you."

"Relax, boyos," Steiner insisted. "That generator's not ten meters from us. That's one reason I

wanted to station us here. We got almost all the Mongrels here with us, and they got their orders: first sign of trouble, they vault that platform and destroy the generator. Just takes a second, they're pretty fragile. Then we're free to scatter."

Ganesha stood forward, and the subdued mutter of the crowd silenced. "My children," he began, "it seems that we live in changing times. This may not be for the best, for change always brings with it distress and an upsetting of the cosmic order. However," he spread his hands helplessly, "who are we as mere mortals to protest? History is a great cycle, and the wheels of the gods turn inexorably whether we will or no."

"Oh, get to the point, you fat windbag," Steiner muttered under his breath.

"Patience," Haakon cautioned him. "Don't want to upset the cosmic balance, now, do you?" Steiner glared and turned away, grumbling.

"It remains for us," Ganesha continued, "to determine how we may, in this transitory life, do well out of this time of change." The platform was rigged with some kind of sound transmission system. Ganesha was speaking in a conversational tone and his voice could be heard at exactly the same volume anywhere in the park. "Here with us tonight are representatives of all the business and fraternal organizations of the lower city." He waved an arm at the men who stood with him on the platform, then at those who stood in the first rank before it, among whom was Steiner.

Prominent among those on the platform was an old man with a powerful, evil face, one-eyed and bearded. He was also missing an arm and had his head bound up in a black turban.

"Who's the hard-looking old character up there next to Ganesha?" Haakon asked.

"That's Rashid, the head of the beggar's guild. He's another one you don't want to cross. In fact, you'd be well advised to stay clear of everybody up on that stand. That's a big concentration of sudden death and misery up there, and they control most of the city. Gang bosses like me are pretty small stuff compared to them." Haakon had to grant a certain grudging respect to that admission. As Ganesha droned on about the ineffable nature of cosmic inevitability, Steiner continued: "Back there in the corner is Harun al Muktar, though that's not his real name. He's the top smuggling fence. Khota Ram is the one in the kaftan. He runs all the big gambling operations. Gambling's under tight government control here, so there's lots of money in it."

"Why the government control?" Rama asked with professional interest.

"The owners of the orbiting resorts swing a lot of influence. They got gambling banned on the ground, so people got to go up to orbit to gamble. Naturally, you got to be well-off to do that, so there's a lot of money in running poor men's games."

This explanation of Mughal underworld life was interrupted when Ganesha began to get around to the meat of his address.

"Until now, the authorities have been content to leave us largely to our own devices, as long as they received their honorariums and we refrained from political matters.'' He glanced significantly at Steiner and a few other men in the crowd. It disturbed Haakon to see a hardcase like Steiner turn pale. ''However, it seems that some of our brethren have chosen to ignore this rule which for so long has given us an unimpeded means of living. These misguided persons have made an unholy alliance with the forces of discord and change. They may have brought upon us disaster.''

Ganesha was addressing the crowd at large, but one-eyed old Rashid was sweeping them with his limited gaze, first fixing Steiner, but then carefully scanning the new faces among the Mongrels.

''Wait a minute,'' Steiner said. ''This ain't what they was supposed to be talking about.'' His face was covered with a sheen of sweat and his neck worked continuously with the movement of busy muscles and tendons. ''They was supposed to—'' His next words were cut off by a sudden barking of police 'bots which floated out from the foliage of the surrounding trees.

''Stay where you are and remain calm!'' came the authoritarian shout from the 'bots. ''We are not arresting you all unless there is resistance. We want to question certain persons among this assembly. Remain calm, and police officers will process you to find these—''

Rama was first across the platform. She hit the little group of men like a bowling ball among tenpins. Two sidewise bats of her hands, without even unsheathing her claws, made a gap through which she, along with Haakon, Jemal, Steiner, and most of the Mongrels poured toward the shield generator. The two generator operators got in one startled, terrified look over their shoulders before she grasped each in a hand and tossed them aside. She picked the generator up, hoisted the compact hundred or so kilos of it over her head and smashed it to the ground, where it lay sputtering until the power died. Overhead, the shield remained intact, the stars still shimmering.

"It was a fake!" she shouted. "The real generator is somewhere else!"

"Stand where you are!" They turned, and there stood Ganesha, a daunting picture of physical presence, backed by a large crew of bulky strong-arm men. "It grieves me, Steiner, my child, but we must restrain you here until the authorities arrive to—"

Without hesitation Haakon attacked, slamming both rock-hardened fists into the massive belly. Calmly, Ganesha locked his massive hands onto Haakon's neck and began to twist. Even Haakon's great strength was to no avail. He was lifted and thrown back like a rag doll, to tumble into Steiner. Both men were knocked sprawling to the ground.

Then Rama was on Ganesha. A pair of vicious slashes sent the huge man staggering back, screaming and bleeding profusely. "Debate cosmic order with the gods, fat man!" she shrieked. Ganesha's backers closed in and she was among them, her taloned hands and feet flashing faster than thought to send men spinning and screaming in all directions.

Jemal slid in by her side, powerblade out. Wherever he saw a weapon, the blade flashed and the weapon dropped as he cut in economical elegance, moving with such grace and precision that his motions seemed almost casual, even bored. Then Haakon and Steiner and the other Mongrels were with them, striking with hands and feet and side-arms until the major opposition drew back, unwilling to tangle with this human dynamo of destruction. The 'bots floated overhead, continuing to yammer their ineffective orders.

"Cease, you young fools!" They turned from their combat-induced stupor to see Rashid, the beggar king, standing inexplicably in their midst.

"If you would live, follow me." The one-eyed, one-armed old patriarch strode through the milling mob.

Rama looked at Haakon, and he shrugged. "Hell, let's go with him. Can't be worse than staying here."

He and the Felid, along with Jemal, Steiner, and such of the Mongrels as were still on their feet, followed the old man through the mob and out to the edge of the park. Everywhere, people were running, batting with ineffective fists against the unyielding walls of the shield as the police 'bots circled overhead, shouting orders that no one obeyed.

Behind a tree near the shield wall Rashid came to a pair of ragged men operating a console identical to the one that had stood behind the speaking platform. They looked up in surprise to see the old man approaching, and behind him a crowd of tough and determined people intent upon escape.

Rashid waved his only hand in a dismissive

gesture. "Go away, you foolish men. You don't really want to die here, do you?"

The men fled instantly, and the old man walked to the console and touched a pressure plate. The shield flickered and dispersed, revealing a dark cityscape beyond. At intervals along the periphery of the park they could see knots of the Sikh policemen, obviously taken by surprise when the shield winked out of existence. The crowd stormed out of the park, sweeping the incomplete police cordon aside in confusion.

"Steiner," Rashid said, in a voice oddly mild for such a vicious-looking old man, "take your Mongrels and disperse. Go back to your territory and lie low until I send you word."

"Let's go, troops," Steiner said, and the leather-clad horde began heading for home. Steiner turned back to Haakon. "You coming with us?"

"I shall take charge of these people," Rashid said.

"Well, good luck, then," Steiner told them.

"It's been an interesting evening, Steiner," Haakon said. "We'll discuss this at some length later."

"Hey, man, this wasn't my fault. I—" He turned as Lorah came up and grabbed at his leather vest.

"Let's go, chief," she urged. "Them police ain't gonna stay loonied for long."

"Well, luck, spacers," Steiner said, and followed his Mongrels into the alleys.

Rashid turned to the little band from *Eurynome*. "And you, my lord of Delius, had better follow me, and that quickly. We have little leisure. I will take you to a place of safety."

"Hold on a minute," Haakon said. "Is there any reason why we should follow you, or feel any safer with you than on our own?" Despite his words, he was walking alongside the old man as they darted between buildings, putting distance between themselves and the park with its confusion and police parties.

"A good question," Rashid said equably. "That of a prudent and cautious man. You should follow me first because you have little choice, being in an alien and hostile city, and second because you have no choice, since the port is sealed and you have no way back to your ship." They stopped at a featureless corner. The sounds of uproar were far behind them, and it was clear that pursuit, if there had been any in the first place, had been shaken off.

"But most of all," Rashid continued, "you must ally yourself with me because I take my instruction from the Lady Maya, and if you would know the secret of the Precious Pearl project, you had better come with me."

"Well, hell," Haakon said, "since you put it that way, let's go." Silently, they disappeared down the darkened streets.

TWELVE

Alexander was bored. The palace had been stunning, at first. The luxuries of the resort and the hunting lodge had paled by comparison. There were whole walls closely studded with precious gems. The rugs here would be wall hangings anywhere else. There was a tub of solid gold filled with Sirian firegems cut in cabochon where you could wallow if you liked that sort of thing. The first day, he had let his acquisitive fantasies run rampant amid this veritable temple to gross materialism. He had availed himself of the abundance of incomparable food and booze, enjoyed the music and incredibly skilled dancers and other performers. There were even scantily clad houris whose only purpose seemed to be the provision of dalliance and gratification for the many noblemen and foreign dignitaries who flocked about the palace. By the second day it all seemed rather ordinary.

By the third, it was dull. He wanted to go home.
He had finally realized that beer drunk from a cup
of cut emerald tasted exactly like beer from a
molyfilm bulb.

"Why do they live like this?" he had asked
Mirabelle late on their second night. "I'm all for
living good, you know that, but just how good do
they gotta live?"

"It has no intrinsic value," she told him. "To
them, it's a symbol."

"What do you mean?" he asked. Abstract reasoning came hard to Alexander, who had always
lived close to his emotions and sensory impressions.

"All this redundant opulence is a symbol of
power, their power over other people."

"But," he objected, "nobody sees it but them.
Who they gonna impress?"

She smiled at him. "Very perceptive, Alex. No,
they're doing this for themselves. To the lower
classes, there's no doubt as to who's on top. These
jumped-up plutocrats have to keep constantly proving to themselves that they're the chosen people. It
also impresses the ambassadors from other systems. Even the Khans of Bahadur can't afford to
live like this. They're saying, 'Bahadur is powerful, but we are rich.' "

So now here he was, sitting on the railing of a
balcony, nibbling at a fruit he had taken from a
tray carried by a servant. No 'bots in this palace. It
was much more gratifying to be served by live
domestics. The rail he sat on was part of a panel
made from a single huge slab of jade, carved and
fretted with infinite hand labor. Idly, he wondered

from which planet they got a chunk of jade so huge. The ladies were off attending some exhibit or other and he was by himself. What to do?

He slid from the railing to the balcony and walked idly inside. He was free to go anywhere he wanted to. He realized with some chagrin that this was mainly because nobody considered him to be quite human, so he was given the toleration people usually accorded to pets. Well, screw 'em, he thought. There were advantages to being ignored. He'd go exploring and see how far he got before somebody started yelling at him.

As far as he knew, the palace was laid out as an immense cluster of interconnected buildings interspersed with temples. The temples were mainly for show. There never seemed to be any kind of religious service going on in them. The buildings were copied after the palaces of ancient India, but they were unobtrusively fitted with all the modern amenities. Invisible force-screens kept in the cooled air while allowing the fragrances of the outside gardens to enter, and elevators allowed access to different floors without the tedium of using the many imposing marble stairways. It was all, he reflected, phony as hell.

The first thing, he thought, was to get out of these overdecorated public rooms and into the works of the place, to rooms marked ''no admittance'' and corridors with guards to keep intruders out. That was where the good stuff would be. Just now, he wasn't quite sure what kind of stuff he was after, but they were here to snoop, so snoop he would.

He decided to try upstairs first. The rooms stayed lavish, but they got stranger the higher he ascended. One was carpeted with living grass and full of long-legged birds. One was full of fountains spraying multicolored perfumes. In another he came across a couple amorously entwined and oblivious to him, lying on a huge, furry couch. Then the couch got up on four stumpy legs while the couple continued to writhe in pursuit of sensual gratification. That, he thought, was definitely a new one. Interesting, but not strategic. He tried a higher floor.

This looked more promising. It was rather plain and undecorated, so probably this area was devoted to business and practical pursuits. He was pretty sure that the service apparatus of the palace complex was concentrated in the subterranean levels. The people he could see up here were mostly in uniform, and the uniforms were not the ornate fancy-dress affairs he sometimes saw below. Here it was mostly coveralls of a single color with rank and other insignia on breast, sleeve, and collar. A small number of them wore arms.

Picking a corridor at random, Alexander dropped to all fours and traipsed along, pausing to stare into open doorways. Nobody ever pays much attention to anything that walks on four feet. He drew nothing but amused looks from the men and women working behind desks or at instruments.

"Someone's pet ape got loose," he heard a man's voice say from a room he had just looked into.

"I thought it was a boy," said a woman's voice

from the same room. That's it, he thought. Keep 'em confused.

He passed out of the area of offices and into something that looked more ominous. Since he couldn't read the local script, he wasn't sure just what this place was, but in several locations he saw posted the pulsing, triangular green plate that meant "unauthorized personnel keep out" on almost every world. This looked promising. Also, there were very few people in evidence. Nothing in his immediate vicinity looked really interesting, so he turned down a side corridor.

"Hey! You there! Stop!" Halfway down the corridor, a man sat behind a curved desk that took up half the width of the hall. A spray of multicolored light on the lower half of his face showed that the desk was a screen and instrument panel, probably a snoop-and-security facility. The man got up and came toward Alexander. He was big and bulky, dressed in a black coverall with silver collar tabs and he wore a holstered sidearm along with a lot of other gadgets on his belt. Everything about him spoke to Alexander of words like "cop" and "jailer."

"Where'd you come from?" the man asked. Alexander gave him a wide, idiot grin and pointed back the way he had come. "Not that, dummy. You came from down below, right? Who do you belong to?" He bent to look at Alexander's neck. "You wearing an ID collar?"

"Don't need one, boss," Alexander said. "I can talk."

"So talk. Who's your owner?"

"Lady Mirabelle. From *Eurynome*."

"Never heard of her or it. Why aren't you with her?"

"Left me in the room. Nothing to do there." Alexander did a quick back flip, then continued. "Climbed out the window. Looking for some fun."

"Well, you won't find any here. Now go back to your owner. If I see you on this floor again, I'll pull your tail out."

"Bye, boss!" Alexander turned and scampered away. He stopped as soon as he was out of sight. Owner, huh? Owner my ass, he thought.

He was alone in a room set into an angle formed by the meeting of two corridors. It appeared to be some kind of lounge area, but nobody was lounging there now. As in most of the rooms he had passed, this one had a window opening onto the outside. He looked quickly around for observers, then jumped to the sill. There were no climbing prospects at this level, but he looked up and saw a band of high-relief sculpture which stretched the length of the building above a row of similar windows. On it gods, Apsaras, Gandharvas, Nagas, Vrikshakas, Yakshis, and an occasional cow or elephant all postured and cavorted to some long-forgotten mythological purpose.

Seizing the bulbous breast of a Yakshi, Alexander hauled himself nimbly up to the carved band and began to work himself along, back toward the forbidden corridor. He moved slowly, aware that someone on one of the balconies below, or just glancing up from a window, might spy him. Each time he thought he caught a hint of movement at a balcony or window, he froze. Among the painted sculpture of the frieze, he was almost indistinguishable when not in motion. His remarkable resemblance to Hanuman the monkey-king made him seem right at home.

Now he was above a window he judged to be well beyond the desk of the dutiful official who had sent him away. Slowly, Alexander let himself down, hanging on by one hand, one foot, and his tail as, inch by inch, he lowered his head so as to sneak a look into the room below. He was ready to jerk himself up and be off at the first sign of detection.

Inside, the room was dim. There seemed to be no inhabitants. Alexander's sense of spatial orientation was highly developed, as was necessary for a subspecies gene manipulated for an arboreal existence. Even so, he couldn't make out much while hanging upside down. All he had was an impression that the room was not like anything he had ever seen before. Cautiously, he let himself down into the chamber. He squatted on the sill, ready to dart out on short notice, as he studied the interior.

For a while, Alexander tried to figure out what it reminded him of. Small, weird animals dangled from the ceiling, dead. They were preserved by some process more primitive than any he had ever seen before, as if they had been opened up, stuffed, and dried. There was a chemical scent in the air of the place, and things bubbled over open flames on tables. He had seen flame used for cooking and heating before, but only as a necessity when roughing it without good equipment. And the containers over the flames looked like glass. He had seen glass, too, on frontier worlds where imports were high but sand was cheap. There were all kinds of other odd stuff too. In fact, the room was incredibly cluttered. Peculiar instruments stood on spindly mounts, sprouting arms that held lenses and prisms. An ancient optical-type telescope gathered dust in a corner. That was another thing. Dust. Apparently, not only were there no 'bots here, but no human servants either. There were piles of old-fashioned books with flip-over pages. That tickled Alexander's memory. Jemal had a few books like that. He liked Old Earth literature. Alexander was sure that was where he had seen a picture of a room like this. It was something to do with a place far back in Earth history where people went around in armor, only it wasn't like armorcloth but in plates, and the plate armor wasn't powered like the military used. Then he remembered that the king in those stories had an advisor or something, whose name he couldn't remember, and the advisor was a wizard, and the wizard had a room like this.

Alexander wasn't really sure just what a wizard was, but he was something like a scientist or a Tesla engineer, only a wizard worked in a much more cluttered place. Silently, he dropped into the room and went to examine things more closely. He found an astrolabe, although he had no idea what it was called, and idly spun some of its bronze rings. A human skull grinned at him from a table and he grinned back. He wondered what so prosaic an item was doing in this strange place. It took him a while to catch on that there were no modern instruments or devices in sight. It had not struck him at first because he was already used to Mughal's relative technological backwardness. Now he realized that, not only were there no talkers or screens or 'bots, there were not even any sources of artificial light, just lanterns and candles that looked as if they were made from real animal fat. Why would anybody want to live like that in a palace like this?

"Hanuman?"

Alexander whipped around. Somebody was standing in a doorway to another room, and he had gotten there without Alexander hearing him. That displeased Alexander, who took great pride in his hearing. The man was an old-looking specimen in a voluminous, midnight-blue robe. His long beard was white, as was the long hair which hung like a curtain from the sides of his bald head. He even *looked* like the old geezer from the picture in Jemal's book.

"Are you Hanuman?" the old man asked. He had a kindly face, with mild blue eyes.

"Sorry to disappoint you, boss," Alexander said, "but my name's Alex. I know who Hanuman is. I seen some pictures and statues. Despite the family resemblance, I ain't him."

"Oh, that's a pity," the old man said. "I have tried for so long to establish contact with the gods. I had hoped that they had sent you as a messenger."

"You want to get in touch with the gods?" Alexander asked. "I met one of them once. Didn't think he was all that great."

"Really?" said the old man in astonishment. "Which god was that?"

"Guy named Xeus. He could be about a thousand meters high when he wanted to. He could make planets, stuff like that. I don't know if he was a real god, though. He put on a good show, that's for sure."

"Xeus! That would be Zeus of the Greeks, and Deus of the Romans, and Dyaus the Sky of the Sanscrit peoples, and also Theos of the Germans! How did you happen to contact him?"

"Well, we sort of tripped over him, actually. That was in the Cingulum. And if you think this place is strange, you oughta see the Cingulum."

"How did—" Then the white-haired man seemed to collect himself. "But, I forget my manners. Please, come into my sitting room. What would you have by way of refreshment? May I offer you some wine?"

"You got any beer?" Alexander asked hopefully. The old man picked up a beaker and handed it to him, full of foamy brew. "Thanks." Alexander had seen so many strange things in his life that it did not seem odd that the old coot had picked up the beaker empty and handed it to him full.

The man gestured toward a chair, and Alexander perched himself atop it, sucking at the foam. The room was only marginally less cluttered than the one they had come in from. The ancient seated himself facing Alexander.

"Please excuse me for not introducing myself," the old man said. "I have lived alone for so long that my manners have departed me. My name is Baibars."

"Baibars?" Alexander said. "I know another

guy by that name here. Baibars the Lion. The king.''

The white-haired man snorted, half in regret, half in disgust. ''That would be my son. A great disappointment to me. I reigned as Baibars of the Holy Cloak.''

Alexander contemplated that over his beer. ''I've heard of you. Howcome you're alive? I mean, howcome, since you *are* alive, he's king?''

''Oh, the family council deposed me. They thought I was not fit to rule. Not that I gave them any great fight, mind you. I was sick of reigning, living amid a welter of fawning sycophants and vicious courtiers. I was ready to retire.''

''Yeah,'' Alexander commiserated, ''I can see how it could get to you.''

''But,'' old Baibars said, ''I would have resisted, if only because the clique that was dominating the council, led by that rascal Jehan of Jahnsi, was trying to forge the alliance with Bahadur, and drawing us into one of their insane wars.''

''Well,'' Alexander said, uncomfortably, ''I don't know. I've had some dealings with Bahadur. Plenty of people have saved their necks or their planets or systems by going along with the Khans. Sometimes they don't have no choice.''

''That I could understand,'' Baibars said. ''I might even have taken such a course myself, albeit reluctantly, had it been necessary to preserve my people. However, this was not the case. A group of noblemen, courtiers and wealthy parvenus saw a way to advance themselves through this detestable alliance, and sought my overthrow. It did not prove difficult. My lifelong studies,'' he waved a fine-boned, almost transparent hand around the room and toward the one from which they had just come, "had already all but convinced the family that I was a dotard unfit to rule.'' He folded his hands across his middle and let his chin sink upon his chest. "I saw no reason to fight it. I needed to be left to my studies, after all. I knew that in them I would find the answer to the suffering of my poor world.''

"No kidding,'' Alexander said, absorbed. Then a thought came to him in the usual roundabout fashion. "Hey, I hope you don't mind my asking, but howcome, since this is the place where the Chelaya comes from and you used to be the king and all, howcome you're so old? I mean, don't take me wrong, you really look great for an old guy, but it's kinda obvious you didn't just now hatch out of no egg.''

Baibars smiled, the curve appearing at the back of his lips as if those muscles had not been exercised in a long time. "How well you put it. No, I stopped receiving the Gilgamesh Treatment long ago. To my enemies it was another sign that I was no longer fit to rule. Who, after all, would voluntarily choose to decline into old age when it could be avoided?''

"Yeah,'' Alexander said, "I was kinda wondering that myself.''

"Some things, I decided long ago, one does not do, even to prolong youth. Youth! What a premium we put on it, yet how few of us had really admirable qualities when young the first time.''

He turned a mischievous glance toward Alexander. "Present company excepted, of course."

"Yeah. Well, look, me and my friends are here to find out about something called Precious Pearl. You know anything about that?" Subtlety was as foreign to Alexander as an inhibited libido. In any case, his friends seemed to be getting nowhere playing their deep, conspiratorial games, so he figured he had nothing to lose by just asking somebody.

"Of course. Precious Pearl was one of my projects. I worked on it reluctantly, because the war party wanted it to advance the aims of their alliance. They actually imagined that they could use the thing and still keep it secret from Bahadur. Men will believe anything if their greed is great enough."

"But what *is* it?" Alexander urged.

"Why, it's the crystal ball, the scrying glass, the voice of the oracle. It's the thing men have sought after for thousands of years, the means of parting the veil and looking upon the naked face of the future." The old man's eyes sparkled and his whole being grew animated.

"No kidding," Alexander said. "Did it work?"

Baibars sat back in his chair. "After a fashion."

"After what fashion?" Alexander asked. He could tell that this was going to take patience. Patience was never one of Alexander's more prominent qualities but he was willing to force himself to it to help his friends out of the rapidly deepening jam they were in.

"I am not quite sure how to explain this,"

Baibars continued, "as it takes a rather specialized education." He favored Alexander with a kindly gaze. "And while I perceive you as a creature of rare empathy and natural virtue, yet I suspect that your background and education have been deficient in such studies as physics, comparative mythology, moral philosophy, and so forth."

"I guess you could say that," Alexander admitted. "My friends might argue about that part about me being virtuous, though."

"Sometimes those closest to us know us least," Baibars said with a look of great sadness. "Be that as it may, I devoted myself to these subjects. I discovered that, in the twenty-second century, a group of scholars on Old Earth had developed a college for the study of such diverse subjects as metaphysics, theology, physics, psychology, philosophy, and so on. The development of Tesla physics in the twenty-first had given great impetus to the study of previously denigrated forms of pure and applied mathematics. All these things were combined into a new field, the Philosophy of Physics."

"Uh-huh," Alexander said attentively. He did not really want a lecture on history. All he had asked was if the damn thing worked. Like any other enthusiast with an audience, old Baibars wasn't going to stop until he'd said his piece.

"Those were unsettled times, with the first great migrations to other planets. There were few at first fit for human habitation. The result was a chain of wars which both stimulated and disrupted human progress. In the welter of wars won and lost, of advancing and retreating armies and fleets, the short-lived college of the Philosophy of Physics was snuffed out, but not until they had produced some truly amazing and alarming findings. Most of their accumulated data were placed under seal in an ancient library. I had found only scattered references to this school until I began corresponding with a fellow enthusiast in these arcane arts, Memnon DaSilva.''

Alexander wagged his ears forward. DaSilva. He had heard that name before.

''DaSilva had discovered the whereabouts of the interred records of the old college. Like all scholars throughout recorded history, however, he needed funding. It was his good fortune that his fellow enthusiast in these arts was a king. I financed his venture, which involved some lengthy negotiations, not to mention some substantial bribes, and he brought back the records, which we proceeded to study and interpret.

''I think I hardly need to tell you that all of my ministers were against this expenditure, but that as soon as it showed signs of results, they all clamored for control and a share of the proceeds.''

''Sure,'' Alexander said. ''I know how business works.''

''Imagine their chagrin, then, when seeing into the future turned out to be useless to them.''

''Huh?'' Alexander said brightly.

''Oh, we learned to part the veil, it is true, but what did we see beyond?'' He paused for dramatic effect.

''I was kind of hoping you were going to tell me.''

"Not one future, but thousands! Millions! An infinity of futures. From each present there branched a fan of futures, each determined by the tiniest shift in the billions of random factors that clatter about the universe. A cosmic ray collides with a DNA chain, and twenty years afterward an idiot mounts the throne of an empire." He cocked a snowy eyebrow at Alexander. "That happens often, even without the cosmic rays."

"You don't have to tell me," Alexander assured him, wondering which cosmic ray was responsible for this particular specimen.

"The device itself is simple enough. It is a product of twenty-first century computer technology utilizing a program made up of abstract energy. Abstract energy technology was much in vogue in those days."

"Is that so," Alexander commented. He'd never heard of the stuff.

"Of course, programming metaphysics into a computer is no easy task."

"I can imagine."

"However, we overcame this—" They were interrupted by an exceedingly loud throat-clearing coming from another room.

"Your Retired Highness, has this little creature been disturbing you?" It was Raj Jehan, and right behind him was the oversized guard who had tried to keep Alexander out. Uh-oh, Alex thought.

Baibars looked up at the intruders with the clear, childlike expression of classical senility. "By no means, Raj Jehan. How good it is to see you again. This enchanting hominid and I have been having a most enthralling conversation. Did you know that he once met a god?''

"And soon to meet more, no doubt," said Jehan, glaring at Alexander. The Singeur grinned back up at him for all he was worth.

"Hey, chief, how are you doing? I got bored so I clumb up here. Me'n this old geezer been having a fine old time, haven't we?" He looked at the old man, who nodded vigorously.

"I fear that his mistress will grow concerned for his whereabouts, Highness," Jehan said. "I shall take him below. I hope he has not tired you greatly."

"Not at all." Baibars looked at Alexander. "Do come visit me again."

"Sure, boss, just as soon—" He wasn't able to finish the sentence as Jehan hauled him through into another room and then out to the corridor. "You could've at least let me say good-bye," Alexander protested. He went on in a conspiratorial tone: "You know, just between us, I think that old guy's a little touched in the head, but he's kind of a sweet old coot. Think I could come back and see him again? He ain't half as boring as most of the people around here."

Jehan hustled him into an elevator. The guard remained behind. "I would advise against trying to see him again. I've given strict orders that you be shot dead if you ever appear on that floor again."

"Well, since you put it that way," Alexander muttered.

"Government business of the most confidential

nature is transacted on that floor.'' Jehan looked down at him with the same unnerving expression as on that occasion on the hunting raft. ''I am sure you would have no interest in such business.''

Alexander wondered why Jehan didn't just kill him now. He could only conclude that it was because he intended to kill him later. Well, Alexander reflected, it wasn't as if he hadn't been in this position before.

THIRTEEN

The lair of Rashid was, surprisingly, not in the heart of the city's slums but in an ordinary-looking warehouse near the port. Somehow the one-eyed beggar king and his hideously mutilated minions looked out of place among the orderly rows of storage levels, among which pallet-rafts moved silently, shuttling shipping containers from ship to storage, from storage to ship. In the midst of this orderly and prosaic activity, the legion of the one-armed, the one-legged, the one-eyed, and the other maimed and ragged, looked positively surreal.

"You will be pleased to learn," Rashid told them, "that your friends are safe, although they are under virtual house arrest in the palace." The beggar king was, incongruously, feeding bills of lading into an obsolete bookkeeping device which appeared to be an ancient computer surmounted by an abacus. His lean, deft fingers would dance across the flat pressure board, then the fingernails would flick out to move the strung beads from one side of the abacus to the other.

"How can you be sure?" Haakon asked.

"Lady Maya has informed me," Rashid answered.

They had been sitting in the warehouse all day, while Rashid and most of his beggars had been out in the city. It seemed that the uproar of the night before had died down as far as the authorities were concerned, but several major gang wars were brewing, and Ganesha's prestige in the underworld community had been severely damaged. The search for the fugitives was still on, but the forces of authority were at the moment too distracted to spend much time on it.

"What about my ship?" Haakon demanded.

"No move has been made to board it," Rashid said. "It is likely that the Admiralty officers in charge have discovered that you have evaded their overrides on your defense systems. They fear the armament your ship mounts." He loosed a dry, rasping chuckle and looked more than ever like the stock villain of a poor melodrama. "If only I could have met you long ago. With your ship, and my beggars and the smuggler's guild, we could have accomplished wonders. You are both accomplished men."

"Are the two we left behind on the ship still there?" Jemal asked.

"According to our people among the customs force, they are. Apparently, there is a third person aboard as well."

"A third?" Haakon said, then: "Oh, Numa. I guess he's taking the opportunity to rest up. He needs it."

"So when do we meet with Maya?" Jemal asked.

"Possess yourself of patience," Rashid told him. "The Lady's plans must mature."

"All this maturing is getting on my nerves," Haakon said. "Ever since we got here, people have been leading us around by the nose with hints and innuendos, and whenever we try to get a grip on the situation, it all just fades away. I'm beginning to wonder if anybody really knows anything."

"I hope you will not think me rude," Rashid said, "if I remind you that it was you who came here, not we who sent for you. If you have been led around by the nose, it may be that your nose is admirably suited to that purpose. Please remember that you could have been killed or imprisoned on any number of occasions since your arrival here, and it has only been through the good graces of my friends that you have avoided that fate." Throughout this oration, Rashid continued to play with his abacus, his words were underscored by the clicking of the ceramic beads.

"That's telling him, Rashid." It was Rama's voice, coming from overhead, atop a pile of plastic-film crates which contained a particularly powerful spice from another of the agricultural Mughal worlds. Even through the hermetic sealing of the crates, the fragrance of the spice seeped out, and Rama had chosen to take a nap amid the splendid odor. She rolled over and stretched, looking down on the little group below. "Our captain is an insufferable man. You must be sure to keep him in his place. I have spent much time striving to disabuse him of his delusions of equality."

"Shut up and go back to sleep, Rama," Haakon said patiently. "You're so much more companionable when you're unconscious." He turned to Rashid. "What's our next move?" He was struck by a sudden sense of déjà vu. It seemed as if he had been saying that, or someone had been saying it to him, ever since they had arrived here.

Haakon intensely disliked the feeling of not being in control of his situation. He had always been a man of direct action: not foolish or thoughtless action, but still a man who did not allow events to control him. It was galling to have to sit idly by while others controlled the pieces on the board. If, indeed, anyone was really in control at all. Haakon was beginning to suspect that nobody had any greater grasp of this situation than he did. At least *they* had time. He and his crew had death devices planted in their skulls, controlled by a man not noted for his patience.

A truly Breughelian beggar came into the warehouse, propelling himself with the assistance of a pair of short crutches. His legs ended in stumps. The grotesque figure progressed to Rashid and handed him a folded paper. Rashid murmured something, and the beggar hobbled off on his crutches and leg-stumps.

Rashid turned to Haakon. "It begins tonight," he said.

"What begins?"

"The operation to get the mutant Chelis plants off-planet, along with the soil samples and bacteria culture."

"Nice of somebody to tell us at last," Jemal said. "I hope you realize we don't have a ship just now."

"That will have to be rectified," Rashid said. "Along with a number of other problems. Our people in orbit will be taking steps to pave the way back into your ship. For us, though, the task will be more complicated."

"You mean getting the stuff into orbit and trans-shipped into *Eurynome*?" Haakon asked.

"No, that, too, shall be rather routine." He waved a hand at the warehouse around them. "Most of the material items to be moved are right here. One of the advantages of dealing with an absentee aristocracy who prefer their pleasures to the tedium of mere work is that they tend to leave business and the civil service to their minions. It is comparatively easy to infiltrate and subvert such a structure. No, our next task will be a bit more of a challenge. I understand you are bored and champing at the bit, so to speak. Are you in the mood for a little excitement?"

"Can't anybody around here form a simple declarative sentence?" Haakon asked. "Is it really so difficult to come to the point?"

"How crude," Rashid said. "Life should be lived as a work of art, not as a mere business transaction or a bodily function. Have you no sense of drama? No grasp of irony or of the niceties of finesse?"

"Oh, hell," Haakon said, "tell it your own way. I wasn't doing anything anyway."

"I shall try to be succinct for the sake of your abbreviated attention span. Sometime tonight, as soon as I receive word from Lady Maya, we shall stage a raid on the palace. There we shall appropriate sundry persons, among them your Mirabelle and Alexander. There. Is that sufficient to break the monotony?"

"Just dandy," Haakon said. "Who are the others?"

"Lady Maya, for one."

"She doesn't need to be rescued," Haakon pointed out. "She's there because she wants to be."

"True, but she refuses to leave without her father. We must bring him out too."

"Hold it," Haakon said, a hand going to his suddenly aching brow. "Her father? Old Baibars? Baibars of the Holy Cloak?"

Rashid smiled. "The very same," he said in the tones of a schoolmaster whose most backward student has just displayed a glimmer of intelligence for the first time.

"But he's dead," Haakon protested, then: "No, I guess he isn't, or we wouldn't be going to the palace to rescue him, would we?"

Rashid increased his benevolent smile. "Impeccable reasoning."

"Anybody else we need to pick up while we're merrily a-raiding?" Jemal asked.

"There are several political prisoners to be freed. Nothing you need concern yourselves about. Your objectives will be the women, the Singeur, and the old king."

"May I ask why we must get old Baibars?" Haakon asked. "I met his son and I must say I wasn't impressed."

"You met his daughter and were very highly impressed, indeed," Rashid said. Haakon acknowledged this with a very slight inclination of his head. "You need Baibars of the Holy Cloak," Rashid went on, "because he is the key to the Precious Pearl project."

"Will he come back with us?" Haakon asked. He was thinking that Timur Khan couldn't complain too much if they dumped a king in his lap. Former head of a valued allied system, at that.

"That shall be up to him, of course," Rashid told him.

"Who'll be hitting the palace with us?" Jemal asked. "Surely there have to be more than just what we have here."

"There will be others," Rashid said. "With their physical infirmities, my beggars can do little within the palace, but there will be other allies aiding us."

"Will Steiner be among them?" Jemal asked.

"Yes. Why?"

"Because I'm not satisfied about what happened back there in the park. I figure Steiner might have sold us out."

"I assure you he is trustworthy," Rashid said.

"I wish my faith in your evaluation was greater," Jemal said.

Rama stuck her head over the edge of the crate

again. "Must we bring back Mirabelle? Let's leave
her there. She annoys me and detracts from the
overall attractiveness of our ship."

Jemal looked up. "Sure you don't want us to
leave Alex too?"

"Oh. I'd forgotten him. Yes, let's leave him
too. He's of no possible value, aesthetically or
practically."

"Both of you pipe down," Haakon ordered.
"Or I'll leave you all behind."

Alexander sat uncomfortably under the twin gazes
of Mirabelle and Maya. Alexander was older than
he looked and had a lifetime of antisocial activity
behind him, but somehow, these women could make
him feel like a kid being dressed down by a teacher.

"You could have gotten us all arrested!" Mirabelle scolded.

"Arrested?" he said indignantly. "We been under arrest since we got here, even if you been
acting like we was guests or something."

"You have a lot to learn about court behavior,"
Maya told him. "Of course we've been under
arrest. Half the people I grew up with here were
prisoners or foreign hostages. You couldn't tell
them from the children of the noble houses or
Princes of the Blood. Often as not you can act like
a guest and they'll treat you like a guest. Mutual
pretense is a part of the game. You overstepped
the rules and put us all in danger."

"Hey, that was your old man I was talking to.
Don't you want to get him out of here? You
should see how he's treated."

"I have every intention of getting him out," she said coldly. "You may well have foiled my intentions." The black diamond in her navel winked in incongrous counterpoint to her words.

"Did you do anything or say anything to give Jehan the impression that you were talking about the project?" Mirabelle asked.

"I ain't no fool, and neither is that old man, even if he acts kind of dotty. But, hell, how do we know old Jehan wasn't listening all the time? Don't they keep the old man under observation?"

"Father can counter any listening or observation devices they may have," Maya said.

"I don't get it," Alexander protested. "You can get around any way you want, but he can't. Ain't it all tied together? I mean, ain't it all part of that physical philosophy stuff he was talking about?"

"Philosophy of Physics. Yes, it is, but it's part science and part magic and part something there are no words for." Uncharacteristically, she fretted for a few moments, searching for words. "I really don't know just how to explain this to you."

"Just take your time and keep the words simple," Alexander told her. "I can be patient when I got to."

"The foundations of science," she began at last, "lie in the principles of experimentation and observation. From the beginnings of modern science in the seventeenth century it became established that, once the form of an experiment was established, any trained scientist, by following the steps of the original experiment, would achieve the same results and observe the identical phenomena."

"Got you so far," Alexander assured her.

"By the twentieth century these concepts were breaking down. Things like subatomic particle physics called into question the old assumptions of cause and effect, and when Tesla principles were rediscovered, all of what was then known about physics had to be rewritten."

Alexander nodded. He didn't know much about physics, but he knew that the Tesla drive was what made space travel possible.

"What it boils down to is that physics is not a single field or science, but many. Some of them have yet to be discovered. From what Mirabelle has been telling me, the people who made the Cingulum had access to at least one brand of physics that has been totally unsuspected."

"Yeah," Alexander said. "She been telling you about the spook tunnels and how they could build their own planets and turn space inside-out? You and your old man would love it there. It's just your kind of place."

"I hope to see it soon. What Father and DaSilva discovered, or rather rediscovered, was a school of physics as different from Tesla physics as Tesla was from classical Newtonian physics. Imagine, for example, a science in which two experimenters, performing identical experiments, reached entirely differing results. Take a simple experiment, one every schoolchild is taught: Hold a rod of copper over a flame and what happens?"

"You get a green flame," Alexander said. "Hell, even I know that one."

"Suppose instead that only males got a green

flame, and females got a red one? Or those over a certain age got a multicolored flame while the young only had solid colors? Or the planet-born saw a blue flame, while those born in orbit had a yellow one, and those born in deep space had a purple flame?''

"That sounds more like witchcraft than a science," Mirabelle said. She sounded distinctly uncomfortable at the prospect.

"Exactly. What I've told you so far is an approximation, an analogy to give you some grasp of what we're dealing with. It's a science of sorts, but we'll be many years in working out just its basic principles. Computers are of no use. Only personal experimentation yields results, and even that must be repeated carefully and often, because the results are subjective rather than objective.''

"Back up," Alexander said. "You lost me there.''

"It's just what I've been saying. The results of suprametaphysical physics depend as much on the practitioner as on the process.''

"I think I'm beginning to catch on," Mirabelle said. "You mean that you can teleport, or whatever it is that you do, because that is your particular talent or affinity? And your father can't?''

"Roughly. Within limits, through the use of a particular mathematical-psychological process, I can transfer myself to a destination without, properly, crossing the intervening space. There's nothing new about the concept. After all, Tesla engines have been doing much the same thing for centuries. The Tesla drive, however, is a mechanical process requiring bulky machinery and force fields and such. This process is largely mental."

"You said 'within limits,' " Mirabelle pointed out with her technothief's grasp of detail. "What limits?"

"I haven't established them all yet, but I know that I can't reach a new location until I'm familiar with it. Remember, the first time I boarded your ship I had to take a shuttle like everybody else. It's terribly difficult to move from one place in motion to another that's stationary or moving at a different rate or in a different direction. Once I'd been there, it wasn't difficult to transfer to your ship from the resort station, because their speed and direction were synchronized."

"What are your distance limits?" Mirabelle asked.

"I don't know. I'm increasing my distance very slowly in my experiments. After all, what happens when I reach my limits? Do I just not reappear?"

"I can see how you'd want to be cautious," Alexander said.

"Can you take anybody else with you?" Mirabelle asked.

"I wish I knew. I can transfer inanimate objects; my clothes and jewelry, for example. I've taken small animals, and they seem none the worse for the experience. But as for taking another human being, I've just never had the nerve to try."

"I guess finding volunteers is a problem, huh?" Alexander said.

"On the contrary. Our movement is full of people who would be more than willing to put their lives on the line for the merest chance of securing a new advantage for us. No," she admitted, "the main stumbling block is my own cowardice."

"How so?" Mirabelle asked.

"Not only am I unwilling to risk the lives of the volunteers, I'm terrified of what the results on me might be. There's an ancient fable, I think it dates back to Earth, about a man who invents a teleportation machine. He experiments on himself several times with success. Then one day an insect inadvertently enters the machine during an experiment. The man emerges part man, part insect. It's a variant on the Faust theme, I suspect, but a sobering cautionary tale in any case. Experimenting on human beings when you don't know all the variables is nothing to be undertaken lightly."

"But you tried with animals," Mirabelle pointed out.

"And I was terrified. Still, I had to nerve myself up to taking the big step. Sooner or later, I'll have to try it with a human being."

"I guess the first time," Alexander suggested, "it better be with someone you really like." Both women glared at him so hard he wilted visibly. "Hell, don't mind me," he mumbled, "everybody says I got no couth."

"And what are your father's particular talents?" Mirabelle asked.

"He has achieved a limited success with psychokinesis, as well as his prescient capability, although that's of very little use except for constructing statistical probability-frames for selecting courses of action. I think it will eventually develop into an extremely valuable technique, but not any time soon. No, poor Father's talents are as undisciplined as he is, I'm afraid.''

"And what of the mysterious DaSilva?" Mirabelle queried.

"He's the one who can tie all this together. Father supplied the backing, but DaSilva is the real scholar. While Father and I, along with a few others, have been toying with the 'wild talents' aspect of this thing, he's been researching fundamentals to put it all on a firm scientific basis. Half scientific anyway. He says that no technology is efficiently exploitable unless you can wield some kind of control over it. You'll be meeting him soon, by the way.''

"Shall we?" Mirabelle lounged back in her luxurious chaise. "And just where is this elusive gentleman?''

"In hiding, of course. Where else? But he and some others will be along shortly to pick us up.''

"Pick us up?" Mirabelle spluttered, for once utterly nonplussed. "Just like that? They're coming in here to whisk us away?''

"Well, it won't be quite as simple as that," Maya admitted. "Actually, it'll be more of a raid. You can expect some excitement. There will probably be shooting.''

"That, we can handle," Alexander assured her. "We been in more shooting scrapes than—well, we been in a lot. Just bring 'em on.''

"Alex exaggerates a bit, but essentially what he says is true. We're accustomed to violent doings. In fact, you might say they are our stock in trade.''

"That's what I suspected. You may have the opportunity to practice your trade soon."

"How soon?" Mirabelle asked.

"It may be tonight. I'm not certain. It depends on when the plant-smuggling operation goes into action. It will be a matter of split-second timing because of the delicacy of the plants. Exactly the right instant must be chosen to move, and once events are set in motion, there can be no turning back. This is a one-shot venture. It has taken years to set up, and if we fail on the first try, we fail for good. There will be no second opportunity. Not in this generation, anyway."

"What would you've done if we hadn't showed up just when we did?" Alexander asked.

"We had other contingency plans, other ships. But your arrival was fortuitous, almost too good to be true: that splendid ship, its early social cachet, its crew of, if you will excuse me, somewhat disreputable professional adventurers, and an unexpected bonus in your case."

"The Cingulum," Mirabelle said.

"Exactly. Making contact with the Cingulum has always been our second priority, right after getting the viable plants off-planet. It seemed truly incredible that both ends could be accomplished with the appearance of a single ship. DaSilva has been doing some work concerning the bending of synchronicity. Maybe it's beginning to pay off."

"I hope my questions aren't getting monotonous," Mirabelle said, "but how does one bend synchronicity?"

"It's another metaphysical concept that's been

dropped and picked up various times. According to DaSilva, coincidence may behave according to recognizable rules. He thinks that if you understand the rules, you may in some way be able to *compel* a coincidence. It's part of a subcategory he calls Jungian physics.''

''Jungian physics,'' Mirabelle said. ''If this gets out, we'll all be obsolete.''

''That's true,'' Maya said. ''We may be in for a new era of sorcery.''

FOURTEEN

"This is our timetable," said the man Haakon
still knew only as Yussuf. They were in a large
side room opening off the main floor of Rashid's
warehouse. There were about fifty people in the
room, some of whom Haakon already knew, the
rest strangers. Steiner was there, leaning sullenly
against an oddly ornate pillar. A number of the
Mongrels stood around him.

"Steiner and his Mongrels, along with the
Eurynome people," Yussuf went on, "will leave
here at nightfall. They will take the old transport
tubes to their station beneath the palace." He traced
the route on a large map of the city hanging behind
him. "For several years now, Rashid's people
have been digging an access from the tubes into
the sub-basements of the palace. To foil detection,
they used only hand tools. As a further security
measure, none of them knew where they were or

where they were digging. Only Rashid himself had full knowledge of the project, so we can estimate at least a ninety-five percent certainty of secrecy in this phase of the attack.''

Haakon leaned toward Jemal and whispered in his ear: "Don't let Steiner out of your sight from here on in."

"I don't intend to," Jemal answered, "but I can't keep track of all his Mongrels."

"This first-in party has the most crucial and dangerous task: to break in, overcome palace security, and free the prisoners, including his former majesty, Baibars of the Holy Cloak." This set off a babble all over the room. Most of those present had assumed the old man was dead. Yussuf rapped on a table for order. "It is essential for the success of all our operations that the old king be taken out. All will be made clear in time.

"The second phase will begin immediately upon receiving confirmation that the attack has successfully commenced. This will be the evacuation operation. Our people have air flitters readied at locations near the palace. One of the Mongrel teams will neutralize, as far as possible, the air defenses of the palace. There will be opposition, though. Some of the aircraft will be dummies to confuse the remaining defenses. Others will be operational, and yet others will be backup. We can expect numerous casualties during both of these phases.

"Once these have been successfully concluded, we will move into the off-world evacuation phase. Transport into orbit of the Chelis plants, the refining bacteria culture, and soil samples have already been accomplished. They will be transshipped into *Eurynome* at the same time as our refugees.''

"It's going to get crowded up there," Haakon muttered.

"They'd better not expect to share *my* suite," Rama huffed.

"How did we get into this?" Jemal said. "I've forgotten."

There was an atmosphere in the room compounded equally of eager anticipation and dread. Haakon could see the anticipation mainly in the younger members—the Mongrels and others with the look of young, dedicated revolutionaries. He realized that many of these people were approaching the end of many years of underground activity, knowing that tonight's action could mean that their years of work and danger had been for nothing. That would account for the dread. He wondered how many of those present had already provided for their own escape in case of disaster. He knew that he certainly would have made such a provision. For the attack team, though, there would be no such option. It was succeed or die for them.

He also wondered how many of those present were traitors or government plants. It was a rare conspiracy that didn't contain several of each. He eyed Steiner. The man was still an unknown quantity. He was equally puzzled by Rashid. Why was a beggar king so high up in the councils of this conspiracy? If anything, the evil-looking, one-eyed man seemed to be the kingpin of the whole operation. Haakon had tried to sound him out on this point, only to be rebuffed. Haakon couldn't blame the man for being cautious, though. It was always unwise to be too free with your secrets with strangers.

"Are we really committing ourselves to this harebrained operation?" Jemal whispered.

"You have any suggestions?" Haakon asked.

Jemal shrugged. "Old Timur's going to pull the plug on us one of these days anyway. Might as well get it doing some good."

The tunnels stretched seemingly into infinity. Once in a while, they emerged from the flickering dimness into a larger blackness, an ancient, un-used station. Sometimes, the tunnels were flanked by walkways, and at intervals the hatches of main-tenance crawlways appeared. In spite of the obvi-ous antiquity and disuse of the system, Haakon felt an odd, illogical trepidation. Subconsciously, he was waiting for a magnetic train to come roaring down one of the tunnels and flatten them all.

Steiner was in the lead, following small, enig-matic marks made on the walls, ceiling, or floor. Haakon knew that most of the marks were dum-mies, put there to mislead investigators. Of the group, only Steiner knew which of the signs were real.

There were at least a hundred in the raiding party. All were armed, some with precious beamers but most with powerblades, hand weapons, or mis-sile weapons cobbled together in workshops con-trolled by the movement. The government's tight control of serious weaponry had made it difficult for even the smugglers to bring in beamers or heavier arms. Several teams packed explosives for the extensive demolitions that were anticipated. They hoped to capture more arms in the confusion of the first rush.

"Last leg, boyos," Steiner whispered. His teeth flashed white in his swarthy face, reflecting the fitful illumination of a glow-plate. "Maybe a hundred paces down this tunnel we come to the new tunnel. Fifty meters up that, it's the last barrier between us and the palace." He turned to the leader of one of the demolition teams. "Got your charges ready?"

"For about the last three years, Steiner." The young man wore black, cottonlike tunic and trousers, belted with a sash that was green in better light. Several others in the group were dressed identically, so Haakon presumed it to be the uniform of another gang. The demolition man looked tough and competent.

"That's good, boyo. Last chance, folks. Anybody with second thoughts?" His hand rested on the handle of a beamer as he scanned the group. He turned to Haakon and grinned. "You want the honor of making the first charge?"

"Sure," Haakon said without hesitation.

Steiner's grin slipped a trifle. It was not the answer he had expected. "Well, if you want it, you got it." He took the beamer from his belt and tossed it left-handed to Haakon. Haakon caught it deftly and tucked it into his boot top. "I'll probably be taking it back off your corpse, so just think of it as a loan. All right, let's stop standing around." He turned and led the way up the tunnel.

Jemal looked askance at Haakon. "Honor, my ass," he muttered. Haakon just smiled. He had been in assaults before, lots of them; ship-to-ship, house-to-house, ground raids, prison breakouts, even, once, an amphibious beach assault. One thing it had taught him was that the first man through the breach had a better chance than those that followed. After their first surprise, the enemy would have the assault point in their sights.

"You should let me have the beamer," Rama hissed. "I'm ten times the fighter you are!" Somewhere, she had scrounged up an armorcloth singlet to replace her leather outfit. It covered everything except her face, her clawed fingers and toes, and her cascading, striped hair.

"Rama," Haakon said, "you're so bad weapons would be redundant. It hardly seems fair to turn you loose on those people with more than your natural armament."

Rama made one of her extensive range of rude noises. A circle cleared around her as she began to emit her disagreeable fighting-scent. Had the armorcloth not dampened it, she might have cleared the tunnel.

Steiner led them into a narrower side tunnel, its access disguised to look like part of the original system. Once inside the entrance, though, it became a rough-hewn passage carved into the raw bedrock of the city. They switched on the glow-plates left there by the diggers, exposing the tool-marked walls and the floor littered with food wrappers and the remains of a multitude of meals consumed in the tedious work of hacking a tunnel in the solid rock.

"Reminds me of home," Haakon said quietly. His palms itched with a flesh-memory of a thousand picks and sledgehammers; the tunnels, quarries, and mines, the brutal labor and the terrible injuries. To this day he did not know how he had avoided being blinded by rock chips. The Bahadurans had not allowed them goggles, or any other clothing, for that matter. He shook himself back into the present.

The tunnel ended at a wall of some concretelike substance. "I hope your people calculated their charges right," Haakon said.

"You saw the diagrams we stole," Steiner said. "Accurate within a hundredth of a millimeter. What could go wrong?"

Haakon grunted noncommittally. It was an inane sort of comment, even for a rhetorical question. These people had never been in a real war. Haakon had seen hundreds of missions. The phrases always used were: "perfectly planned," and "nothing left to chance." It was always a balls-up anyway. Phrases like that always made experienced and cynical soldiers smile sadly.

Steiner gave them their final briefing as the first demo team set their charges. "All right, you all know how it's gonna be. When I give the word, we all go back to the main tunnel. When this wall blows, we come charging in like maniacs. We take a right turn inside the breach and we should be facing a stairway. We go up, and we gotta be ready to blow the door at the top if necessary. Once we're up on the main level, everybody goes to their assigned missions. We've rehearsed it all.

There shouldn't be anybody in the basement to give us trouble, but we can't be sure, so go in ready for a fight."

"Ready," the demolition chief reported.

"Set your timer," Steiner told him. The man fiddled with a plastic box, then nodded to Steiner. "All right, folks, let's go back to the main tunnel. Walk, don't run." He herded them back out of the new tunnel.

"You'd've made a halfway decent briefing officer, Steiner," Haakon said.

"Guess I missed my calling." Steiner sounded a little preoccupied, which was understandable under the circumstances.

The explosion when it came was surprisingly muffled. Most had set themselves for a shattering blast, and the quiet *fump* was anticlimactic.

"Think it blew?" Lorah said, doubt in her voice.

"It blew," Haakon told her. "Let's go!" He went into the tunnel at a cat-footed run, his feet feeling the way among the still-falling rock chips, his eyes slitted against the dust filling the air. He did not slow down when he came to the ragged hole at the end of the tunnel, jumping through and sweeping the room beyond with the beamer, finger poised to shoot.

The room was empty, the light bright after the dimness of the tunnels. It was also full of dust and chunks of concrete. It might have been a palace basement, but it looked like any other basement—a room full of objects the utility of which had long been forgotten. The stairway was where it was supposed to be, and Haakon made a run for it. He took the last few steps slowly. There was a chance that the muffled explosion had not caused alarm above, and he did not want to surrender any advantage of surprise. Gently, he pressed a hand against a pressure plate and pushed. Silently, the door gave way slightly. He turned. "Door unlocked. No sounds of alarm yet."

Steiner waved the demolition team back and climbed up to the top. "We're in luck," he said. Distantly, they could hear the sound of a claxon. "Somebody's awake now. Go!"

Haakon slammed the door aside and jumped through, putting some distance between himself and those crowding through behind. He saw faces turn his way, a number of overdressed and glittering people gaping at this uncouth intrusion into their orderly, safe world.

"Clear out!" Haakon shouted. "Clear out now! This is a raid!"

To underline his words he raked a beam across the ceiling, plowing a charred line through the ornate plasterwork and gilding, bringing two baroque chandeliers crashing to the floor. The action was greeted by a chorus of shrieks, and the inhabitants broke into a panic as the raiding teams sprinted for their assigned objectives. Some of Steiner's people cast flash-and-bang bombs about in order to spread confusion, and others broke discipline, yanking jewelry off paralyzed victims. Haakon turned back to his assigned task. He'd seen experienced troops do far worse.

He charged the length of what appeared to be a ballroom and found the stairway he was looking for. It ascended through the ceiling in an immense spiral, a totally inefficient design for traversing such a short distance, but then, it was there for purely decorative purposes. The inhabitants would use a lift instead. With Rama close behind, Haakon took the first loop of the spiral. The sharp climb and curvature of the stair restricted sight to a few meters.

"Someone coming down!" Rama hissed. Her hearing was more acute than any standard human's.

Haakon stopped, holding the beamer at ready. Would it be guards or panicked civilians? Should he hold his fire in any case? He knew he owed no favors to the local aristocracy and need have no compunction about cutting them down, but the palace was full of servants. Actually, he knew that such ethical maunderings were useless, because when they showed there would be no time for thought and he would act, as always in such cases, by instinct.

He was firing before his mind even registered the uniforms on the men or the weapons in their hands. The first two fell, and those higher up stopped and tried to back up the stairs. It was the most foolish move possible. A quick, aggressive charge down would have overwhelmed those below and swept them from the stairway with few casualties among the guards. Momentum and gravity were on their side.

Haakon was relieved to find that the amateurism of the defenders matched that of the attackers. He vaulted the two bodies and ran into the tangled, disorganized mass of guards who were blindly trying to retreat.

Rama let out a blood-freezing squall, and Haakon stepped aside to let her pass. She hit the packed guards so hard and fast that the few who got off shots hit only the air or their own men. She actually climbed up and over the first rank with a liberal use of her claws and attacked those behind from above.

The action that followed was too swift to follow, but Haakon saw chunks of uniform flying with flesh still attached, and several guards vaulted the rail to the floor ten meters below just to escape. Then the last two or three were showing their backs, running full-tilt to get away.

Haakon made his precarious way over the pile of forms and pushed past Rama, who was checking the fallen for shammers who might shoot them in the back as they ascended. She grabbed a beamer from one and came up behind Haakon, who was slowing as he reached the top of the stair. Those who had fled might be waiting to shoot them as they came into the upper level.

The palace was rocked by a shattering blast. That would be the air defenses being destroyed, clearing the way for the rescue fleet. Haakon jumped out onto the upper level and swept it, with Rama close behind. They saw just the backs of some people disappearing through a doorway. Several other attackers emerged from the stair. Some dashed off on their own missions, others stayed with Haakon and Rama. They proceeded in their assigned direction. In side rooms, they saw men and women, uniformed but unarmed, cowering in shock at this unprecedented invasion.

"Stay where you are and nobody gets hurt!" Haakon shouted. "We have a job to do, and we don't want interference, so if you want to live just keep out of our way." None of those so addressed showed the slightest inclination to hinder them.

They were looking for the wing where Baibars of the Holy Cloak was kept. A separate mission to grab Mirabelle, Maya, and Alexander had been discussed, but Haakon had vetoed it. From all reports they were not locked up, and it would be easier simply to let them join the liberating party when it showed up. Alexander and Mirabelle were experienced at this kind of action, and if Maya couldn't move about as she wished, there was something seriously wrong with her.

They ran to another doorway opening onto a large corridor. As Haakon reached it, an arm protruded through the door and loosed a wild beamer shot which caught one of the Mongrels high on the shoulder. The woman screeched and Haakon kicked out, feeling the snap of the forearm bones through his bootsole. A man cursed through clenched teeth, and they heard the patter of his fleeing boots.

Haakon jumped through, training his beamer on the fleeing man's back, but he did not shoot. "Catch him!" he ordered.

Rama caught up with the guard in two inhumanly long bounds. He was a big, powerful man, but she held him easily with one hand at the back of his neck and the other grasping the wrist of his good arm between his shoulder blades. She marched him back to Haakon, holding him almost on tiptoe.

"You broke my arm," the guard said inanely.

"Next comes the neck," Haakon told him. "We want the old king. Where is he?"

"You go to hell," the man said.

"Twist his arm," Haakon said. "The broken one."

"Third level, room six," the guard said, all the stuffing going out of him abruptly.

"That's not where he was last reported," Haakon said. He nodded to Rama, and she grabbed the swelling wrist.

"He was moved!" the man blurted, sweat beading his brow. "Some kid who was half monkey got into his quarters, and Raj Jehan ordered the old man moved immediately."

Haakon grinned. "Alex. I might've known." He spotted a closet and shoved the guard inside, then welded the door shut with his beamer. "Come on, let's go find the third level."

By questioning the cowed security workers, they found a utility stair off a side corridor and ascended to the third level. Explosions were going off all over the building now, rocking the structure every few seconds as vital targets were neutralized by the demolitions. By now, some of the teams should already be evacuating with their freed prisoners or assigned loot. Haakon could hear the distinctive humming of at least one antiaircraft battery. They hadn't got them all. Then there was a final explosion and the humming stopped.

The whole third level was pandemonium. Guards ran about with guns drawn, some trying to organize a defense, but most intent on evacuation. They were crowding into lifts and down stairways, even crawling out onto ledges in their eagerness to find a place of safety. It spoke poorly for their state of training and discipline, considering that the third level had yet to be attacked.

Steiner caught up with them, ordering his people to spread out and sow more confusion, reminding them not to bunch up into good targets. "They're already getting the other people out down there," he reported. "You found the old king yet?"

"We need to find room six," Haakon said. He grabbed the arm of a fleeing man and yanked him back so hard that he heard teeth click together. He shoved the crystal tubes of the beamer in the man's face and inquired politely: "Excuse me, sir, could you direct me to room six?"

The soothing tones seemed to jolt the man from his panic. "Oh. Why, certainly. Take that corridor," He pointed to the left. "It's the third door on the right."

"Thank you kindly," Haakon said. He jerked his head for the others to follow him. Rama licked blood from her claws as she followed, slit-pupiled eyes darting about in search of enemies.

For all the noise and excitement, there was surprisingly little threat in evidence. The men who had fled up the stairs with guns seemed to have disappeared entirely.

They found room six without difficulty. Jemal tried the pressure plate. "Door's locked," he reported.

Haakon looked at him disgustedly. "Of course it's locked. When you're in jail they usually lock the damned doors."

"Hey, you two," Steiner said, looking sweaty and nervous, "think we could cut out the repartee and get on with it?"

"Stand back," Haakon said, aiming the beamer at the pressure lock. The door opened before he could fire the weapon.

"It took you long enough," Maya said. "Come on in."

"Might've known you'd be here," Haakon said.

"I came up as soon as I heard all the excitement." She turned her head. "Are you ready, Father?"

"I really need my books," said a voice from another room.

"We'll collect them later," Maya told him. "Babi will send them on once we're away. He has no use for them."

"Babi?" Haakon said, hairless eyebrows ascending.

"A childhood nickname for my brother Baibars. After all, when forty or so males in the family have the same name, nicknames are imperative. Are you coming, Father?"

"Babi," Haakon said, bemused. "My God."

"I suppose I am ready now," the old king said, emerging from the adjoining room carrying a small satchel. "But, my dear, be sure to tell Babi that I shall need my sorcerer's paraphernalia as well." He turned his mild, childlike gaze to Haakon. "You must be the Delian viscount my daughter has been telling me so much about."

"She has, has she?" Haakon said, taking the proffered hand. "Well, I'd really like to stay here and chat, but there's an air raft waiting for us, and we shouldn't be late."

"No!" Maya said. "The raft is a ruse. You will take my father out of here through the tunnels, the same way you came in. There will be a special demolition team waiting there to collapse the tunnel after you. Mirabelle and Alexander will be waiting for you there as well."

"Anything you say," Haakon said, "but let's be quick about it."

Maya kissed her father quickly, then turned to Haakon. "If you see my brother on your way out, please don't kill him. He's not evil, just a little stupid."

"Old Babi's safe with us," Haakon said. "As long as he doesn't point anything lethal in our direction."

"I'll see you later then," Maya said. Then she winked out of existence.

"One of these days," Haakon said, "she's got to show me how she does that."

"It would do you no good," old Baibars said. "It is her talent. You, my boy, look more like an agricultural accelerator, the kind who has a special affinity with plants. Have you ever noticed that plants grow more rapidly and fully in your presence?"

"Agricultural accelerator," Haakon said, now thoroughly detached from reality. "It figures." He looked at his gnarled thumbs. "They haven't turned green yet. Actually, rocks have been more my line of work, these last few years."

"Is this really happening?" Steiner asked. "Did

I just see that woman disappear? Am I really hearing these two freaks talk about plants and rocks and sorcerer's stuff?'' The Mongrel chief seemed to be on the point of some kind of breakdown.

Rama was examining her claws. Satisfied that she had cleaned them thoroughly, she said: "Odd things happen around this crew. This is nothing.''

A Mongrel stuck her tousled head through the door. "We gotta get out of here! They getting their heads back on and calling in reinforcements!''

"I better tell the people on that raft we ain't gonna be using it,'' Steiner said. He started for the door.

"You stay with us!'' Jemal barked. "If this tunnel route's been the plan all along, then they were briefed before they left, probably by Rashid. In any case, you stay right where we can see you.''

Steiner turned on him with slitted eyes. "What's the matter, spacer? Don't trust me?''

"I never did,'' Jemal told him.

Steiner glared at him for a moment. "We'll settle this later. No time now.'' He turned to his Mongrels. "Let's throw this place a fish.'' They headed for the stairs.

They made it to the ballroom without incident, although they could hear alarms yowling all over the city. Haakon could scarcely get over his amazement that the security arrangements for the elite of a planetary government could be so lax. He had seen banks that would have been tougher to crack. It spoke reams about the arrogance of inherited power. In all probability, almost all of the planetary defenses were concentrated in orbit.

Most of those still on their feet in the ballroom were white-clad servants, standing uncertainly about, too fearful to make a move. As the raiding party came off the spiral stair and headed for the cellar entrance, Haakon heard a voice behind him say: "Uh-oh, company."

"Hell," Haakon swore dolefully. Advancing toward them was a compact, well-disciplined body of men headed by Raj Jehan. He saw Baibars the Lion in their midst. "It gets serious, people," Haakon said. "Scatter and make every shot count. Try not to kill young Baibars, but don't take any bad chances for his sake." He turned to the old king. "Sorry, but your boy's got to take his chances too."

"Quite understandable," said Baibars of the Holy Cloak. "However, violence will not be necessary."

"I just don't see how that's going to work," Haakon told him. "Unless we surrender, and I don't see that happening, a little violence is in order right now."

Old Baibars closed his eyes and muttered, making cryptic gestures with his hands. When he stopped, Jehan and his group began to turn about, yelling and staring in all directions. "They cannot see us now," old Baibars announced. "It will only last for a few minutes, so we must not waste time."

"Spell of invisibility, huh?" Jemal said. "All right, I'll believe it. Let's go."

The very concept of invisibility had been scien-

tifically disproven for centuries, despite all the
wealth poured into research by military establishments. Now a crazy old coot had made them all
invisible by performing a spell. It figured.

They made it to the basement without being
seen, although they heard a lot of shooting starting
up behind them. Haakon hoped Jehan and his
group weren't just shooting the servants out of
sheer frustration. At the hole they had made earlier
they found Mirabelle and Alexander, along with a
small team of people who had affixed charges to
the impromptu entrance.

"What took you so long?" demanded Mirabelle, fuming.

"We were busy," Haakon said. "If you were
getting impatient, why didn't you just go? You
didn't have to wait for us."

"These dorks wouldn't let us!" Alexander said.
"Besides, we don't know our way around them
tunnels. We'd get lost."

"Where's Maya?" Mirabelle asked.

"She took a shortcut home. I expect we'll see
her when she thinks it's appropriate."

"You people are the talkingest pack of fools I
ever seen," Lorah said. "Can we just get the hell
out of here?"

"Right," Steiner said. "Me'n my people are
clearing out, friends. You wanna come along,
you're welcome to." He stooped and ran into
the entrance, closely followed by his band of
Mongrels.

The leader of the demolition team held up a
control box. "When I get back to the main tunnel,

I'm going to fire these charges. I'd advise you to be there when I do." He followed the Mongrels.

"Looks like we've overstayed our welcome," Haakon said. "Let's be off." They were in the main tunnel when the charge went off. This one was far more powerful than the earlier one, and the concussion knocked several of them down and set all their ears to ringing.

"You all right?" Haakon asked Baibars.

"Certainly. This is most exhilarating. Reminds me of my youth."

"Meaning no disrespect, sir," Jemal said. "But, if you can do the kind of thing we just saw back there, why didn't you just walk out of that place years ago?"

"It is never terribly reliable," Baibars said, carefully stepping around a puddle in the tunnel floor. "Besides, the time was not right. No sense trying to escape until the plants were ready to take off-planet. Who wants to live hiding in some dismal cellar when one can live in a palace?"

"That's sensible," Haakon said.

"Yeah, that's a pretty nice place back there," Alexander said. "If I had to be in a slam, that's the one I'd pick."

"Your view of life is refreshingly uncomplicated, young man," Baibars said.

"He keeps us in touch with the eternal verities," Mirabelle told him.

"Think we could speed it up?" Steiner demanded. "It won't take 'em long to think to gas these tunnels."

"They wouldn't think of doing that with the old king here!" Alexander said, scandalized.

"Oh, yes they would," Haakon said.

"I'm afraid that is true," Baibars said. "Jehan of Jahnsi and his clique would love to utilize this confusion to seize power. It has been done many times before on this planet."

They traveled as fast as they could, limited only by Baibars's advanced years. "I am sorry to slow you like this," he apologized. "If I could levitate like my friend Dmitri Sukesada, I would surely do so."

"You're doing fine," Haakon assured him. "We should be—" He trailed off, reaching for his beamer as they almost walked into a group of men and women standing in the gloom of the tunnel. A light flared and he relaxed. It was Rashid and a pack of his cronies. "Your Majesty," Rashid said.

To Haakon's great surprise, Baibars strode forward and embraced the beggar chief warmly. "Memnon! How good it is to see you again."

Haakon scratched his bare scalp. "Memnon? The name we were given was Rashid."

Baibars turned to Haakon, his arm still about the one-eyed, consummately evil-looking old rogue. "Rashid?" Baibars said in puzzlement. "But, this is my friend and colleague of many years, Memnon DaSilva."

FIFTEEN

"Your shuttle will be departing in approximately one hour," Yussuf said.

They were encamped in an ancient, long-unused port facility that probably dated from the earliest days of planetary colonization. The pads were cracked and densely weed-grown and the towers were tumbling, but simple shuttle craft needed little in the way of sophisticated equipment.

Haakon eyed the clear sky overhead, but that was out of illogical habit. The real threats would be far too high to see. "And you think you're going to get us safely back to our ship in slow, unarmed shuttles?"

"Dr. DaSilva has arranged for your defense from observation," Yussuf assured him.

"Somehow, I'm not terribly comforted. It's bad enough putting our safety in the hands of strangers and flunkies, but you get used to that in the wars.

It's another thing to depend on a pair of witch doctors who make use of mumbo jumbo that would make a tribal shaman blush."

"Dr. DaSilva is a great scientist," Yussuf said. "What he does is not sorcery, it is a form of physics, all the parameters of which have not yet been explored. Haven't you seen enough to know that what they do is real?"

"I've seen enough to know that they don't have it fully under control yet. It's like the early days of chemistry, when it was still half alchemy, or medicine back when they could take your appendix out using anesthesia but still thought bad air caused disease. What good is any system when it's not yet reliable?"

"It may not be one-hundred-percent reliable," Yussuf went on relentlessly, "but it is your only chance."

Haakon had discarded his shirt in the muggy, sweaty heat, even though it was still early morning. His rocklike body was seamed with old scars he had never bothered to have eradicated. He was covered with a sheen of perspiration and was pacing with uncharacteristic nervousness, the weeds with their jagged edges scraping against his boots. "I'm still worried about my ship. They'll have thrown a cordon around her by now. Probably a whole battle fleet."

"Quite avoidable, DaSilva assures me," Yussuf said.

"Easy for you to say. You're not going." Haakon turned to him. "Why is that? Don't you want to get away from here like the rest?"

Yussuf shook his head. "No. It is imperative that the old king and DaSilva leave, and those of us who must establish a rapport with the Cingulum and other resistance groups. But there is much work still to be done here. What we will have accomplished when you get safely away will be the groundwork for the collapse of the Chelaya monopoly and the subsequent inevitable collapse of the present power structure. We will have accomplished nothing if the power vacuum is occupied by another self-seeking group as bad or worse."

They took shelter from the climbing sun in one of the old fuel bunkers, currently employed as a way station for the evacuees. A man looked up from a communication device that had all the marks of a military no-snoop transmitter-receiver. "Our people on Kashmir Three report the presence of a fourth person aboard *Eurynome*. They say no shuttle has approached the ship."

"That will be my daughter Jaga, arriving in her usual fashion," said old Baibars, who was meditating over an ancient text printed on real paper.

"Jaga?" Haakon said.

"Oh, I had forgotten," Baibars said. "You call her Maya, don't you? Actually, she is Princess Jaganmata."

"Doesn't anybody around here go by just one name?" Haakon asked.

"How tedious that would be," commented Baibars.

"How many people are we going to be burdened with?" Rama asked. The immediate action over, her customary bad temper was fully restored.

"I'm not sure yet," Haakon told her. "Don't let it worry you. It won't be for long, and they won't impose on your suite." He didn't add that almost anyone would rather ride steerage with refugees than share a suite with Rama.

Mirabelle was fastidiously repairing her postbattle dishevelment with the aid of a small cosmetic kit equipped with a self-viewer which was far more efficient than a conventional looking glass. Alexander sat by her, looking bored. "This place is too much like where I grew up," he complained. "Too hot and a lot of trees."

"Patience, Alex," Haakon told him. "It won't be long, now."

Jemal got up from where he had been sitting against a wall. Like Haakon, he had stripped to the waist against the heat. "Think we'll get back without a fight?" he asked.

"I don't know," Haakon said. "I—" He cut short when he saw Steiner approaching them and looking belligerent.

"You two satisfied now that I didn't sell you out?" he asked.

"Looks like I was wrong," Jemal admitted.

"Is that all?" Steiner asked. His thumbs were hooked in his belt but his left hand was only a few centimeters from the baroque handle of his old powerblade.

"What do you want, an apology?" Jemal asked. "You don't get one. The day I stop being suspicious I'd better get out of serious work. There were things about you I didn't trust. I make no apology for that. I'm happy to see I was wrong."

"You know, boyo," Steiner said dangerously, "these last few days, it was only my superior's orders that kept me from taking a blade to you."

"Be glad you didn't," Haakon told him.

Steiner turned and glared at him. "You think I couldn't take him?"

Others in the bunker looked apprehensive, but Mirabelle continued applying her makeup, Rama dressed her claws with a metal file, and Alexander continued to scratch something that itched. The rest of the Mongrels had remained in the city, so whatever happened next was between Steiner and Jemal.

Steiner's left hand darted for the ornate handle, but in the same moment, much faster, his right hand dipped into a concealed pocket in his right legging and emerged with a smaller and more modern weapon. No sooner had the right hand emerged than Jemal's left wrist was blocking it, and Jemal's right, with his own powerblade in it, slammed into Steiner's midsection at the diaphragm. If the blade had been powered, the Mongrel chief would have been gutted. As it was, the breath went out of him in a whoosh, and he staggered back to collapse sitting against a concrete wall.

"How did you figure it out?" Steiner gasped, when his breath had returned. "I never had you fooled, huh?"

"It was a good act," Jemal admitted. "You had me believing you were left-handed for a while. It was the cut you got from the Garudas. It came up at you from left to right. Just the kind of cut you'd get from a right-handed man, but only if you were fighting right-handed yourself. If you'd been a real lefty, that cut would've caught you around behind the short ribs somewhere.''

"Never try to fool a pro," Haakon advised him. He grasped Steiner's forearm and hauled the big man easily to his feet. "How about you, Steiner? Are you coming with us?"

"Naw, I got to take care of my people. Besides, I got some Garudas to kill. Maybe Ganesha too. That fat bastard's lived about long enough. Maybe, in a couple of years, things'll quiet down. Shouldn't be any problem to get off-world by then. Thanks for the offer, though.''

"The shuttle is coming," the communications man reported.

"Stand by," Yussuf ordered.

They saw the shuttle before they heard it, an oval speck in the sky, with a peculiar waviness to its outline. "Why is it so quiet?" Haakon asked. "And the way it ripples. Is that atmospheric distortion?"

"Unless I am much mistaken," Yussuf said, "both are effects of DaSilva's masking process."

"Not much of a masking job," Alexander said, "if we can see it from here."

"Naked-eye observation isn't important," Haakon told him. "It's instrument detection that counts. If he can keep us safe from that, our chances of being caught are practically nil."

"Until we get to the ship, anyway," Jemal put in.

"I was trying not to think of that," Haakon said.

"Yeah, boss," Alexander said, "just how we gonna get back aboard *Eurynome* if they want to stop us?"

"We'd better hope DaSilva's got some more tricks up his sorcerous sleeve," Haakon said, "because I'm clean out of ideas."

The shuttle landed on the cracked apron in front of the bunker, still so silent that it seemed to be a faulty holographic projection. Faulty, because it still had the rippling, heat-wave effect that seemed to force the eye away from it. Haakon tried to stare straight at the thing, but stare as he might, his gaze kept sliding toward the edges. It was most disconcerting. Then the masking winked off and he could see it: just a dingy, outdated shuttle that had seen better days. With the masking off, the sound returned as well. They jumped at the subdued hum. After the dead silence, it sounded like a deafening roar.

A pilot Haakon had never seen before lifted the forward blister. "Get aboard and let's get out of here!" he called.

"You heard him," Haakon said. His crew, along with Baibars and several others being sent to establish relations with the Cingulum, filed aboard. Haakon shook hands with Yussuf and Steiner. "Keep your heads down," he advised. "You might've won this round, but you have a long fight ahead. Good luck."

"I'm going to miss you, boyo," Steiner said. "We've had our differences, but you sure kept things lively. I think poor little Lorah's in love with you."

"She'll get over it," Haakon said complacently. "They always do." He turned and boarded the shuttle, and the hatch sighed shut.

"They always get over it, do they?" Rama demanded. Haakon winced. Damn her and her cat ears.

Mirabelle was concentrating on her nails. "Our captain is a notorious heartbreaker, with a girl on every planet. Be grateful you never fell prey to his wiles." She gave the nails another buff and studied the effect.

"It's okay, boss," Alexander put in. "All these legions of admiring females can get to be an embarrassment, but a man like you can handle them."

"You asked for this," Jemal muttered.

"Leaving the subject of my love life for the moment," Haakon said through gritted teeth, "we're left with the tricky problem of getting safely back to our ship. I trust somebody here has some idea of how we're to accomplish this?"

DaSilva stuck his head through a hatch leading to an adjoining compartment. "All is in readiness," he announced. "We shall rendezvous with *Eurynome* in high orbit in approximately two hours."

"High orbit?" Haakon said. "How is she going to get out of the low parking orbit she's in now?"

"She has already left." DaSilva stepped through the hatch. Dressed in a coverall, bereft of turban and beard and cleaned up, only the destroyed eye and missing arm remained as a reminder of the erstwhile beggar king. "Maya has taken her out of that orbit through an amplified version of her own telekinetic talent. There has been much consternation among the Mughali picket ships.''

"I'll bet," Haakon said. He didn't like the idea of someone else moving his ship, even if they did use magic.

"Wait a minute!" Mirabelle said. "Not long ago, she was terrified at the thought of taking another human being along on her ectoplasmic excursions. Are you saying she's now up to taking a whole ship with three other people aboard?''

"As I said, dear lady, this is an amplified process. Electronically amplified, to be precise. It has taken a great deal of time and effort to perfect, working in secrecy, and it is far from true perfection at that, but just as the human voice may be artificially amplified, so may this process."

"The scan lines," Haakon said. "I'd been wondering about that.''

"You discovered that? I might have known. Yes, on one of the occasions when Maya visited your ship, we made use of the electronic process. It was a useful experiment, since we had not yet attempted a transmission of that distance. Had you recorded her earlier disappearance from your vessel, you would have observed only a simultaneous fading of the entire organism.''

"How come we ain't going that way too?" Alexander asked.

"Unfortunately, we have only one apparatus for this purpose. Maya transported it and herself to your ship, and then she used it to remove your ship from its orbit. We shall be compelled to adopt more conventional means.''

"Conventional means?" Haakon said. "That's what you call this? Traveling around in a shuttle that's invisible to detection instruments is conventional?"

"Certainly more so than instantaneous matter transmission."

"Is it really instantaneous?" Haakon asked.

"A shrewd question," DaSilva admitted. "Truthfully, we are not sure. The exigencies of working in secret on Mughal have rendered our tests woefully incomplete. The individual teleportation talent, such as Maya's, is extremely difficult to test in any case, but I suspect that the electronic process is restricted to sublight speeds, like any other electronic wave."

"It won't render spaceships entirely obsolete, then?" Haakon said. He was relieved. That would make him obsolete too.

"Not for a great while, certainly. This study is still in its infancy. It may be like electricity, which was common knowledge for a century before any practical use was found for it."

"We seem to be putting it to pretty practical use now," Jemal commented.

"Yes, if it works as planned," DaSilva said cheerfully. "Of course, putting into use a technology that is insufficiently tested is a notoriously risky procedure."

"Just how many objects as massive as my ship have you successfully teleported?" Haakon asked suspiciously.

"This is the first object of any real bulk we have tried to move." Haakon went pale under his deep tan. Realizing that he had made an undiplomatic statement, DaSilva hastily changed the subject. "By the way, do you have sophisticated regenerative equipment aboard your ship?"

"The best," Haakon told him. "Why?"

DaSilva gestured toward his concave socket. "Monocular vision is most inconvenient. I'd like to grow a new eye as soon as possible. And a new arm."

"No problem," Alexander said. "You think you got troubles, wait'll you see our engineer. He's gotta grow a whole new body. Tesla burns."

"How'd you lose the eye?" Jemal asked conversationally.

"It was government men," DaSilva said. "After Baibars and I refused to perform any more experimental work for the government, they tried to persuade me. One of their persuaders got a bit overenthusiastic and gouged it out. When Maya—Princess Jaganmata as she was then—helped me to escape, it became part of my cover. A fugitive scientist has to be hidden, but another one-eyed beggar could walk openly on the streets and who would take notice?"

"So she sprung you, eh?" Haakon said admiringly, noticing neither Rama's slit-eyed glare nor Mirabelle's quiet, self-absorbed smile.

It felt good to be back in the ship again. There were things to be done; quarters to be assigned for their suddenly burgeoning population. But Haakon had other things on his mind. He didn't for a minute think they were going to get away so easily, without another fight. And he wanted to see Maya.

"Not in my suite," Rama hissed as they passed through the lock. "Nobody in my suite but me! And maybe Numa if I feel the urge, but I think I'm about finished with him now."

"Oh, pipe down," Haakon said disgustedly. "Nobody's moving into your quarters. We don't need the room that bad, and nobody's that dumb, anyway." He glanced around swiftly. What had been done to his ship while he was gone? He could see no changes, but he wouldn't be satisfied until he'd gone over every part of the ship. Except maybe for Rama's suite, which might be unhealthy to approach. And then there was Maya.

In the main lounge he ordered a tequila and lime from a 'bot while he heard Soong's report on the doings while he was absent.

"Quite boring," Soong said. "I spent much of it playing chess with Rand, who is a wretched player. We buttoned up when it became obvious that the authorities on Kashmir Three were of a mind to arrest us, and I demonstrated that their attempted overrides had in no way incapacitated our offensive capability. After that, nothing until Maya's extraordinary arrival and our even more extraordinary removal to high orbit. Is what she says true? Have they really developed some scientific sort of controllable magic?"

"She moved the ship, didn't she?"

"So it appeared, but I could be fooled. Suggestion, hypnosis—I was conditioned against such, but any conditioning is subvertible."

"It's true, all right," Haakon confirmed. "But I'm not sure they have it all that well under control. Even DaSilva admits they're only scratching the surface of this business."

As if on cue, DaSilva emerged from a side corridor. "Do you really live in this spacegoing bordello all the time, Captain? I've just examined my quarters, and they beat any luxury resort I ever stayed in."

"A small thing, but mine own," Haakon said.

"If you don't mind my asking," DaSilva said, "why does the Felid have that suite? It seems to take up about one-fourth of the living quarters."

"When we got the ship, I took the master's quarters adjoining the bridge. The rest drew lots for that suite. It was once the Prince-Admiral's quarters. Rama won."

"And how did you come by such a vessel?" DaSilva asked indelicately.

"I bought it," Haakon lied.

"Ah, yes, of course," DaSilva mumbled in embarrassment.

Haakon found Maya on the bridge. She was fiddling with a contraption she had installed atop the main control console. She looked up and smiled as he came in. "I've just been down to see Father. Thank you for giving him such a fine cabin."

"They're all pretty comfortable on this ship," he said, "as you've no doubt noticed." He looked over the . . . instrument? Machine? He wasn't sure of the proper terminology. It seemed to be a lattice of shiny metal enclosing a structure of clear crystal, but, like the shuttle with its invisibility web, it was difficult to look at directly. If he looked away for a moment, then looked back at it, it seemed to have changed, but he could not say exactly how. "So that's the gadget that gets us from one place to another without the difficulties of known physics?"

"Yes. Along with me. It's of no use without an operator of the proper talent. It's just an amplifier, after all, and it has its shortcomings."

"That I don't even like to think about." He studied her openly. She looked ravishing as always. She studied him just as closely.

"Back when you were raiding the palace," she said, "I never had the opportunity to tell you, but I think you look much better without all the makeup and the false hair."

"You're lying. I look just like an ex-con."

"Maybe I like the look of convicts," she said.

"Well, everybody's got something a little weird about them. Hell, I once knew a woman who liked—well, never mind. I've stashed everybody else, have you picked out a room yet?"

"No, I've been too busy until now, but your engineer tells me that we can't go anyplace for several hours, something to do with readjusting the Teslas due to the new juxtaposition of ship and planet. Why? Did you have a place picked out for me?"

He stepped into the doorway to his quarters. The light came on, revealing the small, relatively Spartan master's quarters. Nothing seemed to have been disturbed. He turned back to face her. "All the other rooms are taken, people doubling up in some. Mine's big enough for two, if you don't mind a little crowding.''

She smiled. "Why, Captain, how gallant of you to share your room. I accept, and I don't mind crowding at all." She walked into the room and turned around, getting its feel.

"Just one thing," Haakon said.

"What might that be?"

He pointed at the black diamond in her navel. "Is that thing surgically implanted?"

"Aren't you going to have a good time finding out?"

SIXTEEN

Maya awoke in darkness, confused about where
she was. That had been happening more often
lately, as she developed her strange talent. She
heard deep, steady breathing next to her and the
memories came flooding back. She smiled and
stretched, then reached out to touch a chrono. The
square face lit up. Still more than an hour before
they could activate the Teslas. In the glow of the
chrono, she studied the body next to her. The dim
light raised the powerful muscles to prominence,
throwing the divisions between them into deep
shadow. She had never seen a body so strong, or
one with so many scars. He looked like a relief
map, and she played with the fancy that she could
read his life and travels from it.

It wasn't such a fancy, at that. It was a well-
used body and face, and one he had chosen, for
his own reasons, to leave in its true condition,

bearing the marks of all his battles and sufferings. She traced a long scar with her fingertip. It ran from the tip of his shoulder horizontally across his massive pectoral almost to the sternum. It was just a thin white line now, slightly sunken into the flesh. She wondered where he had acquired it. War wound? Souvenir of some back-alley brawl with powerblades? The mark of a pit overseer's powerwhip?

She touched another. It was only ten centimeters long, but it formed a thick, raised welt on the heavy triceps. That one had been badly infected. She thought of the pain of receiving such a wound, followed by the days of sickness and weakness as the infection attacked. Even in repose it was the most intensely alive body she had ever seen.

Most of the people she had known in her upbringing had been all surface. This man was all personality and history. In a vague way his mere presence gave her a sense of guilt, the same she had felt when she first saw the cities outside the palace walls and the plantations surrounding the villas. It was a guilt that all her years of rebellion would never erase. To a lesser extent, the others in the crew affected her in the same way. Mirabelle, Jemal, Soong, even truly bizarre specimens like Rand and Alexander and the fearsome Rama. They represented life lived to a peak that was alien to her culture, where all was either effete luxury or nauseating degradation.

There was something attractive about the life they led, something infinitely seductive. Then she remembered the little bomb implanted in his brain.

In all their brains, except for Alexander. No, she had work to do, and that work involved staying with DaSilva and her father and the others on the research team. In the Cingulum. Haakon stirred beside her and awoke. He reached for something on the bedside table and knocked a small object to the floor. Still half awake, he looked to see what it was. On the floor lay a large, black diamond.

"Now you know," she said. "It comes out."

He raised a hand to his mouth. "I think I broke a tooth doing it." He looked at the chrono.

"Still a while yet," she said.

He leaned back and laced his fingers behind his head. "Tell me: Why did you try to discourage us at first? Every time I turned around, there you were, telling me that I shouldn't pursue this matter any further."

"We had to be sure you were what we wanted. You seemed to be almost too good to be true. We looked for an ulterior motive, and of course you had one. Fortunately, it turned out to be one we could live with."

"Are you really going to let Bahadur have the Precious Pearl device?"

"Why not? It's useless to them. Your boss never really believed in it anyway. If the Bahadur royal family is as . . . peculiar as my own, they'll have years of fun trying to make the thing work properly."

"DaSilva says he thinks the device is perfectable," he said.

"Only DaSilva could do it, and he'll be beyond their reach. You might as well give a computer to a tribe of apes and expect them to come up with a power source.''

"Don't underestimate them," he warned. "The Bahadurans may be throwback horsemen right off the steppes, but they can call on the scientific establishments of a hundred subject worlds.''

"It would still do them no good. They would try to pursue it along the lines of traditional physics and scientific method. Only the DaSilva team is even aware of the old Philosophy of Physics school.''

"I wish I could be as confident as you," Haakon said. "But I won't argue. I have to take this thing back if we're to live, and that comes first.'' He thought for a moment. "Speaking of which, there's something we need to talk about.''

"I know," she said hastily, cutting him off. "I've already thought about it. I'm staying with my people.'' She sat up and hugged her knees. "I wish I could go with you, but suicide has no appeal for me. Eventually, Timur Khan is going to push the button on you, and I don't want to be there when it happens. In any case, Rama would find some way to do away with me.''

"Wait a minute," Haakon protested, "she doesn't—''

"Oh, yes she does. She may belong to a different subspecies, but I know another female who's staked a claim when I see one. She wouldn't tolerate me for long.''

Unwillingly, Haakon had to admit that it was true. Even if she wanted to go with him, it would sooner or later come down to Maya or Rama.

Whatever his personal preferences, his crew came first. That had been drilled into him for so many years that it no longer required conscious thought or examination. He touched the wall. A soft glow suffused the room. He rose and went into the refresher to clean up and think. It didn't help.

Jemal and Alexander came up onto the bridge, closely followed by Mirabelle. Soong and Haakon were going over the coded coordinates coming from the navigation console. It was an immensely complicated sequence and it changed from minute to minute. "We've been spotted," Haakon said without preamble.

"How much time?" Jemal asked.

"They'll be in range in ten minutes," Haakon told him.

"How long until the Teslas can be activated?" Mirabelle asked.

"If we're lucky, eight minutes," Haakon said.

"And if we're not lucky?" she asked. Haakon just shrugged.

"Where is Rama?" Soong asked.

"Sulking over something," Jemal said.

Haakon barked into the console. "Rama! Get up here if you're interested in surviving the next ten minutes. We're setting course for the Cingulum right now."

Less than a minute later Rama entered, preceded by an irritated scent. "There was no call to take that tone with me, especially over an open intercom. Our passengers might get the wrong idea." She looked around the bridge, casually glancing through the open door of Haakon's quarters. "Where is your friend with the bejeweled belly button?"

"She's with her father, if it's any of your business," Haakon said. "Now, get over here." He turned to Soong, who was scanning the locater screen. "Position check?"

"Closing fast, and accelerating. Now six minutes to range, about the same for Tesla activation."

"Oh, hell," Haakon said, beads of sweat now standing out on his brow. He punched coordinates in feverishly. "Rand! Can you speed it up any?"

"Sure," said the engineer's mechanical voice over the com. "Last time I tried, though, I ended up with this fancy new suit. You want to try it too?"

"I suppose we'd better take our chances with their beamers," Haakon said. He looked at the locater screen. Imagine sending that many ships out after a single shipload of fugitives. It looked like a whole battle fleet. And there would be no indication when they opened fire. Both the locater and their beamers operated at light-speed. For all practical purposes, the instant the pursuing fleet fired would be the instant *Eurynome* was annihilated. Her shields were no match for such firepower, and even her formidable armament could not slow them down. *Eurynome* was a light cruiser. There were at least six fleet-class battleships out there.

"I don't suppose," Alexander said in a thin voice, "that our friends down there can magic us out of this?"

"Not a chance," Haakon said. "Maya tried a

few minutes ago. Nothing happened. She says it's because we're in a drifting orbit and she's disoriented, for whatever that's worth. That was our last chance. Now we trust to dumb luck.''

"Get your thumbs down," Rand said from the engine room. "We're almost ready to jump."

A final set of unscrambled coordinates flashed on the screen, their color changing from green to orange. A clear plate of neoglass extruded from the console and the five senior crewmen of *Eurynome* each pressed a left thumb against it. This was their key to the Cingulum and all five had to be present to make the jump. Alexander had not been encoded for this function, and Rand, lacking any epidermis, was unqualified. It was a security precaution insisted on by the Cingulum authorities. This way, an enemy had to have all five, plus the coding sequence, to locate the Cingulum.

"Ready to jump!" Rand announced, and they could feel the increasing vibration of the warming Teslas. They were all showing the kind of strain that comes with being in immediate, mortal danger with absolutely no control over the situation. Alexander sat in a corner with his arms and tail wrapped around himself. Haakon sweated. Soong, Jemal, and Mirabelle showed nothing, but they had been schooled in hiding emotion. Rama had her eyes closed and seemed to be muttering prayers in some incomprehensible language. Rama never bothered to hide her emotions, since everyone could smell them anyway. Just now, she smelled terribly afraid.

Haakon had his eyes glued to the locater screen. The fleet was now in range. Then, it wasn't there.

That was all. He took his thumb off the plate. "Made it," he said.

Alexander got up off the floor and brushed himself off. "I knew we'd make it," he said.

"Never had a moment's anxiety, myself," Jemal announced.

"I knew I'd pull us through," Haakon said. "I always do."

"You!" Rama said with unexpected ferocity. "What have you done since we got this assignment? What have any of us done? From the very first we have been manipulated and deceived and led by the nose! Not for one minute have we been in control of our fate, so don't try to play the swaggering adventurer with me. We have been pawns!" She folded her arms haughtily and smelled discontented. "I find this offensive."

"Who the hell are you?" screamed a voice over the com. "Identify yourself immediately or I shall open fire!"

"God," Haakon said disgustedly, "everybody's trying to kill us these days." He hit the transmit plate. "It's *Eurynome*, Scanlon. What's the matter, your identifier broke?"

"Haakon? Of course the damn thing's broke, you know the kind of equipment we've got. What do you want? Every time you people come here, it means trouble."

Maya came in from below. "So these are your good friends of the Cingulum? I'm not sure we shouldn't have taken our chances with Raj Jehan."

"Well," Haakon said, "we've had our problems with them from time to time, but we always work something out." He turned back to the com. "We have a present for your bosses, Scanlon. Call Lopal Singh."

"What kind of present?" Scanlon asked suspiciously. He was floating out there somewhere in a picket ship that was part of the Cingulum security force.

"Tell him," Haakon said, drawing it out and relishing the moment, "that we've brought a shipload of sorcerers"—he got the last words out half strangling with his effort not to laugh—"headed by the ex-king of the Mughal System!" He took his hand off the transmit control and broke into rib-racking laughter. "Oh, God," he said when he was under control again, wiping tears from his face with the back of his hand, "this whole thing would be worth it if we could just see Lopal Singh's face when he gets that message."

Maya looked at him blankly. "You were right," she said. "Everybody has something a little weird about them."

The Cingulum was a vast belt of worldlets circling its primary star in a single orbit. It was a refuge for those fleeing the oppression of Bahadur and it was the most singular place ever discovered in the explored galaxy. It had been artificially created by an unthinkably old and powerful race, and it had qualities utterly at odds with any known laws of physics. Among other things, it could shift positions periodically in order to foil pinpointing by enemies. In order to be accessible to new refugees, though, agents operating in ordinary space were provided with updated access codes and coordinates from time to time. One such set of agents was the crew of *Eurynome*.

The head of security for the Cingulum was Lopal Singh, who now shifted his gigantic bulk in an oversized floating chair in his plain, undecorated office. The chair and his desk were the only pieces of furniture. In spite of its marvels, the Cingulum always seemed to be short of everything. Before him stood Haakon and his peculiar crew.

"I had thought," Lopal Singh began, "that I had already seen every strangeness a man could experience in a lifetime, courtesy of you people. As always, you have demonstrated your ability to amaze me further."

"We always try not to disappoint," Haakon said. "Now, if you don't mind, could you tell us whether your superiors have found our refugees acceptable? If they haven't, would they see to transporting them somewhere else? Because I just don't see what we could do with them."

"Plus," Mirabelle said, "our boss is going to start wondering about our location pretty soon, and we have to get back to him. Timur Khan has even less patience than humor."

Lopal Singh hooked his thumbs in his old-style Sam Browne belt and spoke from the depths of his beard. "My superiors are most happy with these persons, for reasons obscure to me. I pass no judgment. I have been here long enough to know that nothing is too strange to believe, even . . ." he took a deep breath, "a pack of magician-scientists. May God help us all." He looked up at

Mirabelle. Even when he was sitting, his eyes were almost on a level with hers. "Have you received the new codes and coordinates?"

"I have them." After extensive testing, it had been decided that Mirabelle's trained mind was a safer place for the crucial access keys and codes than *Eurynome*'s computers. Before making the Cingulum jump, she would give the computer the needed data. She was conditioned to erase those memories beyond retrieval if anyone should try to force them out of her.

"Then there is nothing more to keep you here." He said it with pointed emphasis. He watched broodingly as they filed out. He always hoped they wouldn't show up again, but they always did, anyway.

Maya was waiting for them at the shuttle dock. As if by common consent the others, even Rama, drew away as Haakon went to her. Neither spoke for a few moments.

"I've seen the inside of Meridian," she said at last. "It's even more fabulous than you led me to believe."

Meridian was a worldlet that contained an enclosed universe, complete with hundreds of complete planets created by the strange race that had made the Cingulum to escape annihilation. Meridian was reality turned inside-out.

"Your father and DaSilva must be happy," Haakon said. "Absolutely anything is possible in there." He fumbled for something else to say, but could think of nothing at all.

"We really didn't have much time together, did we?" she said lamely.

"Maybe just as well. That would make this part even harder."

"I suppose you're right. Well, good-bye, Haakon." She leaned forward, kissed him, and walked away. That was that.

Haakon watched from beneath dangerously lowered brows as his shipmates came back. If one of them made so much as a single snide comment about his abrupt and inadequate leave-taking, he knew there would be bloodshed. However, the only one to speak was Jemal, and all he said was: "Let's go, Hack. Old Timur Khan's waiting."

Timur Khan Bey held the little construction of gold bars and crystal lenses in the palm of one hand. It was a decidedly strange object, hard to look at, somehow. He turned to the line of kneeling figures before him. Their hate showed in every line of their bodies, but equally strong was their fear, and that was the way Timur Khan preferred it. People incapable of hate were useless to him, and people who did not fear him could not be trusted to do his bidding. "So *this* is Precious Pearl?"

"I had it from the lips of Baibars of the Holy Cloak himself," Haakon said. "As you have seen from my report, he constructed it himself, but had only limited success. It was his own opinion that the thing is all but worthless, and his pursuit of its supposed properties led eventually to his downfall." The most sophisticated of Timur Khan's instruments had confirmed the truth of Haakon's story. Fortunately, the Cingulum had conditioning treatments even more sophisticated than Bahadur's truth-detectors.

"Much as I had thought," Timur Khan said. "And you say the old king is dead?"

"Yes, Noyon," Haakon concurred. "There was insurrection in the capital city at the time, something involving a resistance group and the control of some kind of drug plant. We were able to make use of the chaos to infiltrate the palace and question the old man. He was not quite sane, but his story made sense. When the fighting erupted in the palace, we were able to seize the device and escape. He was killed in the fighting."

"Our latest reports confirm your story of civil unrest on Mughal." He turned the device in his hands, but still had difficulty in focusing on it. Functional or not, the thing embodied some unknown technology and should be looked into. When the *Eurynome* crew had returned the day before, he had all but forgotten that he had sent them for this thing. He had more important things on his mind, and the Khakhan had not pestered him about it lately.

"Very well," Timur Khan said at last, "rise and go. Your performance has been satisfactory." They got to their feet, bowed deeply, and turned for the door. "But," Timur Khan said sharply, "do not leave the city. Hold yourselves in readiness. I shall have another mission for you soon."

Haakon bowed and said, tonelessly, "Yes, Noyon."

Timur Khan watched as the door shut behind them. He was pleased now that he had never gone ahead with his plans to liquidate this team. They were good, for subhumans. Very useful.

He tossed the odd little device onto his desk and pondered for a moment, then reached for his bow.

Outside the Black Obelisk the little crew stood, waiting for a transport to take them to the lower city.

"Where to?" Jemal asked. "*Star Hell?* It's always lively down there."

"We may not be welcome down there," Mirabelle said. "They saw us leave with that BT."

"Free spacers!" Haakon said bitterly. "I wonder what Steiner would say if he could see us now."

"Stop feeling sorry for yourself," Rama said. She stretched. "I'm for going to *Star Hell.* The worst they can do is try to throw us out, and I'd like to see them try that with us. Come on, I need some excitement!"

Haakon smiled at her reluctantly. "Hell of a way to talk for a woman in your condition."

She smiled as well and slapped a palm across her stomach, which resounded like a log. As they walked to a settling hoverbus, she draped an arm around his shoulders. "It'll be months before it shows. We can have lots of fun before then." They climbed aboard and headed for Lower Baikal.

Rama settled back in her chair with an uncharacteristically pensive look. "What should we name it?" she said out of nowhere.

"Name what?" Mirabelle asked. "Oh, the baby. Or is it a kitten?"

"It's a baby," Rama said, for once without rancor.

"How should we know?" Jemal demanded. "I don't know about the others, but I've seen exactly two Felids in my life, you and Numa. Felid names are not a specialty of mine."

"The baby will require a nursery," Rama announced. She looked at Soong. "Your quarters should do. The location is convenient."

"What?" Soong protested, for once jolted from his customary serenity. "You have accommodations for a Prince-Admiral and all his entourage. Use one of those rooms in which you store your redundant possessions."

"Speaking of Numa," Haakon said, "what are we going to do with him if he hasn't already jumped ship here?"

"He will stay with me, at least until the baby is weaned and I'm back in fighting shape," Rama told him. "If you try to expel him, things could get violent. Felid males are almost as fierce as the females."

"That settles that, then," Haakon said. He crossed his arms, tucked his chin into his chest and closed his eyes. It would be a typically long, slow, public-transportation ride to the lower city. Around him, the others discussed the possibilities of various names, Alexander holding out for something heroic, Soong favoring something understated. The two women, their usual animosity set aside for once, were discussing, to his intense amazement, baby clothes.

Haakon felt good. Once again he had gotten away with subverting one of Timur Khan's assignments. That was always a deadly business. Once again he had done it without losing any of his people. He was finally admitting to himself just how important that was to him. He had taken this disparate bunch of misfits and outcasts and welded them first into a crew, then into a functioning mission team, and now, finally, into something resembling a family. What had he wrought? Whatever it was, he intended to protect it. It was probably all they would ever have. Yes, by God, he thought, perhaps for the first time in years, I feel good.

CONAN

"Nobody alive writes Conan better than Robert Jordan"   —L. Sprague de Camp